The Future is Mine

The Future is Mine

Vandana Kumari Jena

Ocean Books
Ocean Paperbacks
A Division of Ocean Books Pvt. Ltd.
ISO 9001:2008 Publishers

Published by
Ocean Paperbacks
A Division of Ocean Books Pvt. Ltd.
4/19 Asaf Ali Road,
New Delhi-110 002 (INDIA)
e-mail: info@oceanbooks.in

ISBN 978-81-8430-310-0
The Future is Mine
by Vandana Kumari Jena

Edition
First, 2015

Price
Rs. 250.00 (Rupees Two Hundred Fifty only)

Printed at
R-Tech Offset Printers, Delhi

To

My Son Prakrit

PREFACE

Our childhood was spent with a grandparent or parent narrating a bed time story beginning with, 'Once upon a time....' We have all grown up with the short story, which forms an intrinsic part of our childhood memories. Be it the homespun story, cleverly made up by the doting grandmother, or the classics spun by word smiths, stories always leave an unforgettable imprint on our mind. I have never reached the end of 'Idgaah,' the immortal classic by Premchand, without breaking into tears. Guy de Mupassant's stories leave me with a lump in my throat, while PG Wodehouse with his seamless narratives brings a smile to my lips. Over a period of time, while creative writing has evolved, with traditional novels giving way to graphic novels and the genre expanding to chick lit, erotica, science fiction and speculative fiction, to name just a few, the size of the stories has shrunk, with flash fiction and micro fiction competing with the traditional short story. Fiction can now be written in five hundred words, a hundred words or even less. Sadly, I am told, despite this enrichment, short stories have no takers. Nevertheless, despite discouragement by publishers, I have ventured to write, 'The Future is Mine,' my second collection of short stories.

The short stories in this collection are an eclectic mix, because life itself is multi-dimensional, multi-layered, multi-textured and multi-hued. It defies a pattern. It is a symphony of sunshine and shadows, laughter and sorrow, the mundane and the mysterious. The stories in the collection portray the changing times and values, from the time when bearing an illegitimate child raised eyebrows, to the present when India has become the destination of choice for commercial surrogacy as well as sperm donation. Most of the stories dwell on the plight of women. As a woman, I can understand

and empathize intuitively with women. My protagonists, therefore, are usually strong women. I honestly believe that women are the stronger sex. Yet they are vulnerable as well, with all human failings, foibles and imperfections, because after all, no human being is perfect.

Of the stories in this collection, 'Déjá vu', 'Retribution' and 'Storm Warning' have a hint of mystery in them, as well as a twist in the tale. 'Déjá vu' is the story of a young woman who detests train journeys because of a tragedy in her past. 'Retribution' is what awaits Sabita when she dares to do the unthinkable and embarks on a forbidden relationship, while 'Storm Warning' is the story of a young woman who is convinced that she is being poisoned. 'Long distance Romance' and 'Anti-love' add a dash of humour to the collection. 'Long Distance Romance' is the story of a newly- wed couple, where the hero is in love with his own voice, and even more, with his mobile phone, while 'Anti-love' is the story of a woman who does not have a romantic bone in her body.

The other stories include 'The Tempest', the story of a young girl who made a wrong choice once, and abandoned her love for the sake of her family, but yearns for life to give her a second chance. The 'Tsunami' is the story of a young woman who is plucked by the gigantic killer wave and buffeted around,making her realize how infinitesimal her problems really are, when her very survival is at stake. 'My Own Prison' is the story of a young girl who has to barter her body, albeit differently, for a few dollars more. 'Once Upon A Time in Munnar' portrays the angst of a girl who finds herself abandoned by her own family to secure the future of her siblings. 'The Future is Mine' is the story of a young woman whose abduction by insurgents leaves her traumatized. 'Nemesis' is the tale of a man with a warped mind, who decides to kill his daughters for a longed for son. 'The Unwelcome Guest' deals with the anguish of a father who is unable to bridge the chasm between himself and his bureaucrat son. 'Spider's Web' is the story of a young boy who decides to take law into his own hands and thwart the liaison between his father and his colleague.

Each story, stripped of any pretensions, nevertheless highlights the complexity of human relationships. The stories are meant to entertain and I hope readers will enjoy reading them, and see a slice of their life in the stories.

—Vandana Kumari Jena

ACKNOWLEDGEMENTS

I would like to thank the editorial team at Ocean Books for going through the book painstakingly and for their invaluable inputs. I thank Kiran Soni Gupta IAS, Textile Commissioner, Mumbai, a dear friend and professional colleague as well as a brilliant painter, for generously allowing me to use her painting for the cover of my book. I am thankful to my mother Dr. Padma Srivastava, who has been my role model; my husband Prasanna; my sons Prakrit and Ankit and my daughter-in-law Jennifer Ann Bartlett, for offering their tacit support as well as constructive suggestions.

CONTENTS

DÈJÀ VU

It was a journey like any other. I got inside the compartment, my eyes feverish with excitement. Was it on account of the train journey, which always put me in a kind of dread, was it because Karuna was getting married or for some other reason? I did not know. I sank into my berth in the Rajdhani AC III tier compartment with a smile. I had promised myself that once I started working, I would treat myself to travel by AC first class, just as my grandfather did. 'Dadaji,' my paternal grandfather, having served as an officer of the Indian Railways, was entitled to free Rail Passes while the rest of his family travelled, 'Second Class.' "The Haves and the Have Nots," I used to giggle to myself. I had read Karl Marx and understood the difference well enough. Now with a substantial pay package as a lecturer in a Central University I could afford the luxury of travelling AC 1st Class, although circumstances had compelled me to travel by AC III tier.

I looked at my companions with avid interest. I had read their names on the chart stuck outside the compartment—Madhusudhan Dutt, Robin Banerjee, Tapan Sen, Mr. Raman Sinha and Kavita Sinha. I wondered, Who was Who. The Sinhas were easily identifiable. Kavita was the only other woman in the compartment beside me and she was stuck to her husband as though they were twins conjoined in the hip. They may have been newly married, but that was no reason that she was stuck to him like 'Fevicol,' I thought primly, especially as there were four other occupants in the compartment, who were watching their amorous overtures with voyeuristic delight, as though she was some B-grade film heroine instead of a new bride. I saw an elderly man, almost 60 years old, who looked as though he was Madhusudhan Dutt. His name had an old world-ring to it and reminded me of Michael Madhusudhan Dutt, a renowned poet and one of the luminaries of the Indian National Movement. Next to him was a thin emaciated gentleman, who reminded me of the starving population of Bengal during the Bengal famine, never mind if it had occurred many years before my birth. I imagined that he was Robin Banerjee. I nicknamed him 'Scarecrow.' The third, a rather good looking man sitting across me, who kept a discreet distance away from the newly weds, I guessed was Tapan Sen. Five pairs of eyes were watching me warily. I smiled. I am seldom the centre of attention, but at least three occupants in the compartment seemed to be curious about me.

"Imagine going to Bhubaneswar in the peak of summer," said the elderly gentleman, "One should have headed for Shimla instead." "I really don't like Shimla," yawned the emaciated gentleman, who had increasingly begun to resemble a scarecrow. "It is too crowded, with too many monkeys, give me Darjeeling any day." "He is definitely a Bengali," I thought, "The kind of man who dips a Britannia Marie Biscuit into his tea cup and calls it '*biskoot*.' The kind of man who wears a monkey cap and a *muffler* around his neck and says 'Brrr,' at the first sign of cold, while the rest of us cheer the onset of winter."

The ticket checker came a little while later and proved me wrong on all scores. The older gentleman was called Robin Banerjee, whereas the 'Scarecrow,' was Tapan Sen. The good looking gentleman was Madhusudhan Dutt. His name was so putting off, that I decided to abandon any plans for a train romance. The prospect of a twenty-five hour journey with this menagerie, made me feel that I was in a zoo. The display of Kavita and Raman's ardour, with Kavita looking like a cat who got away with the cream, while Raman displayed a hangdog expression, was getting on my nerves. I took out a novel from my handbag and began reading it. It was the *Da Vinci Code*. I should have read it years ago, but hadn't managed to do so. "You must have seen the movie first," said Tapan Sen patronizingly. 'No,' I said curtly, my nose firmly in the book, "If I ever need to know the story of the movies I watch, I'll search for it on the Internet." "Funny, everyone else I know has either seen the movie, or read the book," he said, getting the last word after all. "Reminds me of the Louvre," said Robin Banerjee. The trouble with travelling in the Indian trains is that everyone thinks they have the right to butt into a conversation, without an apology. I set my book aside. So much for my attempt at keeping aloof. "Have you been to the Louvre?" asked Robin Banerjee. 'No,' I said shortly, "I have not even been to Kathmandu, let alone Paris." 'Touche,' said Tapan Sen, his emaciated face lighting up with a sardonic smile. *"Bhai Sahab, Laddoo khaiye."* Kavita's remark made me smile. She probably hated the attention I was drawing. 'Didi,' she said, "have some," extending the box of laddoos towards me, although I suspect she was at least two years older than me. I grimaced slightly, then felt ashamed of myself, and popped half a Laddoo into my mouth and said, 'Nice,' though the truth is that I detest *besan ke laddoo*. "Myself Kavita, this is my husband Raman," she said before lapsing into Hindi and saying, *"Yeh hamari shadi ka Laddoo hai,"* 'Oh God,' I thought, "Why didn't the newly weds get a coupe for themselves?" *"Shadi ka Laddoo jo khaye woh pachtaye, jo na khaye woh pachtaye,"* This was Madhusudhan Dutt at his trite best. "What about you?" He asked, after a long pause. "Smita," I said, dragging out my name almost under duress. "I am going for my cousin's wedding." "I love train journeys," said Kavita to no one in particular. "I hate them," I said rather vehemently. 'Why?' asked Tapan Sen curiously. For a long time I kept silent. Then I said, "It brings back bad memories." 'Bad memories?' Robin Banerjee asked. "My father died in a train accident. He fell off the train. He died before my eyes. I was five years old at that time." 'Poor Smita,' said Tapan, and placed his hand on my shoulder. I shook a little. I seldom talked about my father. I did not know why I had spoken about him to this group of strangers. Perhaps I had done so because they were strangers.

"I have also witnessed a train accident, when a colleague of mine fell off the train. His brains almost spilled out. He died painfully two hours later," said Robin Banerjee. His voice had become gruff. "I was in the Indian Audit and Accounts Service," he said. Scarecrow raised his eyebrows. "Promotion of course," said Robin Uncle, "I began my career as an Auditor. I spent many happy days in Yarrows, the IA&AS Training College in Shimla. It is beautiful."

"I do not know about that," said Scarecrow, "But I have been a Visiting Faculty in Indian Institute of Advanced Studies in Shimla. My discipline is History." Tapan Sen. Suddenly, the name clicked. "Professor Tapan Sen, renowned Professor of Modern Indian History?" I asked breathlessly. He smiled, gratified that his name evoked such a response.

"I too have a Shimla connection," laughed Madhusudhan Dutt, "I have studied in Sanawar." 'Sanawar?' I began to look at him with renewed interest. Despite his antiquated name, my friend Madhusudhan was definitely worth cultivating. "I am now setting up my business." "Not a tycoon obviously," I thought, "Otherwise he would not be travelling AC III tier." Madhusudhan Dutt was obviously a mind reader. "The AC First and Second Class were fully booked," he said. "I have recently begun teaching Political Science in Lady Shri Ram College," I said, "After completing my M.Phil." The Sinhas had remained silent till now. I wondered what Raman did. He looked as though he ran a ration shop. I was not far wrong. I learnt that he ran a photo studio in Kamla Nagar in Delhi.

For a while, the mood in the compartment became sombre. Everyone seemed to be lost in their own thoughts. Then the waiter came with our lunch. Tomato soup and bread roll was followed by a delicious meal consisting of chicken, paratha, dal makhni, pulao, salad and achar. This was followed by plain yoghurt and vanilla ice cream. "Food for the *God*s," said Madhusudhan Dutt. "Maybe, but obviously not for the old or the ailing," complained Robin Banerjee good naturedly. He took the ice cream from his tray and gave it to me. "I have diabetes," he said, his eyes twinkling, "and I think you can afford to put on weight." I grimaced. I was blessed with the kind of metabolism that I never seem to put on weight. Yet I was reluctant to take the ice cream from him. I was wondering on how to refuse him, without offending him. Then I saw Kavita looking at me enviously. I wondered whether it was the ice cream she wanted or the attention. "Would you like to have it?" I asked. She smiled and grabbing it from my hand, began eating it.

"You are going alone for a wedding, aren't your family members accompanying you?" Tapan Sen seemed to be showing a great deal of attention to me. "My mother died a year after my father, of a broken heart I always think. My Uncle brought me up. I am going to attend his daughter's wedding." 'Oh!' all five were silent. They did not say anything to me but I knew they were full of sympathy. '*Bechari*,' I felt I could hear them say the word, '*Bechari Smita*,' although no one had spoken a word.

"Let us not dwell on sad things," said Kavita, trying to change
the subject, "Let us talk of happier things. We are r married
and are going to Puri for our honeymoon." "Dur tra?"
said Scarecrow, raising his eyebrows, "Ar a
pilgrimage or a honeymoon? There will be
will congregate at the Jagannath temple
at all." "If we get Lord Jagannath's
happy," she said. "I saw the Rat
Banerjee reminiscently, "I got
We saw the surging crowds a
the crowds, but we didn't
we heard that eight pil
he had hoped to dete .
"*Woh log Swarg* *ath*
yatra mein maare pe that
Kavita gets crushed th's Rath.
She talks of death so lig devastating
it is for those who have lo ook at me. No
amount of love showered by and Badi Mummy
compensated for the loss of my pa rew up in the shadow
of their loss. How can one take death ghtly?"

Everyone lapsed into silence after some time. At night as we went to sleep, I got ready to climb up to my upper berth. "Would you like to exchange your berth with me?" offered Dr. Tapan Sen, probably because he was still basking in the warmth of my compliments. "Don't worry, I love the upper berth," I said, as I scrambled up to the top, "I was an athlete in school and college. I may look small but I pack quite a punch." "Stranger things have happened," said Madhusudhan Dutt, looking at my diminutive frame and laughing.

By the time I got up in the morning I realized that the train was late by two hours. It tried to make up on the delay by sudden spurts of speed. By the time the train was about to reach Bhubaneswar, the passage was completely filled, like a pack of sardines. Robin Banerjee was at the door, eager to meet his son, his daughter-in-law and his grandson.

The Rajdhani was going in full speed. We were all standing near the door, which had been opened by Robin Banerjee. Suddenly, as the train rushed towards the station, there was a loud scream and we all saw Robin Banerjee, his arms flaying, falling down the track. His head hit the track and his brains spilled out. I saw his face contorted in agony. I had a sense of déjà vu. I had seen the expression on my father's face. I should have felt sympathy for Robin Banerjee but I didn't. It had taken me twenty years to avenge my father's death but I had done it at last. Nobody in my family had understood why I had refused Bade Papa's offer to buy me an air ticket to Bhubaneswar for Karuna's wedding and chosen to travel by train, and that too by AC III Tier, when almost all my life I had avoided train travel. They did not know that I had learnt of Robin Banerjee's travel plans and it was an opportunity I could not miss. I had no plan. I felt a sense of victory when I stood behind him near the door and nudged him hard with my elbow at his back. I saw him fall, terror in his eyes and remembered the day, more than twenty years ago when I had seen him do the same to my father. I knew that it was no accident because I had heard Bade Papa tell Mummy, "Robin Banerjee has got the promotion which was being given to your husband Sameer earlier." Had it been jealousy or greed which had made Robin Banerjee do what he did? Or was it because he could not help giving into temptation? I had no idea. Neither did I know, nor did I care. But when I had seen my mother sob her heart out before the lifeless body of my father, I knew that I would avenge him and her one day, even if it took me a lifetime to do so. In my book, the only justice was, "A life for a life." I had done just that. I had spent twenty year of my life, unable to get a decent night's rest. At last I had earned the right to sleep in peace.

□

LONG DISTANCE ROMANCE

On the day of my engagement, on 11 August 2000, when my fiancé and I exchanged rings, little did I know of my spouse-to-be's obsession with rings of a different kind. Pyromaniac I had heard of, but phonomaniac? A fortnight later when we got married, my father made the fatal mistake of sending me a small cellphone as a parting gift, to keep in touch and to confirm that my Prince Charming had not turned into a toad overnight. Papa must have pursed his lips, when the next morning instead of hearing his darling Vandana beti's dulcet tones, he heard the bridegroom's nasal ones. But husband dear had begun his married life with the belief that I, and all my material possessions, belonged to him, for better or for worse. Within two days, the cellphone became so much a part of him that I wondered if the vow of "Till death do part us," had been taken with me or with my cellphone.

After marriage, I began to learn new things about him. Not only did he love himself, he was even more in love with his voice. He loved to hear it morning, noon and night. Having been a student of mass communications, he loved to communicate. That he always did not have a ready audience before him, did not deter him. If, in the film *Deewar*, Shashi Kapoor had dismissed Amitabh Bachchan with the one-liner, '*Mere Paas Maa hai*,' Sanjay in a minor variation of the theme, would have said, '*Mere Pass Cellphone hai*.' Money of course was of no consequence, partly because communications, not calculation had been his forte. Just four days after our marriage, I got a call from him. 'Vandy,' he said, "I'm speaking from Nirula's Pastry Shop, what kind of pastry do you like?" While many a woman would have melted with love, at the sound of her husband's voice, I was busy calculating the cost of the call. At eight rupees per minute, the pastries would come in expensive if I didn't decide quickly. "Pineapple pastry please," I hissed. "Speak loudly," he bellowed, "I can't hear you." "I said, pineapple pastry," I yelled. "There aren't any," he replied. "In that case doughnuts would do," I said. "Plain ones or chocolate ones?" he asked. 'Either,' I said, knowing that brevity, is indeed the soul of economy. A minute later I got another frantic call. "Oh my God, I don't have my wallet on me, someone has pinched it, or maybe I have dropped it." The possibilities were immense and my husband was about to describe each of them in detail. "I'll look for it," I yelled as I cut down the phone. "I'll call you up later," he muttered. I looked for the wallet everywhere and finally I spotted it, on the bedside, where he had obviously replaced it with the love of his life, the cellphone. Five minutes later he rang up again and was pleased to know that he and his money had not parted, not just yet anyway.

That evening I told Sanju that not buying pastries had cost us 80 rupees. He was hurt. "Here I am, yearning to hear my wife's voice and all you think of, is money." "Do you know," I began cuttingly, "At the rate at which you are going, we will get a bill of five thousand rupees at the end of the month," "Oh my God," he said, and then suddenly he cheered up. "Since your father gave the cellphone, won't he meet the bills as well?"

The next evening, while we were sitting on our lawn, nursing a *nimbu pani*, our neighbour dropped in, her huge Labrador in tow. "I'll get you a drink," my husband said, an epitome of chivalry. For one dreaded moment, I thought he would ring up on the cell and ask the servant for one. But better sense prevailed. Apparently, even Sanju knew the cost of lemons. He left the cellphone on the table and went into the house. Mrs. Bali suddenly twittered like a bird and asked me the way to the restroom. I led the way to the loo. A few minutes later we returned. Tiger was sitting placidly by the table.

"Where's my phone Vandy?" asked Sanju on his return. "It was here, on the table." I said. "It isn't there any longer," he said,

"Well I knew it was a mobile but I didn't really expect it to run away," I said facetiously. He almost broke into tears at my retort. "This is serious. How could you leave it alone and go? It's not even insured," he said. "Well, neither am I," I retorted. This time he glared at me and I realized that any more of my humour and my marriage would be on the rocks. "Somebody has pinched it," he said, "This is a matter for the police." "This has happened because of you," he said darkly, while waiting for the police to appear, "You were jealous of the mobile." "And what do you think I did, practice voodoo?" I hissed. Mrs. Bali was enjoying herself. After all she had the rare privilege of being the sole witness to our first matrimonial battle. Just then the police arrived. "Spoilsport," I heard her mutter under her breath as she bid us Goodbye. "I don't think the cellphone is stolen," said the inspector after hearing Sanju. "The telephone couldn't have done a Houdini," said Sanju. "But no one could have taken away the phone while the dog was here," countered the inspector. He pursued his lips like Sherlock Holmes and said, "Strange, why did the dog not bark?" "Because someone known to him had picked up the phone," both Sanju and I uttered in unison. "Dial the cell number," said the inspector, "And let it ring." I went inside and dialed the number, while the inspector and Sanju prowled around the lawns. They began to hear a faint sound nearby. It came from the adjoining garden. And then realization finally struck them. The cellphone, small enough to rest in my palm, now rested in the abdomen of that monster Tiger. A smile spread across the face of the inspector. "There Sir, your mystery is solved." 'But,' wailed Sanju, "How do I retrieve the mobile?" "Well, if it had been a thief," grinned the inspector, "Hum usse ugalva lete" (We would have made him vomit it out). On that humorous note, he left us. Only, like Queen Victoria, we were not amused.

We went to Mrs. Bali's house immediately and narrated our tale of woe. "Ah my poor Tiger," she said, her face going red, "I wonder what will happen to him now?" She rang up the vet while Sanju kept pacing up and down the drawing room, wearing down the carpet, much like an expectant father.

"Your dog will survive," said the vet. "What about my cellular phone?" hollered Sanju into the receiver. "It will probably come out the next morning," he prophesized. Now it was Sanju's turn to seethe. He could not imagine an overnight separation from the cellphone. He looked beseechingly at the neighbour. "Can't you induce vomiting?" he urged. "Why don't you give it a try?" she countered.

"Vandy," said Sanju "Are you willing to give your right hand for a cellphone?" I gathered his meaning, he was asking me to put my hands into the jaws of death. "I really can't," I returned sweetly, "As I said before I'm not insured." "Well neither am I," he said, "and remember I am the main breadwinner." I was stumped momentarily. "All you have to do is tickle his throat, with a feather of course," he added hastily, seeing me glare. "And you do not have to worry about your being incapacitated," he continued in his wheedling tone. "You're already married." "But will not remain for long," I returned, "If this conversation continues." "And it will be difficult," I said relishing the turn the conversation was taking, "To get married once again, minus a hand." "That will be a problem," he muttered nastily, "Even with both your hands intact." Just then Tiger, his stomach full, put his head down to sleep. Now we understood the wisdom of the old adage, "Let sleeping dogs lie."

The next day, at the crack of dawn, Sanju was ready to go. "Come on," he said, walking stealthily, "We are going for a walk." But there was certainly no romance in the morning air. We were to follow Tiger on his morning rounds. I am a dog lover of sorts. I have lived with a German Spitz. But a Labrador, I realized, is a class apart. Not for him a little jog around the park before his morning ablutions. He went for a five kilometer run everyday. Tiger ran like an Olympic runner along with the servant, while we huffed and puffed behind. "Sanju," I said, sweat pouring down my face, "If anything happens to me I want you to know I have written my will in your favour." 'This,' he said, quelling me with a glance, "Is not the time for words but for action." I saw that his eyes were glued to a banyan tree. Beneath the tree a mini hurricane was in the offing. Tiger was letting off a big whoosh. Along with the sound and fury came out the remnants of his Last Supper. Two pair of eyes stayed glued to the scene after Tiger had left. We heaved a sigh of relief, when we saw the outline of the precious mobile. "Vandy, pick it up," ordered Sanju. "You forgot the magic word," I said. 'Oh,' his brow cleared, "The word Please?" 'No,' I clarified, "The word I'll." Without another word, he pulled out a pair of plastic gloves from his pocket, picked up the cellphone and dropped it in a polythene packet.

Once we came home, he began "Operation Cleanup." He cleaned it with a damp cloth, not once, but twice. Then he smelt it and almost gagged. 'Nothing,' he said, "Will make me touch this again." An hour later he bleated, "Can't we get another one?" Then I had a brainwave. I liberally sprayed my husband's favourite perfume Fahrenheit on it. He froze in shock. "You've half emptied the bottle," he said. "It's for a good cause," I retorted. Later I went to the cellphone shop. "This cellphone has only limited features," I said, "For that," he smirked, "You would need a more expensive model." I paid the extra amount and opted for a more expensive model. The shopkeeper took the phone, smelled it suspiciously, and said, "Why does it smell different?" "Oh does it?" I asked innocently, "I didn't know, this is our first cellphone you see."

We brought a new model that evening. It is not only better. It is bigger. Hopefully, Tiger would find it quite a mouthful, if he repeated his antics. Sanju was touched by my gesture. Papa was not. "You didn't find my gift good enough," he mourned, "So you exchanged it." The time had come to tell him the truth, the whole truth and nothing but the truth. So we did. 'What,' he chuckled, after hearing our tale, "Do you think happened to the old mobile?" "I'm sure it was sold," I said. We all laughed. So if in recent times you have bought a cellular phone which reeks of Fahrenheit, it is time for you to freeze. And if after reading this you say, "Oh shit," I for one, will not blame you.

□

RETRIBUTION

It was a slow death, Sabita thought, guilt assailing her as she looked at the still body of her blind mother-in-law, but it was not about her mother-in-law that she was thinking. Waves of grief flooded over her, covering her like a shroud, which covered Amma now. It had begun in a moment of weakness and continued ever since. She looked at Anuraag's photograph on the drawing room wall. What did he know about moments of weakness, what could he, he who lived the life of a hermit, a saint, reclusive, alone and beyond temptation? How could he understand? "He couldn't," she shuddered, "Not now, not ever." She then saw her brother-in-law Raghu standing beside her. But he was not looking at the body on the ground. "I have informed him," he said to her in an undertone, almost whispering the words in her ear. Shanti, the maid shuffled into the room just then. "Take away the cups," Sabita said mechanically, almost oblivious of the small crowd of neighbours who had gathered, on hearing the news of Amma's death. She could feel Raghu's eyes bore into her back. She turned to look at him. His eyes seem to burn in his face…they reminded her of a train emerging from a dark tunnel, its lights burning bright, of the bright embers of a freshly stoked fire, of dark and passionate nights, of rumpled silken sheets, of the warm feel of naked bodies lying back-to-back, their ardour spent, as if in denial of the proximity of a few moments ago.

"It's over," she said, mouthing the words softly to herself and to him. 'Never,' he hissed, "I can never let you go." "This can't go on forever," she pleaded with him that night, when everyone had left, and she and he were left alone, with the body of her mother-in-law in the drawing room. She tried to blot out the image of Amma, accusing her and Raghu saying, 'Kulachini, kulta,' to her and Raghu pushing Amma violently, and Amma collapsing on the floor…Amma dead. "It was an accident," she said to herself, her eyes closed, almost unmindful of Raghu's mutterings. They had been careless, forgetting that Amma was blind, but not deaf, she may not have seen them, but had heard them. "You're mine," Raghu had said, taking possession of her body and leaving her yearning for more, "I'll never let you go." And Amma had heard.

When had it all started? She shuddered to think about it. Was it when her husband Anuraag had left her within a year of their wedding to go to Dubai, where his childhood friend Prakash had found him a well-paid job, leaving her behind with an old, blind mother-in-law and unmarried brother-in-law? "A five-year contract?" She had blanched at the very thought, while Anuraag had shrugged philosophically and said, "Think of the money I will earn." Or was it the night when she had slipped and twisted her ankle and Raghu had picked her up and carried her upstairs, putting her gently on the bed and caressing her ankles, until a strange languor had crept over her and the faces of Anuraag and Raghu had blurred and he had taken her with a passion that had at first alarmed and then excited her, playing with her body like an ace musician with a stringed instrument, making all her pent up longing burst forth?

"When he comes home, you will have to choose between us," said Raghu. 'Choose?' she laughed dementedly. "I am Anuraag's wife," she babbled, "It's his *mangalsutra* I wear, and if you say anything about us to him I shall deny it." 'Even,' said Raghu, his eyes glittering strangely, "If I tell him about the mole on your thigh and the mark on your back." She blanched on hearing him speak. "You wouldn't, you couldn't," she said, wavering between supplication and admonition. But she knew he would. And that man, her husband, ironically named Anuraag, who seldom wanted or needed love, would never understand or forgive them. She had to do something about Raghu, she thought, especially now that she knew about his incredible strength. Today it was Amma, tomorrow it could be her turn. But what could she do?

She thought of her mother-in-law once again, whose body lay cold in the drawing room. She thought of the relations who would come for the cremation, of Anuraag's voice, thick with grief, telling her over the phone, "Wait for me, I'll take the next flight and come home."

When Anuraag returned home, he seemed as grim, as taciturn, and as forbidding as he had on their first night. 'What,' she wondered, "Would he say if he knew the truth?" "He would kill me," she thought with certainty, looking at his gaunt face and his lean brown hands, "He would put his fingers around my neck and choke me, slowly and painfully, until I lose every breath in my body."

After his return, Anuraag took care of everything, the cremation, as well as the *Chautha*. She felt the days pass in a haze. "What will happen to me?" she wondered, "While Ammaji was alive it was alright, but after her, Anuraag cannot let me live in a house alone with Raghu." A part of her body trembled in protest. That, it said, is what I want, I really want, but I can't have.

She knew similar thoughts were churning in Raghu's mind. She could not ignore the strange glitter in Raghu's eyes. Anuraag did not know it, but there was no way Raghu was willing to let her walk out of his life, the girl he had seen and loved, but who his mother had got married to his elder brother instead. He knew that he would rather kill his brother first than give her up.

After the *Chautha* was over, Anuraag called Raghu at night and said, "Could you get the car filled up with petrol? I have to meet some people tomorrow before I leave." 'Leave?' Raghu's voice had a sudden lilt to it. Was it possible that Anuraag would go away to Dubai without Sabita? He had hoped too soon. "Before I leave," Anuraag said, looking straight at Sabita, "We need to talk." Raghu took the car keys from Anuraag and began to form a plan in his mind. When he returned after filling up the petrol, he was ready. He opened the bonnet of the car and began fiddling with it. "Hey, what are you doing?" called Anuraag from the window upstairs. Raghu looked up, his face red with guilt. Then he relaxed. Surely from the first floor, Anuraag could not have seen anything. "Dada, I was checking the car for you," he shouted. Anuraag smiled, "What a caring brother I have," he shouted back.

Sabita entered the kitchen and began searching. She had to do something about Raghu, before she had her talk with her husband. She needed to buy time, she could not afford to have a confrontation between Raghu and Anuraag, not before she had found a way out. 'Opium,' she thought, "It induces sleep." She had been giving it occasionally to Amma. She would have to think of something else tomorrow. She brought Raghu a glass of milk and saw him gulp it down in one go.

"Raghu, I received an urgent call just now, I want you to go and drop this parcel at Jacob's Inn today." Anuraag's request shocked Raghu. 'Today?' he could see sweat break out on Raghu's face. "But you said you would be going tomorrow," muttered Raghu, "Besides it's getting late." "Take Sabita with you," said Anuraag. Sabita looked at her husband in surprise. "Does he suspect something?" she wondered, trying to read his face in the dark. "I want," she said, dropping her voice to a mere whisper and clutching his *kurta*, "I want to be alone with you. You wanted us to talk, remember?" "Obey me Sabita, just this once," Anuraag said, his voice flat. He saw the stricken look in her eyes, and then he thrust the parcel in Raghu's hands and saw Raghu reluctantly open the car door. If they were innocent, they had nothing to fear, Anuraag thought, as the car left the gate.

"I shall make Raghu stop at the first turning," thought Sabita, "I don't care what reasons I give, after the glass of opium laced milk, soon Raghu will not be in any state to drive." "I shall drive till the end of the road, and then stop the car, pretending that there is engine trouble, I know that the brakes will fail." thought Raghu, as he drove the car. He wondered why his eyes suddenly felt so heavy with sleep. He saw the truck coming before him, and Sabita's loud screams, as he tried vainly to press the tampered brakes.

The news of the crash came soon afterwards. Anuraag reached the spot on Raghu's motorcycle, and saw the car in flames. From the upstairs window, he had seen Raghu tamper with the car brakes, but he had expected Raghu to stop the car midway and return home on some pretext. He had not expected them to die. Perhaps Raghu had left it until too late. "Could it have," Anuraag thought with a twinge of guilt, "Really been an accident?" He thought not.

He heaved a long sigh. His dear mother, now dead, had given a hint him of what was happening, through a letter written by the maid Shanti. "Amma," he thought sadly, "Had been blind but not deaf." He had planned to talk to Sabita about the divorce. He did not know that it would end this way. He would have to stay back to tie up all loose ends, take care of the cremations and put up the house on sale. He looked at his open ticket in his hand and smiled. Within two weeks he would be back in Dubai with his precious Prakash, to whom he really belonged.

□

MY OWN PRISON

Not all prisons come with iron bars, locked doors and a high security wall. They are prisons nevertheless. The house I live in is one. It is a yellow, double-storied building with two dormitories, one large hall, a common room and an office. But it isn't a Working Women's Hostel. For me, it is a prison or a cage. I came here six months ago and I know I will get reprieve only four months later. But when I leave, I will not go scot-free. I will take the scars of the prison along with me. I look at my softly curving abdomen. I am five months pregnant. "Naina," the Warden calls out to me. I walk into the office. I see a man on the computer screen in front of me. He is talking to the Warden, on something called Skype. "So how is she?" he asks the Warden. The doctor, who is present, answers instead. "She is fine," she says eagerly, a tad eagerly, I think, though he is not talking to her.

I can feel his eyes following me. He turns his eyes towards me and I can feel his eyes raking me, even as he asks routine questions. "So Naina, how are you?" he says. "I am fine," I say shortly, although the Warden glares at me. I know she thinks I should be more polite. This man is paying me well for the job. And he is the father of my child. Sorry, he is the father of the child I carry in my womb, for the sake of money. "So the baby has started moving, has he?" he asks, his eyes focussed on my face, as they go down and linger on my breasts, and then move to my increasingly distended abdomen. "And the baby kicks, does he, like Ronaldo?" he laughs. I laugh uncertainly as well. I do not really know who Ronaldo is. I guess that he is someone who kicks. William did not stipulate a high general knowledge as a prerequisite, when he was looking for a surrogate mother. He just wanted someone young and healthy. And who could be younger and healthier than me? I am 19 and a virgin. If I was on the marriage market in some Islamic countries, I would fetch a high bride price.

"Put your hand on your belly," he commands. I want to bristle with indignation, but I know I can't. One lakh rupees of William's are in my bank account. The balance money needed to pay off the loan on our house in our village. "Now tell me, is the baby kicking?" he asks. "Yes it is," I say and wince, as indeed the foetus kicks hard. A smile spreads across William's face. It makes him look younger and nicer somehow. I am a little afraid of him, this man I have never seen, whose child I carry. "Single men should not be allowed to have children," I argue later. "Why not, if he can pay for them?" asks the doctor, "In any case, they are not using your gametes. You have nothing to fear. You are not the biological mother of the child."

Nothing to fear, she says. I know that I have everything to fear. I fear the thought of the delivery. I have never had a man touch my body. I have never had a man undress me. I have never felt the touch of male flesh. And yet, I will give birth to a child in four months. I do not really understand everything about a marriage and the first night, although I have heard Chachi and my other Buas giggle about it in the past. I remember how Manu had looked at me yearningly and I had pushed him away every time saying, "Not before our marriage." That was long before Amma died in the soap factory because of a machine malfunctioning and before Baba got run over by a bus, leaving him bed-ridden. It was before the Lala came to collect the money we owed him, on the loan we took from him, for constructing this house. That was before Sheela Bua told Baba about the Hostel in Mumbai where they would pay me two lakh rupees to have a baby. "Before marriage?" I had shouted, "I am not a whore," and they explained about surrogacy to me. "No man would ever touch you," they said, "It would be like the Immaculate Conception, like how Jesus Christ was born."

I know how Christ was born. I have been to school. I have passed Class XII. One day I had hoped to go to college. But that was before Baba had his accident.

Most mothers are thrilled with the wonder that is growing inside them, but not me. For me, things are running in reverse. I will become a mother long before I become a bride, if I become a bride at all that is. I look at myself and wonder. I will be a mother soon, though the child will not be mine. I know that they have used the gamete of a female donor. But right now he is thriving inside me. The doctor explained to me that the baby is inside a sac, which contains amniotic fluid, this child of William and a woman neither William nor I know. The child I will carry for nine months and will give away later.

In the hostel where I live, everything is restricted. We watch serials only for one hour every day. We often hear sermons of famous Swamis on different channels. "To keep our minds healthy and pure," I am told. I would like to watch action films like *Once Upon a Time in Mumbai, Gangster* or horror films like *Raaz*, *Raaz-II*, and *Raaz-III*. But the doctor says it is not good for the baby. And the doctor's word is final.

I have nausea every day. I throw up every morning and evening, even though the first trimester of pregnancy is long over. I eat everyday even after I throw up, because the payment I receive is linked to the growth of the foetus. I am told that if the baby's birth weight is more than 3.1 kilos, I shall receive Rs.10,000 as bonus. Perhaps I need not hand over this money to Baba. I could save it for my wedding. I could buy a red silk *saree* with *zardosi* work, like the ones I see in magazines, and dress up like a real bride. Manu would be in raptures if he sees me like that.

There are many questions which plague my mind. What will happen if something goes wrong during my delivery? What if I die? What if a caesarean section is required? I will have a scar on my body. A long vertical or maybe a horizontal scar, a dead giveaway that I have been a mother. I have seen Shanti Tai with that scar on her abdomen. Does Manu know where I am? Will he wait for me? Will he believe me when I tell him where I have been these past few months? Will the birth passage be loose after delivery? Will he suspect me of promiscuity?

There are questions and questions whirring in my mind. Everyday there are questions. Sheela Bua says I am lucky. In circumstances like mine, I could well be in a red light area for years, with a series of men as lovers, till I lose track of time and men. They would all become a blur, men who see me not as a woman but a piece of flesh.

I want to rebel against fate. I was born to be a girl, a beloved, a wife and then a mother. But for me, motherhood comes first.

Sheela Bua says I will be doing something noble by carrying this child. It is *"Punya ka kaam,"* according to her, giving birth to a child for someone childless. But her statement does not answer any of the questions that plague me. But I also have questions to you Baba. Why was I born a girl, Baba? And why was I born poor?

☐

SILENT NIGHT

The Collectors Conference was over at last. As the Valedictory Session ended, Charu heaved a sigh of relief. It had been difficult for her to keep her eyes open during the closing session. She wondered if it was the enervating heat, or the richness of the lunch, which was responsible for her near somnolent state. She remembered the lunch she had taken in the Shiv temple in Koraput. She had sat cross-legged on the floor, with all her colleagues and protested mildly as ladleful of rice, *dal*, *aloo baigan tarkari*, *ghanta tarkari, chutney* and, *papad* was served again and again, till she had wanted to curl up and sleep on the *chatai* itself. Slowly she walked out of the large hall where the conference was being held. She smiled as she saw the cars lined up outside the portico. Many of the collectors had planned to leave for their districts straight from the conference venue itself. She smiled as she saw Abhay's wife, her one year old baby in her arms, frantically looking for him. Further away, Vineet's wife, six months pregnant, was leaning by the car door, awaiting his arrival. For a moment, she felt something tug at her heart. All her colleagues had someone waiting for their return. There was no one waiting for her. An emotion, somewhat akin to self-pity, began to engulf her. Then she shrugged her shoulders and smiled. Everyone knew that she was married to her job. She could not imagine being just a housewife like Abhay's wife, with her life being just an eternal wait for her husband. She knew that if she juggled a job and a career, she would be able to do justice to none. And she was a perfectionist. She could bear nothing less than perfection. She slid into her car and returned to the Circuit House. She needed to rest. She had an eight hour long drive before her the next day.

When Charu arrived in the Circuit House, she slumped into the armchair. But even the A.C. in the room could not make her shed her listlessness. She decided to have a bath. "I must enjoy this old bath tub one last time," she thought as she entered it and let the warm water soak into her and draw out every vestige of tiredness from within her. Feeling refreshed, she stepped out of the bath, her long hair coiled on top of her head, and vigorously rubbed herself with the oversized towel which hung on the rail. "The towel is meant for someone who is at least six feet," she laughed to herself, "Someone like Abhay or Vineet, not for someone like me who is a diminutive 5 ft. 2 inches in height."

After her bath, she wore a cotton *salwar kameez* and suddenly the years rolled away from her. She looked and felt as though she was still in her teens. She looked at her watch. It was just 7 p.m. But she knew that she was the lone occupant of the Circuit House. All her other batchmates had been housed in the PWD Guest House. She was the only privileged one in the Circuit House, because she was a woman. This time she would have preferred company. Evenings could be very lonely. No one knew that better than her.

The lights went off suddenly and the room was plunged into darkness. 'Power cut?' Charu wondered, her eyebrows puckered. 'No,' she thought, shaking her head, "Probably a fuse had blown." She remembered watching the T.V. news at the same time the last evening. She looked out of the window. She could see the street lights. Suddenly, she felt an urge to feel the night air. "After my bath, I don't want to get soaked in this heat," she thought as she picked up her flashlight, opened the door and walked out.

The doorman saluted her smartly as Charu stepped out of the Circuit House gate into the street. She felt the wind blow onto her face. The monsoon was about to break. And about time too, she thought. It had been so hot and humid during the day. She began to walk slowly along the road. The road was deserted, except for a car parked at the end. The driver had put up its bonnet and had bent his head down. "Engine trouble," she ruminated. She knew nothing about cars, she laughed to herself. She knew nothing about most things mechanical. She walked slowly on the road, and then her eyes became riveted on the driver. He was oblivious to her presence, so engrossed was he in sucking out petrol and filling it in a jerry can. Suddenly, he lifted his head.

A sort of rage began to build within her. A rage that began as a constriction within her chest, and then began squeezing her ribcage. If she didn't know it better, she would have said that she was about to have a heart attack. She was scrupulously honest. Honesty was the badge she flashed around before everyone. She hated corruption. And yet her driver, her own driver Karan, was pilfering petrol from her official car. The rage which was constricting her suddenly erupted. She knew what she had to do. "Karan, just wait till we return to the district," she said, anger making her voice rise. He looked at her for a long time. He was guilty and yet there was something bold and brash about him. He seemed almost insolent when he said, "I am sorry Madam." He spoke the words as though they had no meaning and as though he was rendering the apology simply because, under the circumstances, the form had to be maintained. There was no iota of guilt on his face, she fumed, although she knew that even a heartfelt apology would not have mollified her.

"Come back to the Circuit House immediately," she said and without waiting for a reply, she began walking back. She could see the lights burning inside the Circuit House. "Thank God, the lights are back," she thought, "It would have been difficult to pack in the dark."

Once she reached the Circuit House, Charu ordered a quick dinner and rang up her subordinate in the District Collectorate. "I plan to suspend my driver," she said tersely, "Please have the order ready in the morning." 'Sir, Madam,' spluttered the voice at the other end, "Please do not travel at night, it is already late." "I am not afraid of the dark," she retorted.

An hour later she left Koraput by road. The driver started the car and almost as a reflex action switched on the car stereo. Her favourite song, '*Aa Bhi Jaa...Aa Bhi Jaa*,' by Lucky Ali began playing. Normally, she enjoyed the music. But today she was in no mood for relaxation. "Stop it," she shouted, and the driver turned around in surprise, on hearing the rage in her voice. He switched off the music immediately.

As she leaned against the backrest, Charu realized that her back had begun to ache. She could feel sharp needles of pain stabbing her back. "Long hours of travelling by car on bumpy roads have taken toll," the doctor had diagnosed, when she had visited him. She shrugged her shoulders in resignation. It couldn't be helped. The doctor had advised bed rest. But for her, work came first. She opened the car window and saw the star-studded sky. "The stars glitter like diamonds in a jewel case," she thought and then smiled as she realized how prosaic her simile was. "I am no poetess," she shrugged to herself, "I am a bureaucrat." She continued to look out of the window. She had never travelled on the *ghat* road in the dark. It was a different kind of experience. The moon seemed to glide across the sky. The moonlight seemed to have wrought magic in the air. She felt the tension ease a little. Suddenly, the car came to a halt. "Madam *torch hai*?" Karan asked. She reluctantly handed him the flashlight she always carried, in anticipation of an emergency.

"The car is too hot," he said, coming back to the window, "I need some water for the car." "Come on, didn't you carry any?" she asked. "You were in such a hurry Madam," he said quietly, "I simply forgot."

Karan then picked up the empty jerry can and went in search of water. "Where would he find water in the dark?" Charu wondered. She had no idea at all. This was not a well-traversed road. This was not her district either. She had come here only to attend the Collector's Conference. What madness had possessed her to undertake this journey at night? What madness indeed?

She recalled with dismay that the People's War Group (PWG) had attacked a post near Raigarh, not far away from where she was stranded. Her junior colleague had warned not to travel at night, but she had not listened to him. She never did listen to anyone. She was bold, confident, brash and headstrong. Now she added a new word to the list. 'Foolhardy.'

Suddenly, the skies opened up. Charu looked at the sky in surprise. She had never been able to get over the monsoon in Odisha. The lightning zigzagged crazily across the sky. The thunder rolled and rumbled loudly. She saw the rain splash hard against the windowpanes and splatter noisily on the car roof. Where there was silence a moment ago, now there was mayhem. She shrugged to herself and then shivered slightly. Earlier, to her, the monsoon had meant just a few showers of rain in July, which was over even before she found time to take out her synthetic *saree*s from her steel trunk. Suddenly, the downpour seemed threatening. The monsoon she had longed for, had arrived with a vengeance. She thought she saw a pair of eyes shining behind a bush. What sort of an animal was it? She thought with a shudder. A leopard? A bear? A wolf? She could feel the hair at the nape of her neck begin to rise. She felt goose pimples all over.

Then, at a distance, she saw someone walking towards the car. For the first time in her life Charu felt vulnerable, extremely vulnerable. She was not just an officer. She was also a woman. The words began to hammer in her mind. A young woman at that. And who knew better than her, about the crimes against women? The one thing she longed for now, was the warmth of her own bed and the security guard at the gate to ensure her safety and security. Why had she decided to return at night? She thought, cursing herself. To hell with the petrol. Who bothered about the theft of a few litres of petrol?

And then she saw him more clearly, as he walked towards the car. Karan's shirt was beginning to cling to his back. He looked at her and began to smile. She had never really noticed how wolfish his smile was. Then he walked towards her side of the car. She saw the look in his eyes and knew what he wanted. She saw the muscles rippling beneath his chest. Looking at him she guessed that his chest was rock hard. And then he opened, not the front door near the driver's seat, but the door next to hers. She stiffened in her seat, closed her eyes and started chanting mantras soundlessly. "If he dares to touch me," she thought, "I shall kill him."

"What can I do?" Charu thought to herself, keenly aware of her own vulnerability. Could she resist a man who was over six feet tall? All he had to do was to pinion her down on the seat with one hand and take her. Her shouts would be of no avail, for no one would hear her. There was no one walking on the road. And there were no vehicles nearby.

Rape. It was only a word she had heard. Now she was going to be a victim. "Not if I can help it," she thought to herself, as he opened the door. "What do you want?" she shouted at him, her voice hoarse. "Nothing Madam," he said, looking surprised at hearing her scream, "I want to take my towel and clothes, which I have kept underneath the front seat." So saying, he dunked his head and brought out the shirt and pant rolled in a towel and beneath a tree, his back towards her, he took off his shirt and began to dry himself with a towel. In the moonlight night, she saw his torso, with the muscles rippling, as he scrubbed it vigourously with a towel. She was unable to draw away her gaze from his body. At last she turned away, disgusted at her own behaviour.

Minutes later he was dressed and back in the car. This time when he switched on the stereo she said nothing.

It was 6 a.m. in the morning when they reached Ganjam. At ten o'clock Charu was back in office. Her instructions to her subordinate had been carried out meticulously. The suspension order of Karan was inside a file marked, "Most Urgent." She looked at it for a minute. "This was what I wanted, wasn't it?" she thought to herself. Just then Karan entered the room. 'Madam,' he said, folding his hands and looking chastised, "Please give me one more chance. I have three small children to look after." A minute later, the insolent grin was back on his face.

She saw his receding back and suddenly felt very tired. This was not the first time he had done it, she knew and this would not be the last. But suddenly she did not care anymore. For a moment she re-lived the nightmare of the night before, when her imagination had taken wings and filled her with dread. She was glad to be alive and safe. She took out the suspension order and tore it into shreds.

□

ILLUSIONS

Sita stood in the kitchen, chopping onions with mechanical precision, watching with satisfaction the growing mound of sliced onions, even when tears rolled down her eyes. Prateek entered the kitchen just then and said, '*Chalo Ma.*' 'Where?' she asked, taken aback by his sudden request, even as she put the wisps of hair which had fallen onto her forehead, back into place. "Oh Ma, Don't you remember? We are going to buy a new computer today." Ever since Prateek had learnt that his father was entitled to a computer loan under a new scheme launched by the Government in 1995, Prateek had been pestering his Dad for one. Two years later his father had agreed to Prateek's request and applied for a loan. "Well then go with your Dad, I know nothing about computers," she said, turning back to the chopping board. "Ma, Papa is insisting that you come along," Prateek cajoled.

"Oh well," she muttered aloud. She knew that Prateek's father was insisting on her accompanying him, so that if anything went wrong later on, he would say that as she was present, she was equally to blame!

"Give me a minute. Let me change my *saree*," she murmured. "No, the *computer mela* will close if you delay any longer," Prateek said. "Okay then," she said, running a comb through her open hair and tying her hair into a knot, "Let's go."

Prateek was almost jumping with joy at the prospect of buying a computer, and the twelve year old's enthusiasm began to affect her as well. As she sat in the car, their latest acquisition, whose purchase had been possible only because the price of second-hand cars had crashed and had begun to match those of new motorcycles, she heaved a sigh of relief at the thought that the days of riding pillion on her husband's scooter, with Prateek sandwiched between them, were finally over. She had always closed her eyes on these journeys, terrified on seeing the buses speeding towards her, as if ready to mow her down. For once she was enjoying the car ride, taking in the large billboards, advertising the latest films. Her husband drove carefully, the **L** sign displayed prominently at the back of the second-hand Maruti. She looked at her feet and felt a twinge of alarm. Her *chappals* were frayed at the edges. She had no time to change into her newly bought *sandals*. She then noticed a treacherous streak of turmeric running across her cotton *saree*. "Oh heavens," she muttered aloud, "Why did I ever listen to Prateek?" Suddenly, the car came to a stop outside a signboard which read 'Essex Farms.'

"You two go ahead, I'll meet you in half an hour," said her husband, before leaving. She looked at his retreating back in astonishment. He was leaving the purchase of the computer to her and Prateek? What was wrong with him? She relaxed when she saw Prateek enter the iron gates with great confidence, stride straight ahead, and then turn left toward a gaily-decorated entrance gate. "Prateek are you sure this is the venue of the *Computer Mela*?" she asked hesitantly, "There are too many people wandering around." "Of course I'm sure," said Prateek confidently as he took her by the hand, "I came here with Papa yesterday." She heaved a sigh of relief. Prateek and his Dad had probably shortlisted the models. She was here only to help them make the final decision.

"*Aapko kahan jana hai*?" the guard at the entrance gates rudely blocked their entry and asked. His eyes looked them up and down insolently. She was only too aware of her slippers, with their frayed edges and her turmeric streaked *saree*. "*Yeh Seth Kamal Kant ke bete ki shaadi ka reception hai*," he said condescendingly. "It is obvious," his manner seemed to imply, "That you can't be his guests." Prateek's face fell, not because of being belittled himself, but because the humiliation to which he had just subjected his mother. It did not matter that their destination was not the wedding reception, but the *computer mela*. They both knew that the guard had let the people before them enter, without asking them any questions. Prateek turned away from the gate, his shoulders drooping dejectedly.

Suddenly, a well-dressed young man with hazel eyes and curly hair strode towards them. 'Ma'am,' he said cheerfully, "Hindi Ma'am." 'Sanskrit,' she said softly and his face cleared, "Yes of course, Sanskrit Ma'am. Don't you remember me? I'm Nalin Kant. Shri Kamal Kant's younger son. You taught me Sanskrit in Class VIII." "Well Nalin, I'm afraid we've come to the wrong place," she confessed, "I thought this was the venue of the *Computer Mela*." "The Mela was held on these grounds yesterday, today it has been shifted inside the Hall," he said, "But while you are here you must bless the newly weds." She automatically started delving into her purse, hoping desperately that she would find at least five hundred rupees in it, but he understood her dilemma. "All they need is your blessings," he insisted.

Soon she was standing beside the beautiful blushing bride and the handsome groom and later sipping a coke and chatting with Nalin, while Prateek moved around happily on the lawns, digging his teeth into a succulent chicken tikka. A little later Prateek tugged at her *saree* and said, "The *Computer Mela* Ma, it will really close down if you delay any further." She broke away and said, "Nalin, I really must leave now." "I'll see you off," he offered as he walked with her upto the gate.

Prateek and she then went into the Hall where the *Computer Mela* was being held and Prateek chattered away about the merits and demerits of each model. She heard him absently, smiling to herself, her mind far away, and when he demanded to know her opinion, she happily endorsed the model Prateek had chosen. They reached the entrance gate of Essex Farms just as Prateek's father brought his car to a screeching halt. She slid into the front seat with a shuttered look on her face.

"Ma, I didn't know you had friends in high places," said Prateek curiously, "What were you two talking about?" She smiled vaguely and said, "This and that." What had they been talking about? She, with her photographic memory, had asked Nalin almost casually, “Which school did you study in Nalin?” “St. Columba’s,” the name had slipped out of Nalin’s lips before he realized it. “I teach in Kendriya Vidyalaya,” she had smiled. He had the grace to blush. “How did you guess?” he had asked her curiously, “You must have taught hundreds of students.” “I teach Physics,” she had said quietly, “Not Sanskrit.” He had almost done a double take on hearing this. Then she had asked him the one question that had been bothering her, “Why did you do this Nalin?”

“I was standing near the gate, when I heard the guard questioning you,” said Nalin. “I saw your son’s face crumple. I saw your face turn red. I could not bear to see you humiliated. So what if you weren’t my Hindi teacher. You reminded me of her. It’s just a chance I took.”

“Papa. Papa, do you know Mummy has taught the business magnate Kamal Kant’s son?” Prateek asked his father, his eyes shining. It had actually taken the shine off his recently purchased computer. “Thank you,” she said silently to a young man with hazel eyes and curly hair, “For protecting our dignity, saving our pride and for keeping my son’s illusion intact.”

□

THE TSUNAMI

Anu sat on the Marina Beach in Chennai, soothed by the vast expanse of sea before her, an incredible blue which seemed to stretch endlessly. The sea had a strange effect on her. She could feel the pull of the water, a strange magnetism which could draw her into its fold. She loved the sea in all its moods, Calm as a windless morning or choppy and turbulent like a tempest in fury. All her problems seem to shrink into nothingness, whenever she was at the beach.

For a long time she sat there, picking up a handful of sand and letting it slip through her fingers, like an improvised hourglass. She looked up at the sky, an infusion of blue and yellow, with streaks of grey and felt strangely rejuvenated. The sound of noisy footsteps broke into her chain of thoughts. She saw a bus parked by the roadside. A stream of children were disembarking from the bus and rushing onto the beach. She saw their white and red uniforms, with red cardigans and blazers and screwed up her face, trying to remember which school they were from. God, it had been five years since she had left India. Five years was a long time.

She got up and walked along the shore, away from the hordes of children, some of whom were shouting while playing with a ball. Others were playing Frisbee, and some others were simply running on the beach, their feet leaving tiny imprints on the sand. She wanted to get away from them. She needed solitude. Last night had been hectic. She had eaten her Christmas dinner with Sarah, her only Christian friend in the city. It had been a lavish meal, with chicken, potatoes, rice pulao, green *salad* and plum cake, washed down with white wine. “Sorry there is no turkey,” Sarah had shrugged, “It costs Rs. 2000.” Anu had sipped the wine, letting it give her a warm glow which had made her a little more talkative than usual, and left her with a mild headache in the morning.

She kept walking on the beach, and stopped when she saw a big shell, a luminescent shade of pink. Picking it up, she wiped it with the corner of her *tee shirt*. She saw a shrimp scurry alongside, before burrowing itself in the sand. Seeing the burrows on the sand she thought whimsically that the entire beach seemed like a giant sieve. Finally, she reached a solitary rock on the beach and sat on it, conscious of its dampness, which would no doubt leave an imprint on her jeans. She sat watching a boat with a big yellow sail sailing on the sea, fishermen perhaps, out in the sea for their first catch of the morning. She toyed with the cellphone in her hand. It was silent. She had brought it with her nevertheless, just in case he called.

She saw the wave when it came, a large foaming wave, reminding her of a hooded King Cobra. The white foam glistened in the winter sun, like sparkling crystals. She smiled. Undoubtedly, the wave would drench her, when it came to her with gigantic force. It would spray her with the foam, drenching her clothes. She didn’t mind getting wet. Her jeans were rolled up. Her T-shirt was old and faded.

The wave, when it came near her, took her by surprise. The snake had turned demonic. The wave was gigantic. The white foam had turned brown and the wave yawned and opened its gaping mouth, while she sat paralyzed on the rock, even as she heard children scream and run away from the beach. Then like a giant killer, it plucked her from the rock in a single swoop and sucked her into its vortex.

She heard the roar of water all round her and felt her hair being pulled away from her scalp. She experienced the drumming in her ears, as the salt water gushed into them. It was no gentle wave. It was a killer tidal wave. Much later she would learn what it was The Tsunami.

The end. Was this the end? She had said the same thing to herself a week ago when she had barged into Rajesh’s office and seen him coiled around Nina. Instead of being abashed or feeling guilty he had blustered, "It's over Anu, our marriage is over. I can't carry on like this anymore. I love Nina." With these words Nina, his secretary had found her rightful place on the chessboard of their lives as his white queen and said 'Checkmate' to her dreams. The black queen had been banished. No. The black queen had decided to bow out of the game. "I am returning home," she had said, not wanting to argue that five years of marriage could not be written off so easily, not wanting to plead for another chance to make their marriage work. How long did it take to pack a suitcase, toss in her clothes from the almirah, pick up her handbag and move into a friend's house? How long did it take to buy herself a ticket to India on the next available flight from O'Hare Airport in Chicago? She had done it within a week.

She didn't have to explain her sudden arrival in India to her folks in Chennai. She didn't even have to tell them the truth. All she said, when she arrived from the airport at 2 a.m. in the morning was, "I wanted to surprise you during Christmas!" No one was really surprised by her unexpected arrival. She was known for doing the unexpected.

"Stay calm," Anu told herself as she was tossed and buffeted around by the waves. Her life was not over then. It could not be over now. "Stay calm," she repeated to herself, trying to control the rush of panic, the sense of helplessness, the desire to give up on life, which threatened to engulf her. Her swimming instructor's lessons came back to her. "Take a deep breath and lie calmly on your back in the water. Tilt your head all the way back so that your ears are just under the surface of the water. Spread your arms out to your sides like an airplane. Do a light flutter kick with your legs. Relax. Breathe normally." It was impossible to do all that. It was impossible to breathe normally when her heart was thudding in her chest and her rib carriage was constricting her. But she tried. It was her only chance of survival.

Slowly she began to experience a sense of buoyancy. She left her body loose and began to float. But where was she? She had no idea. "Think cheerful thoughts," she said to herself. "This is not the sea. This is a bed. A water bed." Her dream bed, which she had yearned for but never purchased. "Too expensive," Rajesh had shrugged and refused to buy her the one thing she had set her heart on. A bed where love making would be like making love on the waves. She thought of Rajesh and involuntarily her lips curved into a smile. She thought of their love making, that feeling of euphoria, which began as a slow fire in her limbs, stoking flames which reached her heart, her head and her pelvis. She thought of the aftermath, cuddling in the nook of his arm, the warmth of the sun filtering through the window during winter mornings, turning the world into a golden molten liquid. She closed her eyes. The water had turned cold. The skies had darkened. Was it night time? Her cellphone was lost. Water clogged and rain soaked, it would lie on the beach somewhere, and she would be unable to talk to Rajesh when he called. If he called.

Lucky Rajesh, she thought to herself. He would not need a divorce now. Her poor parents. She imagined them, both her mother and father searching the Marina Beach in Chennai for bodies. She imagined her mother, turning around the bodies on the beach and murmuring, "Anu Anu…" and her father, a defeatist droop to his shoulders, saying, "Come back Janaki, do you think anyone could have survived this killer wave?"

Anu closed her eyes. The reality she faced was too grim. Her chances of survival were very slim. She sought escape in fantasy. She became a mermaid who had been swallowed by a large whale. She was waiting for her saviour to cut open the whale and rescue her. She was a fairy princess who lived underwater in glass palace where the ogre had confined her. She suddenly remembered that this is what he called her, 'My fairy princess.' She was just six years old. He was the prince, who lifted her and carried her over his shoulders, who tickled her and made her laugh. He was the prince. No, the ogre, who introduced her to games, "Just between 'you and me.' We won't tell Mummy, will we? She will not like it." He was the ogre who took her into the attic and undressed her when her mother had gone to the temple and her Dad was at work. He was the ogre who slobbered over her with wet kisses, like her bulldog Danny, and said, "Do you like it? like it? like it?" his body touching her in places where no one else did. He had died two years later, in a motorcycle accident and everyone had cried including her mother and father and wondered who would take care of Anu now that her father's younger brother was dead. She had not known what had been happening to her until as a fourteen year old she had read, for the first time, about molestation, rape and child sexual abuse.

No one knew of the enormous sense of guilt she had carried all through her teens. "It's my fault, it must be my fault, I must have deserved it, I shall deserve whatever bad happens to me in future." This became her mantra. It was guilt which had let her allow people to trample all over her, and allowed Rajesh to say, when she had caught him with his white queen Nina, "I cannot help it, Anu, if you are frigid."

Anu woke up hours later, still afloat at sea. The sun was up. Where was she now? In the Bay of Bengal or the Indian Ocean? She was still drifting like a piece of driftwood, now on the verge of exhaustion, her energy dissipated. She never knew she would reach a point when she would actually welcome her end. She decided that she would not cry now. She had not cried when Rajesh had shouted, "Over, it's Over," as though marriage was a tennis match they had been playing.

Just then Anu saw a boat surging towards her and grabbed it, only because she was afraid that it would collide with her. But she managed to hold on to it. She waited for helping hands to bring her on board. But no one came forward. Slowly and painfully, she raised herself and then crawled into the boat. She saw a yellow and white sail on the boat. Was it the boat she had seen in the distance while sitting on the beach? She did not know. But this was not a fishing boat. Perhaps someone had gone sailing that morning. There was no one on the boat. They must have toppled over, or perhaps the wave had simply plucked them from the boat, as it had plucked her from the shore. She searched the boat and found a blanket, wrapped in polythene. She stripped off her clothes, which clung to her like a second skin and wrapped the blanket around her. Her teeth started chattering, whether from the cold or from fear, she did not know. Hunger began to gnaw at her. Her lips were parched and dry. She rolled her tongue over them and felt her cracked lips. For how many days has she been afloat? She had no clue. She had lost track of time. Slowly, she clenched her lower lip and began to lick her blood.

She did not realize when she had dozed off. When she woke up she had a blinding headache. She was dehydrated. She felt drained of energy but raised herself on her elbow and spied a bottle which had rolled away. She opened it, smelt it and touched the liquid. Water. She began to drink thirstily and then realized that she needed to ration it. She let a few drops of water roll down her parched throat. For the first time, she realized that she had a chance of survival. She smiled.

She was rescued by a passing boat which brought her to Nagercoil. One day later her mother and father were by her bedside at the city hospital. "You're alive," said her mother, in a voice which said that she had begun to believe in miracles once again. A week later she was discharged from the hospital.

When she was back at home in Chennai, she received the call she had been waiting for. "It's for you," her mother smiled, "It's Rajesh." "Where was Nina of the silicone implants, the talon-like nails and the purring smile?" she wondered. 'Anu,' said Rajesh, his voice raw with emotion, "You don't know how much I missed you." She shook her head. Nina was definitely not by his side. "Thank God you are alive," said Rajesh, sounding overwrought, "It was only after I thought that I had lost you that I realized how much you mattered to me. Let us forget what happened in the office. Please come back to me."

She thought of the sun drenched mornings and the cold nights she had lived through, in the preceding week, when she had been at one with the elements, the stars, the sun, the moon and the wind. Before them Rajesh and Nina were no more than mere specks in the ocean. The future did not hold any threats for her anymore. There was something elemental about the Tsunami. It had taken its toll, she learnt in the hospital. Thousands had died in India, many more had died around the world. But she had survived. She had survived three days of battering at sea, while battling for her life. It had hurt her body but cleansed her soul. It had taught her about the limitless dimensions of life. “Come back,” said Rajesh once again, “I can’t live without you.” “But I can,” she said to Rajesh, before putting the phone down.

□

THE TEMPEST

The New Delhi Railway Station was overflowing with people. She found it difficult to keep pace with Amit as he strode onto the platform, looking curiously out-of-place in it. She thought, "His place is at the airport lounge, where he can rest on the leather sofa, flick the ash from his lighted cigarette and relax. Not among the jostling crowd." She virtually had to run, to keep pace with Amit. It was easier to keep the coolie in sight, who lumbered ahead with her suitcase and strolley bag.

'AC First Class.' Amit's voice held unconscious snobbery as he gave directions to the *coolie*. Once she would have mistaken it for class. "*Yahein aayegee Saa'b*," the *coolie* informed Amit as they waited for the train to arrive. The smell pervading the railway station then hit her. The smell of the talcummed baby who had burped and spilt milk on his father's shoulders, the smell of the lady who was enveloped in a cloud of deodorant, which contrasted sharply with her unkempt hair and unwashed neck, the smell of samosas fried in rapeseed oil, which the vendor carried on his head, the smell of spicy chole, boiled in soda, garnished with onions, slivers of ginger and slit green chillies and above all the smell of sweat which hung heavily in the air. There was something very comforting about people, she thought, and being part of the crowd. It helped ease the tension, which always existed between Amit and her. "Wait here," said Amit as he disappeared towards the notice board, to check out her reservation. "You've got the small coupe," he said with satisfaction on his return, "You are sharing it with someone called Priya."

The train was twenty minutes late. "We are fifteen minutes before time as it is," he said angrily. She heard his raised voice and looked away. She had been taught by her grandfather to reach the railway station well in time, while Amit preferred to catch a train at the last possible minute. "You know how much I hate waiting at the station," he muttered, taking out a cigarette from his pocket. "I had suggested taking the flight, you know," she said mildly, "Especially as this is a two night journey." "You know I hate flights," he retorted. She shrugged her shoulders. Amit's job took him away very often, on many flights, all over the world. Perhaps he had a fear of flying, but that had not prevented him from leaving home almost every month. This was the first time she was going away from home, ever since he was posted in Delhi, and that too to Trivandrum. What perversity had made him insist on her taking a train? And why had she agreed to his suggestion? She had no answer to that.

The train entered the platform at last. Amit strode confidently into the AC First Class compartment and opened the coupe marked 'C.' He was surprised to find that it was already occupied by a man. He had a thin sensitive face, with flecks of grey on his temples. His glasses kept slipping off his nose, which he absent-mindedly pushed back. "I think ours is the lower berth," said Amit, his voice acquiring an aggressive tone, which it usually did when throwing a challenge. "That's right," said the occupant mildly as he continued to read a magazine.

"Shall I open your suitcase for you?" muttered Amit, not looking at her and without waiting for a reply he opened it and took out a bed sheet and pillow. She knew that the Railways would supply their own sheets and pillows. But she also knew why Amit was doing so, he wanted the other occupant to go to the upper berth immediately. The man however refused to take the hint.

Instead, he looked pointedly at the instructions on the compartment wall, which clearly stated the bed should be folded between 6 a.m. and 9 p.m.

Amit followed his gaze and had the grace to blush. He then stood looking helpless, looked at his watch and asked, "Are you carrying any magazines?" She shook her head. "I'll get you some," Amit said, glad to escape from the coupe, which had suddenly become claustrophobic. He returned five minutes later, with an arm load of magazines. It took her one glance to see that she had read all of them. They had stood in the magazine rack for days. But he had never known that.

"When will you be back?" his words, uttered casually, hung in the air. "I don't know," her response was automatic. But he seemed surprised and looked questioningly at her. "It all depends on Papa's health," she reminded him. He seemed to have forgotten that her father had suffered a heart attack and was now to undergo bypass surgery. Perhaps Amit was thinking of other things, like their last fierce quarrel.

Amit looked at his watch again. "Please go before the train starts," she urged him. He left, relieved to make his escape, with just a cursory glance at her. She wondered whether he would miss her at all, or would he feel an overwhelming sense of relief at her departure. The train gathered speed as it left the platform. She had a long journey ahead of her, two nights and one day. The flight would have taken her four and a half hours. But arguing with Amit was impossible. She hadn't wanted to argue with him anyway.

She settled back on the berth, immersed in her own thoughts. Her life need not have been the way it was. She had wanted to spend it differently, with the man of her choice, with a man who loved her. "I want to marry him," the moment she had told her father this, all hell had broken loose. "Who, that loser? No never," her father had said in strangled tones. "But he isn't a loser, this is he wants from his life. To bury himself in books, to teach, to write a book that touches your heart and mine. His poetry drives me to tears. I can sit at his feet and listen to him for hours. He may never be rich but I know it in my bones that he will become famous. And I know that we would be happy together."

But she never spoke these words. In her father's book, the daughters of businessmen did not marry teachers. They married rich. They were decked in gold and diamonds. In her father's world, daughters did not argue with their fathers, especially when they were second among four daughters, with two sisters yet to get married. In the world in which she lived, daughters bowed their head and accepted their parent's *diktats* as their destiny. She was a model daughter and so did she.

Five years of marriage were enough to teach her what was true unhappiness. Five years which began on her wedding night, when Amit stumbled into bed and snored. In a way, it was a relief, but it was also a disappointment, because it signified rejection. It was a relief because although she had taken the *seven pheras* around the sacred fire with Amit, it was Ranjan in her consciousness. Whenever Amit took her she had only to close her eyes and imagine that it was Ranjan and Amit's brutality would become passion, the violence urgency, the lust love. Luckily, Amit did not expect any response or ardour from her, because she knew instinctively that in his book wives were expected to suffer love making passively, without responding to it.

She suddenly aroused herself from her reverie and looked at her watch. It was just 8 p.m. There was still a long time to go before she could settle for the night. There was a perfunctory knock at the door and then the ticket collector entered the coupe. "Your name caused much confusion," he said humorously to her fellow passenger. She hung her head and blushed. Obviously, Amit had created a fuss and taken up the issue with the ticket collector. Her co-passenger smiled and said, "My name is Priya Ranjan actually."

Half-an-hour later there was another knock on the door and a waiter came in. 'Dinner,' he announced, in that sing-song voice waiters always assume while serving food. The waiter attached small tables and served tomato soup in large bowls along with soup sticks. The waiter looked at both of them curiously. She took a sip. The soup was delicious, with butter floating on top. She saw Priya Ranjan dip and then crunch a soup stick in the soup bowl.

"Going home?" he asked her conversationally. 'Yes,' she said, "How did you guess?" "Well since you left your husband behind, you could only be going home." "What is your name?" she asked, 'Priya Ranjan,' he said although he had mentioned it to the Ticket

Collector a few minutes ago. She appeared to be shocked. "I knew someone by that name," she said evasively. "The name does not have a very happy association for you, does it?" he said shrewdly, "Why do you say that," she muttered. "I saw your reaction when you said the name," he responded. She knew that he was very perceptive. She fell silent. She toyed with her soup, but he ate it with apparent relish.

The waiter entered the coupe once again with the next course. *Parantha subzi*. "Not for me," she demurred. But when the waiter brought chicken biryani, she relented. Each grain of rice was done to perfection and the chicken was tender and succulent. Her neighbour was eating it with great relish. "You know," he said suddenly, "I've never travelled in AC First Class before," 'Really,' she said, "One would never have guessed." "Now you are snubbing me," he laughed, "I can't afford it, but this is a special occasion."

"Let me guess, the publication of your first novel?" she hazarded. "How did you guess?" he asked, and she laughed. Then she felt silent. She had never felt so light-hearted in years. She felt as though she had shed the cloak of seriousness which surrounded her. This is how it had been with Ranjan.

Make belief. She and Ranjan had indulged so much in make belief. "That isn't real life," said her best friend Mala. "Life isn't just witty lines and humour. It is much more."

Not like the other world she now lived in. The world of the perfect marriage. She knew all about it. She remembered the red tell tale mark on Amit's shirt, which was not made by her shade of lipstick. Her confrontation with Amit. Her finding the packet of condoms in his air bag and her recalling his assertion that he hated using them. Her leaving them prominently on the drawing room table, to tell him she knew, but receiving no explanations and no answers.

The rancour. The hatred. The fear. Was this how her future would be? His life packed with half-truths and lies, with bottles of rum, packs of cigarettes and packs of beer. Was this how their life would be? An arid, air-conditioned one, full of lies? With their lives intertwining only at night. Once a week.

She remembered their last quarrel. She had rung him up in his hotel room, after learning of her father's heart attack. A woman had answered the phone at 2 a.m. in the morning.

She has confronted him on his return. He had sneered and said, "So what? You're hardly in a position to talk. I know all about you and Ranjan." She remembered her stunned disbelief at his accusation and her fervent denial about their physical relationship. He had said cryptically, "How do I know?"

The dinner was over, but soon after a man entered the coupe, bringing the bed sheets, pillows and blankets. He started making their beds. "*Baahar toofan aa raha hai*" (there's a storm outside) he said conversationally. "*Bahut baarish bhi ho rahi hai.*" (It's raining heavily too). After making their beds he left.

She got into bed and pulled the blanket upto her chin. She heard her co-passenger move out of the coupe. Must be going to change, she thought. She shut her eyes.

After some time, the door slid open. Her co-passenger entered the coupe. The crisp *kurta-pyjama* suited him. He turned off the light.

For an interminable period, he stood still. Then he was beside her, pulling her to him. "I didn't want to do it this way. Not here. Not like this. But I've waited too long. And we have such little time."

Two nights and a day, she thought, as she traced his dear familiar face. So long she had dreamt about this, about holding him, touching him and loving him.

She didn't know what lay ahead. What if her father died? What if he didn't? Would she have the courage to leave Amit? At least her younger sisters were married, she thought wryly. She could no longer be accused of ruining their lives.

Once she'd made a choice. A wrong one. But she had been young. Just twenty years old. She was older now and capable of tackling life.

She turned her thoughts to Ranjan, whom she had met accidentally a few days before. With him she had felt as though she had come home. She had mentioned her travel plans to him, hoping that he would join her. Nights of anticipation followed. Also of dread, at the thought of transgressing the bounds of her marriage.

Outside, the storm raged on. Rain lashed. Thunder rolled in the distance. As she arched her body to meet his, she knew it could never match the tempest that raged within her.

□

SPIDER'S WEB

I had a nightmare that night. I woke up, drenched in sweat, my heart pounding and my pillow wet. I slid out of bed and went quietly out of my room onto the front door and then slowly walked down the stairs. God I needed air, I was beginning to suffocate. Anger raged in my body like an erupting volcano. 'Witch,' I said aloud, 'Witch.' From a distance, I heard footsteps. Hers. I saw her jogging down the road towards India Gate. I glanced at my watch. It was five o'clock. There was not a soul in sight, on that cold, winter morning. I took up a stone, polished it with my pullover and hurtled it with all my might at the Red Maruti Deluxe on the road. The stone hit the windscreen and plopped down onto the gravel. I ran towards the car and saw the glass begin to crack…in concentric circles…like a spider's web. Or like the contour lines in my atlas. I was excited. Revenge. I had taken revenge. I had destroyed the one thing close to her heart, her car. I remembered how excited she had been when she had purchased it. Wicked woman.

Wicked, a home breaker, a tramp. I knew what I was talking about. I had read her letter to Papa. Of course, Papa did not expect that I would enter his room and rifle through the contents of his briefcase. Nor could he imagine that I could even hazard a guess about the combination. And I hadn't a clue really. I would never have guessed that the number of the combination was 983. It was my friend Babloo who had told me that it was possible to turn around the numbers and hear a special clicking sound when the actual numbers tumbled into place. I had merely wanted to check it out. So when Papa was away and Ma was taking a nap, instead of preparing for my Physics test, I had decided to see if Babloo's theory worked. It did. As the briefcase had swung open, I had instinctively gone through it and seen the blue envelope. It had taken just one page to make my world collapse. The letter was addressed to Papa by Smita. I spat out her name. Smita, the woman who lived upstairs, who worked in the same office complex as my father, who went jogging around India Gate and who drove her red Maruti to work. A shudder passed down my frame at the thought of my poor mother, oblivious of it all, her spectacles perched on her nose, spending her time correcting answer scripts.

And Smita, that witch, calling Ma '*Bhabhi*,' while carrying on an affair with my father, dropping in occasionally to borrow sugar or to return it or simply to chat with Ma on Saturday afternoons. Now I knew why she was in and out of my house so often.

At 9 o'clock, I was standing at the balcony when I saw Smita Sinha walk towards her car. She was dressed in a crisp pink *saree* with a black border, and a pink blouse to match. I saw diamonds glittering in her ears. I had never seen diamonds in Ma's ears, even though she too was a working woman. Ma's salary simply went in paying bills and buying things for the house. I now knew where Papa's salary went.

"Oh No," Smita Sinha screeched as she saw the damage to her car. I saw my father rush down the stairs, his briefcase in hand. "What's the matter?" he asked. "Oh Mr. Mathur, some one has shattered my windscreen," she sobbed. "The ruffian," said Papa, gnashing his teeth, "If I knew who he was, I would give him the thrashing of his life." His anger seemed to calm her down. "Never mind," she said fatalistically, "These things happen." "Must be some urchin from the servant quarters. These people…" she let her voice trail off. "Ah well, I am sure the insurance will pay for the damages," said Papa philosophically.

"But how do I go to office?" she asked suddenly. "Come on, I will drop you in your office, don't forget that we work in the same office complex," my father murmured. I gnashed my teeth in anger. I had not realized that by smashing her car, I would bring my father and the witch closer.

I went back into the house, looking crestfallen. My mother was sitting in the drawing room, with answer scripts littered on the table. Her glasses were perched on her nose. Strands of grey escaped from her loosely made bun. For a fraction of a moment I thought that I couldn't really blame my father if his interest wandered. The next minute I chided myself for my disloyalty. I thought of my mother being chained into the kitchen where Papa had neglected to put an exhaust fan. I had seen Ma, her blouse drenched in sweat, making *mathri* and *vadas* for evening snacks, when all Papa was doing was carrying on an affair with Smita.

'Ma,' I said, "your hair has begun turning grey, why don't you dye it?" "Why! Don't you like your mother because she is getting old?" she teased. "It's not that," I said, putting my arms around her, "But Papa may not like it." "Your Papa never liked anything about me but I refuse to change," she retorted, sprawling a little more into the sofa. I could see the rolls of fat on her midriff and wondered what Papa thought of that. Papa who went to the gym for a workout, who went to Lodi Gardens for jogging, who thrived on soups and salad, who was so different from Ma.

I was out on the lawn playing cricket when Papa returned from office and Smita slid out of the front door of the car. I hadn't realized that Papa would give her a lift on his return as well. I saw her clutch her briefcase and Papa say, "Leave it, I will bring it up." Papa's gesture merely fuelled my hatred towards her.

As I saw them climb the stairs, laughing together, I realized that I had never seen Ma and Papa laugh together. I had not seen them talk much to each other. I had seldom seen them go out together. Yet here was Papa, laughing light-heartedly, his face lit up like a 100 watt bulb. "Hi Rahul," Smita Sinha said, seeing me in the corridor, "See I have got something for you." She opened her purse and fished out a bar of Amul Chocolate. I understood instinctively. Amul Chocolate. A gift for someone you love. She must have bought it for Papa, not knowing that he was a borderline diabetic. And now she was passing it off as a present to me. Her gesture merely fanned the flames of my anger towards her.

"There must be something I can do to put a stop to it," I thought. "Get her out of the way somehow. Permanently." That night as I lay in my room, I covered my face with a bed sheet and thought. In order to plan, I had to know her routine. I knew she was very health conscious. She went for a morning walk at five a.m. in the morning. And it was still dark until then. I began to keep a check on her. Every morning at five a.m. her door would open and she would climb down the stairs in a rush, her rubber soles making almost no sound. She would return by five past six or ten past six. I tried to formulate a plan. The simple plans were the best. And I knew I had thought of a perfect plan. I hoped I could execute it as well. I had been watching 'The Omen,' on TV that night, which had given me the idea of leaving a toy on the top of the stairs, when she went for a morning walk at five a.m. in the morning. Accidents were known to happen.

At precisely five o'clock, I heard her begin to bolt her door before locking it. I rushed down the steps and switched the mains off. The staircase, well-lit a moment ago, plunged into darkness. I crept back slowly to the first floor. There was complete silence upstairs. She must be wondering whether to go down, or return to her house. I had not thought of this eventuality. A little later I heard her footsteps in the corridor. I thought of the little toy I had placed strategically on the top of the staircase. I hoped that she would step on it and stumble.

I heard her piercing scream and was one of the first persons in the apartment building to run out, in time to switch on the mains without anyone noticing. I found her crumpled in a heap at the bottom of the stairs. Dead. Quite dead.

I was a murderer. A murderer at the age of twelve. I felt nothing at the thought, nothing at all. No guilt. No regret. No gloating. No exultation. What had I done after all? Just placed a toy on the staircase. Any one could have dropped it by mistake. As for the lights, they went off and came on in Delhi all the time.

The arrival of the police unnerved me momentarily. "Whose toy was it?" asked the Inspector, once everyone had assembled downstairs in stunned silence. "It was mine," I admitted, looking at the toy motorcycle in the Inspector's hand. "I must have dropped it while coming down the stairs, after playing with it on the terrace," I said, tears springing into my eyes, "Oh! Inspector, I am responsible for her death." "It was an accident," murmured the Inspector kindly, patting my head, "You are not to blame." Turning towards Ma he whispered, "Madam, see to it that he doesn't feel guilty about the accident."

I waited at home to watch my parent's reaction to her death. Papa was upset, but not unduly. 'Poor Smita,' he said, "She was a good neighbor. You will miss her Jyotsana." 'Yes,' Ma nodded, "I make friends very rarely and she was a friend." I looked at Ma pityingly. How little did she know the truth about Smita, I ruminated.

Six months later, I received a shock. Papa and Ma came and sat by my bedside. She held me and said, "I don't know if it will come as a shock to you Rahul, but your Papa and I are getting divorced." I couldn't believe my ears as I heard the dreaded words. "Why? Why?" I repeated the words again and again, my face ashen. Again it was my mother who spoke. "We were just an incompatible couple. We had irreconcilable temperamental differences. We could have divorced years ago, but we didn't, for your sake." "So why do you need to get divorced now?" I whimpered. "Because now your father has found someone else," said my mother gently "and once our divorce comes through he wants to get married again."

"Who is she?" I asked, my throat turning dry, "Whom does Papa want to marry?" "No one you know," again it was Ma who answered, "it is a colleague in his department called Smita."

That night, when my mother came to check on me, she saw my pillow wet. She thought it was natural under the circumstances. She hugged me and said, "There is no need to be sad Rahul. I am glad, I am really glad that it is over. I had become tired of this life of pretence." But she did not know that my tears were not for her. They were for myself and the burden of guilt that had begun to eat me up. And the long years of pretence that lay ahead of me.

I had a nightmare that night. And the next night. And the night after that….

□

CHARADE

The drumming in her head grew louder. Shweta felt the tension headache come on. She knew that it was anxiety which was causing her headache. Her eyes were fixed at the door, waiting for the doorbell to ring. She sat in her room, mentally rehearsing what she would say to Sameer. "What would he say?" she wondered, when she heard the doorbell ring. She opened the door, her face tense. "What is it," Sameer asked, "What's the matter?" 'Sameer,' she said, her voice faltering, "I have a problem." "What is it?" he repeated, his voice concerned. "Sameer," she whispered, "I'm pregnant." She saw the colour drain from his face, and her stomach muscles tightened in fear. Her fate seemed to hang in balance. What would he say? Would he say, "It's your fault, you said you would take care of things?" Would he gently suggest abortion as the way out. Or would he say, and she almost felt a gut wrenching pain at the very possibility, "Whose child is it anyway?" No he couldn't say that, Shweta said to herself, they had been in a physical relationship for two years now. Then she saw Sameer make an effort to smile. "We'll get married of course," he said, putting his hand into hers. "Oh Sameer," she said, bursting into tears, "But you said you wanted to wait till we had saved some more." "Shweta I would have liked to wait," he grinned, "But apparently the little one did not." He put his hand on her shoulder, pulled her gently from the bed and said, "Let's us go out and celebrate."

"I'm sorry," said Shweta, as they sat in the tiny restaurant across the Working Women's Hostel where she stayed. "For what?" he asked, ruffling her hair gently. "For upsetting your plans," she confessed. No one knew better than her that he wanted to save for at least three years, so that they could have a house and a car of their own when they began their married life. She had agreed with him. Part of her earnings as a lecturer and most of his savings from his corporate job went into saving for the future. Life had become quite Spartan, but he had assured her that the sacrifice was worth it. Shweta was besieged by fears and insecurities since as a Management Executive, he was required to tour frequently.

Shweta looked at him anxiously, seeking reassurance. Sameer looked into her eyes and said, "Shweta in a way I am glad that we are getting married. This relationship had been less than fair to you. You have been so patient about it, putting your dreams on hold, and not complaining at all." She saw the concern in his eyes and broke into a fresh bout of tears, thinking that if he had said all this a year ago she wouldn't have felt so insecure. For a year, she had been assailed by doubts which plagued her constantly. "What if he changed? What if his feelings changed?" Feelings were transient anyway. What if one day Sameer said, "Shweta, this relationship isn't working out anymore, we are growing apart," or "Shweta, I am sorry, but I have found someone else." She knew that he loved her but the fact that marriage was not a part of his immediate plans had torn her apart.

"Vinnie, what do I do now?" Shweta asked Vinnie anxiously the next day, as she sat in Vinnie's one bedroom apartment. "What do you mean?" Vinnie raised her eyebrows. "Sameer has agreed to marry me but what shall I do nine months later when the baby doesn't come along?" Shweta persisted. Vinnie laughed and said, "Shweta if you could fake a pregnancy, why not an abortion as well?" Shweta shuddered, "I don't think I could." "Why not?" retorted Vinnie, "Miscarriages happen every day."

"Shall we have a registered wedding?" Sameer asked Shweta a few days later. She looked at him in surprise and realized that he was concerned about her and had suggested a low-key wedding, so that their relations would not count the gap between their wedding and the birth of their child. "If only you knew the truth, Sameer," Shweta thought, guilt burning down her throat like a corrosive poison. "A registered wedding would be just right," she said wanly.

Their wedding was attended by a handful of people. It took just a few signatures to pronounce them man and wife. What had changed, she wondered, when she shifted into Sameer's apartment, except that she had given up her room in the Working Women's Hostel and now shared his cupboard as well? If she was not delirious with happiness, it was because she knew that she had built her happiness on a lie. Sameer attributed her lack of enthusiasm to her delicate health.

Two weeks after their wedding Shweta went to Meerut to visit her parents. From there, she rang Sameer up and sobbed, "Sameer, I am truly sorry, but I have aborted the baby." "I am coming down immediately," he said, and true to his words, within two hours he was in Meerut. He found Shweta pale with exhaustion and anxiety. She saw Sameer's face crumple with grief, his eyes looking tortured at the thought that she had lost the baby. Sameer's grief was genuine. Hers was fake. What could she say to him? "Never mind Sameer, we shall have more children." Or could she confess, "Sameer there is no need to grieve, this is not really the death of your dream child. This is merely the price I extracted from you for sharing your bed before marriage?" She couldn't tell him the truth because she lacked courage. He held out his arms to her and suddenly she was clinging to him and crying because of her lies, her deceit and also because of his faith in her.

Five years later as she sat on the front lawn of her house, she thought contentedly that life had been kind to her. Sameer had risen in his company and was now a General Manager in Hindustan Unilever. She was now a permanent lecturer in Delhi and had just submitted her Ph.D. thesis. Their happiness was marred by just one cloud. They had no children. She felt as though the Gods had finally extracted revenge from her, for the charade. He was however, not troubled at all by the absence of children. He knew the children would come one day. Shweta's anxiety turned into guilt when they celebrated their fifth wedding anniversary and suddenly she wanted to consult a doctor. "I shall come with you

Shweta, for your complete medical check-up," Sameer offered immediately, willing to allay her fears. Dr. Chabbra, the gynaecologist offered to run a series of tests for them. Once the results were in, she called them over. "It is bad news I am afraid," she said to them, her face serious. Even before she said it, Shweta could gauge from the bleakness of her expression what the verdict was. "Sameer I am afraid the tests show that you are sterile," Dr. Chabbra murmured, saying something about the possibility of his having contracted mumps during adolescence, which had left him sterile. Shweta closed her eyes on hearing the doctor, feeling the tears sting her eyes. She knew this was divine justice or divine retribution. But she heard Sameer say "That's impossible doctor. Five years ago Shweta was pregnant, in fact that is why we got married earlier than we had planned." He turned to look at Shweta for confirmation. She hung her head, unwilling to look into his eyes and utter that lie which he wanted to hear. "Shweta had a miscarriage later," he said in answer to the doctor's unspoken question. The doctor sat in tight- lipped silence, her face judgmental and her expression grim. It did not take a genius to guess what she was thinking, thought Shweta, her heart sinking. The gynaecologist looked at Sameer with pity. An unexpected pregnancy and a convenient abortion. She had seen many cases like that. "It is medically impossible," she told Sameer. "Whose child were you carrying?" her eyes accused Shweta. Sameer walked out of the room in silence, his shoulders hunched.

'Sameer,' Shweta said hesitantly, as they got into the car, "It was a charade. I had faked the pregnancy only to marry you. I was afraid that one day you would tire of me and leave. I wanted to have strings to bind you with. I later faked the abortion as well." "You believe me, don't you?" she asked, her voice raw with anxiety. His shoulders were hunched, his eyes were bleak and infinitely sad. She saw him mouth a silent 'Yes.'

But she knew, that despite his answer, he would always be besieged by doubts and there would always be times when he would look at her and wonder.

□

OF HOPE AND DESPAIR

The silence in the car seems deafening. I look at Sneha surreptitiously as I drive. Her lips are set in a straight line. She is looking straight ahead. She does not give me even a sidelong glance. Her dimples, which I love, are not at display. Her high cheek bones seem even more prominent than before. She looks stern, stiff and unbending. This is not how an eighteen year old should behave. I would have preferred to see her with her head thrown back, eyes crinkling with laughter, either on the cellphone or glued to her iPad. That is how our earlier journeys had been. But those had been shopping trips, or weekends spent at a resort, or a night at the movies. We didn't have the question 'what if?' hanging before us.

My stomach is tied up in knots. I can almost feel my heart thudding loudly. I know what is plaguing me. I am afraid. What if my fears turn out to be true? I know that it will break Sneha's heart. I can almost see her dreams crumble and come crashing down. For the past eighteen years I have tried my best to see that her eyes never fill up with tears and I have almost succeeded in my task. But after what I am doing to her she may just end up hating me.

I steal a glance at her once again. Her hazel eyes are staring straight ahead. I don't think anyone in my family had hazel eyes. Nor in Hemant's family. Himanshu too has hazel eyes. That is where it all began. My doubts, fears and suspicions. When Sneha spoke about bringing Himanshu home I was initially very apprehensive. No woman wants her eighteen year old daughter, who had just started college, to have a steady boyfriend. Male classmates are welcome, but a steady boyfriend? Images of a pony-tailed hunk, dragon tattoo emblazoned on his forearm, a rolled up joint hanging from his lips, rose before my eyes. It was the stereotypical image of a hippie of the 1970s, no one I had met in real life. In the event I was happy to meet Himanshu. He was good looking, clean shaven with shampooed hair and clean nails, wearing a T-shirt, jeans and sunglasses. He had no tattoo. He smiled at me while I scrutinized him. Sneha frowned unhappily. She was not happy with my scrutiny. But one had to be careful with teenagers. I saw Sneha and Himanshu sitting together on the drawing room couch and smiled. They were like two peas in a pod. They liked Hindi film music, loved cricket, enjoyed reading detective fiction, liked *pizzas* and hated *pumpkin* and *brinjals*. When he left I said, "You and Himanshu are so similar." "Like is boring," I teased her, "Opposites attract." "Just as you and Dad did," she countered. I laughed in response. Yes my husband and I were poles apart in our thinking, upbringing and approach to life.

When Himanshu came home a month later he was without his sunglasses. I saw his hazel eyes, and his dimples which flashed prominently every time he smiled. I was struck by his similarity to Sneha and could not control my doubts. I fell silent, my face ashen. Sneha looked at me suspiciously. "Out with it Mom," she said, "What is bothering you?" My heart started pounding. We were treading on dangerous grounds. I did not know what would be wiser, to keep my doubts to myself or bring them out in the open. Finally, I told her about my apprehensions. I was afraid that she and Himanshu were siblings. She was astounded. "How is that possible?" she said, "Unless Papa had an affair. Or you did?" Her words were a slap across my face. My eighteen years old had accused me or my husband of infidelity.

It was time for revelations. I didn't know how to tell her. 'Sneha,' I said, "I have to tell you something." The words sounded ominous. "You were born ten years after our marriage." She looked bored. She knew all this. This was history. "Well we had problems," I said. "I know," she said, 'Fibroids?' My eighteen year old had immediately attributed the problem to me. "I had no problems," I said defensively, "Your Dad did. Major problems.

The doctor advised sperm donation due to your Dad's low sperm count. Nineteen years ago sperm donation was not well known. Hemant baulked at the idea. He was appalled that I could even think of bearing another man's child." "Over my dead body," he said, "I will never allow you to have another man's child. For me, it will always be a bastard." I wanted to experience all the joys of motherhood. The pangs of birth, bouts of morning sickness, yearning for strange kind of foods, the first kick of the baby in my womb, the onset of labour pain. I had been deprived of it for so long. But Hemant was not willing. "We can adopt a child from the orphanage if you want," he said. But I did not want a made-to-order baby. Then Hemant suddenly died of meningitis. "If only she had a child," lamented my mother, "She could have kept busy." That is how the idea came to me. I asked the doctor for donor sperm. In 1995, sperm donation in India was virtually unheard of. But thanks to the doctor at the fertility clinic, I became pregnant. Sperm donors in India have to remain anonymous. I never knew who your biological father was and I didn't care. After you were conceived I pretended that you were Hemant's child. Thankfully, you were induced three weeks before the due date, due to my supposed hypertension. No one suspected that you were not Hemant's child." "Sperm donation? What do you mean?" said Sneha, looking disbelievingly at me. "How innocent you are," I said, as I began explaining the process to her. "I know all about it," she cut me short, "I also know of the Niyog pratha in Mahabharata. Weren't Dhritrashtra, Pandu, Vidur and the Pandavas born that way? In the film *Eklavya* weren't Saif Ali Khan and his sister Raima Sen born as a result of natural insemination?" I looked at Sneha and wondered, "Do all teenagers know so much trivia?"

Sneha had never met her father, she knew that she was a posthumous child, for her I was both her mother and father, yet she was squeamish about the idea of having a sperm donor for a father. I remained silent. "So what?" she said, once she had grasped the circumstances of her birth, "What has it got to do with Himanshu?" "You both look similar with hazel eyes, dimples and high cheek bones," I muttered, "What if you share the same biological father?" Sneha began laughing. "Mom do you realize how ridiculous you sound? There must be lakhs of boys and girls with high cheek bones, dimples and hazel eyes. We couldn't all be siblings, could we?" 'Well,' I said feeling foolish, "I once saw an episode of the serial 'Boston Legal' in which the lawyer's client's daughter and her boyfriend both turned out to be born from the same sperm donor." Sneha groaned, "Talk of Life imitating Art. Mom you don't know how strange you sound. You saw a serial and expect this to happen to your daughter. That was reel life. Do you realize the odds of that happening in real life?" 'Well,' I said defensively, "Can you ask Himanshu?" "What should I ask him?" muttered Sneha, "Should I ask Himanshu if he was born of a sperm donor? Do I look crazy? I am wondering how to tell him about my birth and of his reaction." "Well if he loves you...." I left the sentence incomplete. Sneha brooded over my revelation about her birth and finally gathered courage to meet Himanshu. She came back deliriously happy, after Himanshu told her that he was concerned with her and not her birth father. Himanshu had told her that his father had worked in an advertising agency and his mother was a banker. They had divorced when he was young.

I met Himanshu's mother by chance during the College Annual Day Function. She was stern and plain looking and had I not known it I would never have guessed that Smriti Ghosh was his mother. "All the good looks in Himanshu's family come from his father," I chuckled to myself. I was lucky that I was beautiful and no one commented about Sneha's lack of resemblance to Hemant. I told Himanshu's mother about Himanshu and Sneha. Apparently, although Himanshu spent most of his time with Sneha, he had not told his mother about her. Was it because she was possessive about him? I wondered. Himanshu's mother saw them coming together into the auditorium and gaped. Apparently, she too was struck by their dimples and hazel eyes. "I must tell you that I had conceived Sneha through sperm donation," I told her after sometime. "I left my husband," she disclosed, "After I discovered that he was a sperm donor. I baulked at the idea of his fathering children of other women. I felt betrayed. We were living in Pune in the 1990s. I left Raj and subsequently we divorced.

Raj then moved to Delhi. I learnt later that he died in a bike accident. I have been transferred to Delhi only three years ago."

So there was no man I could turn to for confirmation about Sneha's birth. For a moment, I felt a pang on hearing about Raj's death. Sneha had lost the chance of meeting her birth father, if indeed he was her father. I knew that there was only one way of finding out the truth, by going to the Fertility Clinic to which I had gone for Sneha's birth. Dr. Kaul, the fertility specialist, listened to me carefully, but like Sneha cited the odds of Himanshu and her being siblings. "Himanshu's father lived in Pune. You lived in Delhi," he pointed out. But I had my arguments ready, "He later came to Delhi. I don't know at what point of time." Dr. Kaul quoted to me the Confidentiality Clause in the Form I had signed. He argued that the records of Sneha's birth were over 18 years old. He added that he was retiring after three months. He accused me of being a frustrated middle-aged woman, coming in the way of my daughter's happiness. I listened to his tirade in silence. Then I told him that I could not let Sneha and Himanshu get into a relationship if they were half-brother and sister. Dr. Kaul had to help me find the truth. He argued and said that there must be many men with hazel eyes, dimple cheeks and high cheekbones. "Not all of them would be sperm donors," I argued. At last he relented and said that he would see if he could trace the records and find the identity of Sneha's birth father.

Days turned into weeks and weeks into months. I thought he had forgotten all about it. And then the phone call came. Dr. Kaul had called me and Sneha over to the clinic, but he did not disclose anything over the phone. Tension is writ large on Sneha's face and mine as I drive over to his clinic. What will it be? A clean chit for Sneha and Himanshu, or the end of her dreams? Are my suspicions right or unwarranted? Has Dr. Kaul found records of the sperm donor? Or has he failed to do so and wants to match Himanshu and Sneha's DNA? Will the testing of DNA tell him if they share the same biological father? The tension is killing. Sneha's fate lies in balance. I can only keep my fingers crossed and pray.

□

FANTASY

She woke up to the sound of waves lashing on the shore. The rhythmic sound of the waves, coming and then receding, had a mesmerising quality to it. The salty tang of the sea breeze exhilarated her. She yawned and then rubbing away the last vestiges of sleep from her eyes, stretched languorously like a cat. This was her last day in Goa, the day where she had to decide her future. Last night her mind had been in a terrible turmoil, but today she was enveloped in a cloak of peace, for she knew what she wanted out of life and she knew that her decision was right.

Her ruminations were interrupted by a knock on the door. Room Service. Moments later a liveried waiter with a tray brought her a cup of tea. Sipping it appreciatively, she closed her eyes and thought of the tumultuous events of the last few days. Too much had happened too soon. A kaleidoscope of images flashed through her mind. Sumit flashing fire, when she told him of the modelling offers she had received. "You want to take up modelling? You want to do ramp shows? You want to be a pin-up girl? You want to be every man's fantasy?" He made it sound sordid and she knew what the bottom line was. "It's me or your career. Choose." But choices were so difficult to make. Life could not be decided by the roll of a dice, and who knew which way the dice would roll?

"Sumit, It's an opportunity of a lifetime. And it won't last forever. A model's professional career-span is so short, its barely five years." The words remained glued to her throat, they never rolled out. She could not tell him what all this meant to her. It meant emerging from the shadow of her successful, elegant careerist mother, making a transition from a gawky pimple-faced bespectacled girl into a svelte sophisticated young woman. It meant a silent reaffirmation in herself and her abilities, as well as the financial independence, so necessary for the future Sumit and she were planning to carve for themselves. But she remained tongue-tied. Sumit, whom she had known for years, who was her neighbour and friend, seemed to be a man possessed. Jealous. That's what he was, she realised intuitively. Jealous and possessive. He felt that she was his possession, to be hidden from prying eyes, to be kept in safe custody, and locked up.

Was this the life she wanted for herself? Would all her ambitions remain unfulfilled? She wasn't sure of what she wanted from life. So when her parents spoke about the 1992—All India Medical Conference being held in Goa she had jumped at the chance. She needed space, lots of personal space. She needed to distance herself from Sumit to think objectively. On the journey from Mumbai to Goa by steamer she had stood at the upper deck, watching the emerald green waters, calm and unmoving which stretched endlessly. She had wondered why her own life could not be that smooth. The tempest which had raged in her life overwhelmed her. Seeing the setting sun, looking curiously like an orange ball of fire, dip into the horizon, she suddenly recalled the belief that if you make a wish just when the sun disappeared, the wish was bound to come true. She closed her eyes, screwed them up tight and prayed silently, "Oh! Lord, let me find happiness." Opening her eyes and turning back, suddenly she collided with someone standing behind her.

"Oh hell!" he swore softly and she saw his pair of glasses fall onto the ground, followed by his camera. 'God,' she muttered stricken, "I hope it isn't damaged." "Lady," he said, his voice oozing sarcasm, "I wouldn't know, I can't see without my glasses." She stooped to pick up both the camera and the glasses and found that the camera thankfully was unharmed, though the glasses were broken.

She did not know what sense of impishness made her dip into her purse and fish out her pair of glasses, which she carried just in case something happened to her lenses, and perch it on the nose of a virtual stranger, "Ah, I see light," he said, and turning to her he added, "Are you an Ajanta figurine come alive, or an ophthalmologist in disguise?" 'Neither,' she laughed, "I am just a student." "At least we see eye-to-eye with each other on the question of glasses, the power of my glasses is also minus three," he laughed.

And then, of all the prosaic things in the world, they discussed myopia, its onset and progression. Sitting on the deck, the saline breeze blowing on to her face, completely oblivious of the fact that the breeze had ruffled her carefully done up hair, she continued to talk to him, uncaring of the passing time. She learnt to her surprise that he was a doctor and when she teasingly said, "Doctors should marry nurses," he smiled and said, "When are you joining the nursing profession?" "I won't," she said, her chin jutting out, "I want to be a model." There, she had said it. "Fine, but a model's career span is limited, what after that?" He had unknowingly thrown back her argument at her. When she had said, "I'll get married," he had argued, "Well what after that?" She realised that he was one of those men who did not have any quarrel with modelling as a profession and did not expect women to be mere appendages to men, but individuals in their own right.

As they disembarked, he kept her pair of glasses, having learnt that apart from her contact lenses she had another pair of glasses, and promising to return them to her hotel within a day. The next evening he was at the hotel, a new pair of glasses in a metallic frame perched on his nose. She thought that was the last she had seen of him, and she was glad. She was not in the mood for casual flirtation, let alone something serious. She had no thought of him in mind when she entered the Basilica of Bom Jesus to see the mortal remains of St. Francis Xavier. Peering at the casket, she was aware of an impatient movement behind her, and she shifted hastily, nearly colliding into the man standing behind her. "Don't make it a habit will you," he laughed, "I don't have another pair of glasses, and I can't see without them." She turned crimson, and wondered if he had followed her here, but blushed at her assumption when he turned and introduced her to his friends who had accompanied him. The unexpected meeting did enable him to ask her out the next day, while promising to show her Goan cuisine. True to his promise he took her to the Mangesh Temple and then to a small restaurant where she had Pork vindaloo, Goan fish curry and Prawn balichao. Talking to him she found it easy to talk about her fears, her childhood and her parents.

Rajesh Sinha. That was his name. He met her in her hotel the next afternoon. "Doesn't the seminar last the whole day?" she asked. "It does," he admitted and then said that having read out a paper in the conference he felt he deserved a rest.

Swimming with him at the beach, seeing half-clad tourists being baked lobster pink, trying kaju feni and wrinkling up her nose at it, she told him about herself, her ayah dependent childhood, her parents who had all the money in the world for her and no time, and even of Sumit and their last quarrel. "He's jealous," he said complacently, "If he really loves you he will let you have your own way." But she knew Sumit. His word was law. He was indulgent as long as he had his own way.

Within seven days, she felt she had known Rajesh for a lifetime, yet she was unprepared when he proposed to her. "We hardly know each other," she said and he argued, "You've known Sumit for ten years and yet you say that you hardly know him." She knew that he was right. "I need time," she said, and he smiled and said, 'Tomorrow?' She acquiesced because she was leaving the day after.

That night, in the solitude of her room, she thought of Rajesh and his proposal and tried to visualize what life would be after marriage with him. Rajesh had specialized in orthopaedics and worked as Assistant Professor in a medical college. She could imagine him tired after a long and gruelling day at the Operation Theatre, with no patience to spend an evening out with her. On the other hand, she thought, he is loving, caring and liberal in his outlook. While she was ruminating she was interrupted by a phone-call. 'Room 205,' asked the receptionist, "Call from Delhi," and then Sumit was on the line. "Missing me?" he asked, as if nothing had happened between them. "Huh, Huh," she said, and then added bitterly, "I hope you haven't forgotten everything." "I haven't," he said abjectly, "I was jealous. I'm sorry Sapna, but I always took you for granted. Only when I realized that I was on the verge of losing you that I realized how much you mean to me." And with that the phone went dead. She tossed and turned the whole night and had drifted off to sleep only in the early hours of the morning, her mind in a complete turmoil. But she had woken up fresh, at peace with herself, knowing what she would tell Dr. Rajesh.

....

She heard the sound of footsteps on the staircase and heard the doorbell ring. She heard the bolt being turned and then her mother's weary voice say, "Hullo doctor." She heard him say, "And how is she?" and her weary response, "As usual." He said, "I have some good news for you, I had written to the Institute for Orthopaedically Handicapped and they have promised to give her a wheelchair." She could imagine her mother's care worn face brighten up, as she passed him a cup of tea in the chipped bone-china mug, along with a plate of glucose biscuits. She then heard him say, "It is not right for her to remain locked up in the room the whole day. Why don't you rent a house on the ground floor, a two bed-roomed house with a garden, so that she can see the sun, feel the air and enjoy the sunshine." Her mother's voice turned bitter. "Houses with gardens cost money, and I am barely able to survive on his pension. Because of her condition, I cannot even take up a job as a school-teacher. She killed her father, and ended up with her legs crushed. How I wish she had died instead." "Don't say that," said the doctor, "Don't you think she must have regretted it." "He was looking forward to the Conference in Goa, it would have made a nice change from Delhi, but she had to quarrel with Sumit, and crash the car," her mother said and began sobbing. She listened to her mother's tirade in stony silence. How many times had she relived that night? She remembered her desire to accept the modelling assignment, which would bring her both the financial and psychological independence she needed, and Sumit's unexpected anger, which almost broke up their relationship. Her driving her father to the station in anger, her dear absent-minded father, who was unaware of the tension within her, which robbed her of her reflexes when she saw the on-coming truck. The doctor's diagnosis, which spelt the death-knell of her dreams and Sumit's total indifference to her plight.

She could hear the doctor shuffling his feet uncomfortably and saying, "Now let me see the patient." He entered her room silently. 'Sapna,' he said gently, "Sapna beti, how are you today?" She clenched her eyes tight and turned her back, pretending to be asleep. 'Sleeping,' he said aloud, with complete understanding, willing to play along with her in this little charade. He touched her twisted legs and saw the book by her side. A book on Goa. "I'll take you to Goa one day, even if I have to carry you on my back," vowed Dr. Rajesh Sinha silently, looking down at the daughter of his best friend. He thought of Sumit with anger, who had never visited her even once, not even in the hospital, when he had heard of her loss of legs. A pretty girl Sapna. No. Not a pretty girl but a paraplegic who took refuge in dreams and was forever lost in her world of make-belief, as an escape from the tormenting reality.

With gentle hands he ruffled her hair. But she still did not turn, unwilling to see the pain in his eyes and to let him see her tear drenched pillow.

□

THE PRICE

There was a stench of death in the house. Ravish shook his head, waving away the thought from his head. Death had no smell. Maybe it was not the smell of death after all, but the smell of blood. Maybe it was the smell of putrid flesh. He looked at his father-in-law's face and winced. He had seen death before. His own father had died a decade ago. Died in his sleep. But he had never seen the brutality of death. Someone had taken a blunt instrument and struck Babuji on his head. Babuji's head had caved in. Blood had seeped out and along with it his brains.

The police had arrived even before he had been able to drive down. The body was being taken away. The stunned silence of an hour ago had been replaced by loud wailing. The shrill sounds of women weeping at the top of their voices began to annoy him. Was this genuine grief, he wondered, or a public display of grief? Then he looked at his mother-in-law, her hair flying all over her face, her eyes wild, her shrill screams coming as though from somewhere else. She was not faking grief he knew. She was genuinely devastated. How much was it because of love and longing for her husband and how much was it because of the fear of the future was a different matter altogether, but whatever the reason, there was no disputing the fact that her distress was genuine.

Maya entered the room just then. Her eyes were red from crying. She was heartbroken, Ravish knew. His thoughts flew back to the past. He remembered that just six months before when he had been transferred from Manipur to Bhubaneswar he had received nothing but a hero's welcome. Babuji had been waiting at the entrance of the Arrival Lounge of the Airport, a marigold garland in hand. Maji had a bunch of red roses in hers. Suddenly, everything was forgiven. Maya was forgiven the fact that he was a Vaish from UP and not a Brahmin from Orissa. He was forgiven the fact that he had been allotted a tough cadre like Manipur. Maya, their smiles said, had chosen well after all.

Babuji's chest had swelled with pride when he had been posted as Collector Cuttack. He had savoured the news for long. For the next five years, he knew, he could show off his I.A.S. son-in-law to his relations and friends.

It was a month later that his father-in-law had come to Cuttack to visit him. He seemed intimidated by the sprawling Collector's residence, the acres of land dotted by palm trees and the pond behind the house. Ravish smiled to himself. His stock, he realized, had risen some more in his father-in-law's eyes. "I had always seen this house from outside," Babuji had muttered, "I had never been inside." Ravish had laughed. It was then that his father-in-law had begun to mumble something. "An appeal is pending with you," he had said, "I wonder if you can do something about it." It must have been the long arm of coincidence at work, Ravish had smiled to himself, because that was the case he had finished studying just the day before. The petitioner had been a clear victim of injustice and he had intended to redress the petitioner's grievance. But he had no intention of discussing the case with his father-in-law. "I'll see what I can do," is all he had said in return. Babuji had smiled a trifle ingratiatingly and added, "He is a relation." 'Oh God,' Ravish had groaned to himself, "Not this. I hope Babuji has no more cases to recommend." He had not linked the big basket of fresh fruits Babuji had sent with the case at all. Nor the *saree* Babuji had given to Maya on Durga Puja.

It was almost two months later that Babuji had made a simple request for transfer. Again he had smiled ingratiatingly. "Here it comes," Ravish had thought to himself, and sure enough Babuji had begun to mention the travails the family had to undergo, after the male member of the family had been transferred outside. He had heard it all before. An ailing mother, stricken with paralysis, a working wife and a daughter of a marriageable age. "Only you can help," Babuji had stuttered, "An order from you can solve all their problems." He imagined the supplicant coming to Babuji one morning and saying, "Only you can help." He imagined Babuji's chest swell with pride. His 'Jamai babu' his son-in-law was the Collector. "I cannot disappoint the old man," thought Ravish. "Well if the rules permit," he said half-heartedly. "You are the Collector," said Babuji to him, "You are the king of the district."

"King of the district," Ravish rued to himself, "But with pockets almost empty by the end of the month." He had hated himself when Maya's face fell, when he told her brusquely that he could not give her the ten thousand rupees she needed to buy gold filigree earrings. "But you are the Collector," she had parroted and he had said brusquely, "My take home pay is twenty-five thousand rupees." Maya had never raised the issue with him again.

Babuji's requests had not ceased with the passage of time. He had, Ravish said to himself, almost begun to dread Babuji's visits. At times he would request for a gun licence. At other times it would be a request for house allotment. Yet at other times it would be a request to help someone to get employment as a casual peon. "Babuji is a true social worker," he had gibed to Maya one day and Maya had smiled in return.

Almost four months later, while coming out of his Office Room unexpectedly one day Ravish had overheard a man telling another "Oh! he will get the land allotment order in his favour. He has approached the Collector's father-in-law."

His steps slowed down automatically. He pressed his body against the wall. He hoped that the two people, engrossed in their conversation while walking down the stairs, would not turn back and look.

"It works very simply," the man said. "Saab works through his Babuji." He could still remember his hand tighten in rage, as he stood with his body pressed against the wall. He recalled the sheer anger he had felt at the allegation, the burning rage which seem to scorch him. He wanted to race down the stairs, pull the man by his hair and hit his head against the wall. How dare he make allegations about his integrity and get away unscathed? He who had never taken a single *paisa* from anyone. He wondered why he did not bellow at them and ask them to stop.

Ravish knew the answer to that one. There was a doubt plaguing his mind, a doubt which had popped into his head the moment he had heard the two men speaking. But he knew that he had no means of knowing the truth. He had gone home in humiliation and in mortification. He had no idea how easy it was to besmirch his reputation. "Why, in Manipur," he muttered to himself, "Where they demanded money from corrupt officers and even killed them, nobody ever demanded money from me. Everyone knew that I was honest."

Maya had been delighted to see him return home early. As he slumped on the sofa she said, "Bapa has sent me this gold filigree set," and showed him an intricately carved necklace with matching earrings and rings. For a moment he had been struck by the exquisite workmanship in gold. The next moment he had begun to be plagued by doubts. "Oh really," he had said, "Babuji seem to have become rich rather suddenly." "His pension has increased," she had said, but her voice had faltered. 'Oh,' Ravish had said, his eyebrows raised, "And yet I cannot get you the same on my salary…" he had left the sentence unfinished. Maya had begun to look distressed. "He must have sold off some land in the village," she had said lamely. 'Land.' The word began to reverberate in the air.

Land allotment. Ravish remembered the last weekend when his father-in-law had casually mentioned the land allotment application which was on his table. It had appeared to be a genuine case. He had seen nothing devious in it. Perhaps Babuji was being genuinely altruistic. Maybe he had got confused. Maybe the men were talking about someone else. Maybe this allegation of money was all a lie. There was only one way of knowing the truth. All he could do was wait.

It was just a few days later that Babuji had inquired about the award of a contract to a firm. Only three tenders had been received. Babuji was recommending some firm. "Theirs is the lowest tender," he had said. "How do you know?" Ravish had asked, "They have not been opened yet." Babuji had merely smiled in return. Ravish had promised to help. Babuji had gone back looking pleased. And yet when the tenders had been opened he had rejected the lowest tender and recommended the second lowest one, in view of the past performance of the firm, their financial viability and the fact that the difference between the two was marginal. His recommendation had been approved and the contract had been awarded to someone else. A week later Babuji had died. "This is the price Babuji had to pay for my action," Ravish thought guiltily.

The SP arrived soon after. "Did your father-in-law have any enemies?" He asked. "Not that I know of," Ravish said, shaking his head. "If it was Delhi I could have blamed it on the Pardi tribes," said the SP worriedly, "they are supposedly a criminal tribe and they kill before they loot. The way his head is crushed in seems like their handiwork. But this is Bhubaneswar not Delhi. And surprisingly nothing of great value was stolen." "Except a few trinkets of Maji," murmured Ravish.

Ravish thought of the events of the last few weeks. A wave of guilt began to engulf him. If the two men had to be believed, Babuji had taken money. His death proved it. Yet there was nothing he could do about it.

His mother-in-law was still crying. He shrugged his shoulders. At least Maji would have no financial worries, he thought cynically. Babuji had seen to that before he died. A moment later, he was repentant. All this was conjecture on his part. What was the truth? He knew he would never know for sure.

□

NIGHTMARE

I had a nightmare tonight. And last night. And the night before that. In my nightmare Nikhil stood at the foot of my bed screaming, "Murderess, murderess, you killed our child, you did, you did." Then Abhishek's face, curiously bloated, swam before me. 'Ma, Ma,' he whined, 'Ma, Ma.' The sounds were transformed into a sheep's bleating and suddenly Abhishek became a little lamb who was being led to a slaughter house, where I wielded the knife. I woke up in cold sweat and instinctively put my hand across the bed. The bed was empty and the sheets were unwrinkled. Nikhil's springy black hair did not rest on the pillow. I knew he would be curled up on the sofa in the drawing room, his face turned towards the back rest, his back towards me. His posture was symbolic of his rejection. He had been this way for the last one week. I could bear this rejection. What I could not bear was the implacable look in his eyes, which could shut me out of his world and create an irrevocable barrier, which no tears of mine could melt.

Abhishek was dead and I was responsible for his death. For Nikhil that was the only reality. Abhishek had been critically ill and was on a drip. The drip was going too fast, which led to high fever. And all through it I slept. 'Slept,' Nikhil's voice rose hysterically when I dragged out my explanation, "You slept Anju, when you were to keep awake, when you had to give him his dose of antibiotics at midnight? How could you sleep Anju, how could you?" I could not answer his question. But it wasn't really a question. It was an accusation. "Now you can sleep as much as you want. No one will disturb you," Nikhil had said. I stretched my hand, trying to touch him, to ease his pain, but he recoiled from my touch. Dr. Anant, Abhishek's pediatrician looked at me, but his eyes did not condemn. Perhaps he had seen too much pain in his profession to pass judgments on others. "Perhaps it was for the best," he said hesitantly, "Perhaps both of you can begin again." 'Best?' Nikhil seized upon the word, "My son died due to Anju's negligence and doctor, you say it was for the best? How can you say that? She killed him. Anju let him die because Abhishek was handicapped. She did not want my deaf-mute child." "Not your child alone Nikhil," Dr. Anant said firmly, "He was her child too." Laughter began to bubble in my throat, hysterical laughter which threatened to spillover, but I stifled it. Who knew that Nikhil would react to Abhishek's death this way? Abhishek's death had created a void between us which no grief, no tears and no remorse could fill. The bond between Nikhil and me had been so tenuous that it had snapped at the first pull.

"I'm sorry," Dr. Anant said, awkwardly shuffling his papers before rising to leave. Sorry for what? Was he sorry for Abhishek's death or Nikhil's outburst? I saw Abhishek's face on the pillow, his hands clenched into fists, his eyes closed. Dead. Quite dead. I felt a wave of a nameless emotion sweep over me. Was it grief or relief? I did not really know. We had discovered his handicap only two months ago. The placid baby who lay in the baby cot, alert eyes watching the mobiles hanging from his cot, or the posters on the bedroom walls, was actually deaf. "He's such a placid child," a friend who came to visit us after Abhishek's birth had murmured, "Even the whistle of a pressure cooker doesn't disturb him." Nikhil and I had smiled, he with fatherly pride and I with an artificial smile stuck to my face. But when one night, the thunder rolled and Abhishek slept through it all, we suspected. And when Nikhil shook a rattle behind Abhishek's ear and Abhishek still did not turn, we knew.

"Anju, it's alright, it's not the end of the world," Nikhil had said. But I had known even before the ENT specialist had confirmed, that there was no hope. Abhishek, my deaf-mute child, would grow up in a soundless world, where all noise would be blotted out. Perhaps Abhishek was this way because of the medicines I had taken during pregnancy. Perhaps he was deaf-mute due to reasons which medical science had not begun to fathom. Perhaps it was retribution. My life had been shattered after the diagnosis, while Nikhil had held Abhishek tight as if he would never let him go. But now Abhishek was gone. The next three days after Abhishek's death were spent in silence, but not before Nikhil had his say. He said, "You let him die, when you realized that his world would remain soundless. His world of silence became a burden to you. Abhishek became a stumbling block for your career." "That's a lie," I screamed, my face white. "Don't bother to deny it," said Nikhil contemptuously, "You did not want my child, if you had your own way, you would have got rid of it. Once you learnt that he was handicapped,you rejected him." "Such perception, Nikhil," I wanted to scream, "But for all the wrong reasons." "Anju, our bond is gone," he said, when I tentatively suggested that we would have more children, "Our marriage is over. You are free to go wherever you want." He did not spell it out, but I knew who he meant. "I want you, just you, and no one else," I wanted to scream, but Nikhil had nothing left to say to me.

'Rajan,' that was the name Nikhil had left unspoken. Hysterical laughter bubbled within me once again. If only you knew the truth, Nikhil. But the truth is the one thing I can never tell him. On the eve of our marriage Nikhil had asked me, "By the way, who is Rajan?" When I had looked stricken, he had misunderstood and said, "Forget it, let us put the past behind us," and I had been too shocked to tell him that there was no past. Rajan and I were friends, inseparable friends in Banaras Hindu University during our BA and MBA. We were friends as well as rivals, but we were never lovers. We spent most of our waking hours together in libraries, in lecture halls, outside tea stalls and inside college canteens. I had wanted more from our relationship, I confess, I had wanted much more. My eyes spoke volumes and had Rajan wanted to see it, he would have seen love in my eyes but he never did. And my love for him, remained unrequited. My parents, who had neither welcomed nor frowned upon our relationship but accepted it with characteristic nonchalance, brought Nikhil's marriage proposal to me, when I was selected as a Management Trainee in a multinational firm.

"I'm getting married," I told Rajan in flat unemotional tones. I wonder how I had expected him to react. Maybe I had hoped that he would hold my hand and say, "I will never let you go." Rajan looked at me for a long time, without giving me a clue to his feelings and then he asked, "Are you happy?" "A marriage and a career, what more can a girl want?" I said in a loud voice. And that was that. Rajan did not say anything thereafter. "Look at me Rajan, say something," I willed him to react, but Rajan's face remained impassive. My marriage took place six months later and before I even got to know my husband, Nikhil left for Harvard on a three-year fellowship, leaving me behind to pursue my career in India. "I'm afraid Nikhil, to live alone in a city like Delhi," I said, for Nikhil's parents were in Bangalore and mine were in Varanasi. But Nikhil believed that everyone needed space to grow and bloom, and he did not want to uproot me, for a matter of just three years. Soon after marriage he left me and went to the US. Living alone in Delhi was a nightmare for the first two years, with me alone, in a big house in Delhi.

Aching for Nikhil and for a family life, trying to throw myself into work to keep myself busy and not succeeding. Learning the hard way that work does not compensate for lonely evenings and lonelier nights. Not being able to keep in touch with Nikhil who was a terrible correspondent, not hearing his voice long distance because I had no phone and had to go to the landlord's house to receive his calls. Entering an empty house every evening. Living for two years on scrambled eggs and toast, coffee and toast, soup and bread and Maggi noodles, because I found cooking a chore. Missing Varanasi, the town in which I grew up, missing my home, the maze of lanes that make the Vishwanath *galli*, the serene Ganges where moisture laden breeze lapped my face. Missing all this in Delhi, which was a *jungle* of cement and concrete. I could feel loneliness tiptoe from behind me and seep into my being. Having just music for company, music and books, and the

Doordarshan channel on the television with its Sunday feature film, *Chitrahaar* and *Rangoli*. And of course my thoughts. And occasional depression, especially after the demolition of the *Babri Masjid*, while worrying about my relations who lived in Ayodhya and elsewhere. That is how I spent the first two years after marriage.

And then one afternoon, while I was ambling along the market place, I met Rajan. He was just the same, wearing a *kurta* and *pyjamas* and carrying a *khadi jhola*. He looked like an NGO representative rather than a marketing whizzkid. 'Anju,' he shouted enthusiastically, "How are you, and where do you live?" I waved unenthusiastically towards my house across the road and he said, "Won't you invite me for a cup of coffee?"

Coffee? Once I had expected to do just that. Iron his clothes. Cook his breakfast, lunch and dinner and even polish his shoes. But he had not known that, or perhaps he had guessed my feelings and pretended not to know. Perhaps he had not been willing to bear the burden of love.

I made coffee for him and brought it for him on a tray, but just as I passed him the coffee cup my hands began to shake. The hot and scalding coffee spilled all over his *kurta*. I hurriedly pushed him beneath the shower and hunted for Nikhil's *kurta* for him to wear. Rajan came out of the shower, his chest pink from being scalded. I was besieged with guilt. It must have hurt him but he bore the pain stoically. I had met him after years and had caused him pain. I brought a tube of Burnol and began rubbing it on his chest. Suddenly, he caught hold of my hand and asked, "Has life been treating you kindly?" And the dam within me burst. "Damn you, Nikhil, damn you," I thought, and I cried all over Nikhil's *kurta* which Rajan was wearing and Rajan cradled my head on his lap and rocked me gently. And then it seemed the most natural thing in the world that he would make love to me, and for the first time in my life I felt his lips on mine and I closed my eyes and it was Rajan no more but Nikhil and it had been a long, long time since we had made love. 'Nikhil,' I murmured huskily, but Rajan didn't hear.

After it was over Rajan got up from the bed and without quite looking at me said, "I'm sorry." But I saw his eyes, which mirrored not just shame, but another emotion. It took me a long time to identify it. Contempt. "My wife wouldn't have done this," he seemed to say. Then he walked out of the house and I stood beneath the shower for hours, trying to cleanse myself and make myself whole again. I wondered what would happen if Nikhil ever knew about this. Nikhil who had suspected me of having a past. The non-existent past had spilled into the present. I promised myself that this would never happen again. I would be everything Nikhil ever wished for in a wife.

Then the unexpected happened. Nikhil's father succumbed to a heart attack and Nikhil, an only child, returned to India a year before schedule, without obtaining his degree. Nikhil took the death of his father stoically, but I could see his underlying grief. Within days of his return I found it growing within me, the one mistake that threatened to destroy my life. He guessed that I was pregnant and was delighted. "How happy Papa would be," he said, not seeing me cringe with fear. He was warm and affectionate, and caring. He was also extremely perceptive and immediately saw through my fears, which he attributed to the wrong reasons. "Promise me, promise me, you will bear the child," he would say, and I, exhausted by the rigours of my job, the home and the pregnancy, could only nod weakly. But he was so solicitous, he cut down on his tours, his partying, his foreign trips, and that is when I fell in love with him. He was no stranger who had married me and deserted me months later. He was my only love. "Oh God," I prayed during my pregnancy, "Let the child die."

Abhishek was born premature and sickly, and to my mind tainted. He first had jaundice and then septicemia. How I hoped that he would succumb to the illness, but he survived. Nikhil tried to see in him an image of himself, but I could only see Rajan's features stamped all over him. I turned the other way whenever the baby was brought to me. Despite Nikhil's entreaties I did not extend my maternity leave and left Abhishek to the care of ayahs. I tried to lose myself in work, in meetings, in tours, in professional challenges, and Nikhil saw me as an over-ambitious, career woman, caught in the vortex of professionalism at the cost of her home and child. When we discovered that Abhishek was a deaf-mute, I thought it was divine retribution. "Rajan, do you know what you have done?" I said silently. Then Abhishek fell sick with severe bacterial dysentery. "He needs hospitalization," said Dr. Anand. But Nikhil wanted to look after him at home. "Remember each dose is crucial for him. Make sure the drip is regulated. If it goes too fast he may develop high fever and collapse," said Dr. Anant. But Nikhil was afraid of cross infection in the hospital and was sure that he and I could manage to look after Abhishek at home. He left me to keep a watch over Abhishek till midnight, after which he planned to take over. I had a flask of coffee by my side and a best seller to keep me awake. But I, an insomniac, who tossed and turned at nights in bed, just closed my eyes and slept that night, and drifted into my world of nightmares. At times Abhishek was a millstone around my neck, pulling me down. At other times he was a deaf-mute giant who squeezed my neck, as though it was an over-used tube of toothpaste, till the saliva dribbled from my mouth down my neck and I died.

It was three o'clock when I woke up from my sleep that night. Nikhil was frantically trying to ring up Dr. Anant while Abhishek's face had turned crimson with high fever. Dr. Anant came minutes later and gave him a life-saving injection, but it was too late.

Then began Nikhil's tirade and his silence. I would have thought that Abhishek's death would have brought us closer, but Abhishek, that deaf-mute child, had pulled at Nikhil's heart strings so hard that Nikhil could not get over his loss. Nikhil has turned into a wall of stone at the loss of his son. What if he learns the truth? Will it ease his pain? Will he understand my agony, my dilemma, my guilt, which made me sleep when Abhishek was dying? Will he forgive me? I think not. I can almost see his face crumple with disbelief, anger and hatred. "Murderess, Murderess," he had screamed in my earlier nightmares. 'Adulteress,' he will scream in my present ones. His love for Abhishek will turn to revulsion. He can learn to live with grief, but can he live with hatred?

Nikhil's shoulders are bowed with sorrow. He mourns Abhishek. He thinks of me as a callous, ambitious, career woman, who discarded her handicapped son, who wanted him dead because he was a deaf-mute. This is a lie, and the lie is destroying me. But the truth will destroy me even more.

□

THE ENCOUNTER

The drive to the venue of the function, the Jacaranda Hall at the India Habitat Centre, was very long. As I sat in the chauffeur driven Ford Figo, watching a host of emotions flicker across Rati's face, I could feel butterflies flutter in my stomach. I had a celebrity sitting beside me, but one who charmed everyone with her unpredictability. It was her unpredictability, and even worse her brutal frankness, which unnerved me at times. She turned to me, her face almost entirely devoid of makeup. "Come on Rati," I had argued when she was getting ready, "You must put on at least some make up. This function is being held to felicitate you and you know that all the cameras will be focussed on you." "Are you afraid that I would look like a famished lizard?" she laughed, shaking her plait from side-to-side, leaving me gaping at the simile. She did have a long face with sharp, angular features. The press called her face arresting. But it was her eyes, which were at times smoky and at times smouldering, which captivated everyone.

Our car came to a stop at a red light. An urchin weaved his way through the maze of cars and rapped on the window. The driver shooed him away. 'Stop,' said Rati peremptorily. She then dug into her 'museum,' as she laughingly called her bag, and hunted for change. Irritated with the delay she was causing, I took out a five rupee coin and thrust it in his hand. There was no grateful 'thanks,' from Rati. Instead she pouted and said, "Why did you give him the money, I was supposed to give it to him!" The urchin turned back on hearing the exchange and she dipped into her purse once again, fished out a bar of Lindt chocolate and handed it over to the urchin. His eyes widened with delight when he opened the cover and saw the chocolate and I saw him dig his teeth into it and savour every morsel. "Really Rati," I reprimanded her, "That chocolate must have cost a fortune." "Three hundred rupees," she said nonchalantly. "You shouldn't have wasted it on the beggar," I said. "It is something he will remember all his life," she said dreamily.

Escorting Rati to the function began giving me jitters. Her unpredictability was well known. I was never sure what she would say next. And today she seemed to be more moody than usual. Being her friend and knowing her ever since my college days didn't help. Working in Lifelong Publishing, the publishing house which had published her books, only made things worse for me. I could not excuse myself from this escort duty. Both the publisher and Rati expected me to be at her beck and call whenever she was in town. I thanked God that she lived in Kolkata and not Delhi. A huge crowd had gathered at the venue to receive Rati. I could see many people holding garlands and flowers in their hands. After all, her latest novel had made it to the international best-seller list for six months. "Imagine what will happen if there is a human bomb amongst them," she whispered into my ear, smiling impishly as she got out of the car and walked towards them. "You are not the Prime Minister of the country," I said angrily. She dimpled in return.

A renowned poet came forward to receive her. Seeing him at a distance, I whispered, "Do you know who he is?" 'Sure,' she giggled, "His parents produced more tragedies than Shakespeare." The poet escorted her towards the Jacaranda Hall, and then she was on the dais. But I discovered that I was being unduly apprehensive. Rati was brilliant when she gave her speech. When she read out passages from her novel, the words fell from her lips as though a turbulent waterfall cascading through the boulders, at times smooth and flowing and yet at other times loud and noisy. All the while she spoke she had the audience enthralled.

I was not surprised to see her being mobbed by autograph seekers. Suddenly, I saw a plump, middle-aged woman, with a prominent double chin, dressed in a heavy *Kanjeevaram saree* and wearing a chunky diamond necklace come and stand near her. "Hi Rati," she said with the ease of familiarity of an old acquaintance. Rati turned towards her and said, "I'm sorry, I don't seem to remember having met you…." "Surely you know me. I'm Neeta Upreti from your school, Loreto Convent, Lucknow." "I'm sorry," Rati said apologetically, "But I passed out from St. Mary's Convent, Allahabad." "But you did study in my school earlier, didn't you?" insisted the woman. "School? Which school did you say it was?" asked Rati, her forehead furrowed, "Yes I think for a few years I did study there." "You must remember me!" said Neeta in a high-pitched voice, making a lot of heads turn, "I was your classmate, I was the only girl in school who distributed imported sweets and chocolates for my birthday. Everyone always waited eagerly for my birthday."

Rati now looked almost distressed. She frowned and said, "I'm really sorry, I don't remember anything. I seem to have an extraordinarily poor memory for faces, anyway it was all so long ago." "That is just not possible," asserted Neeta Upreti while the entire crowd avidly watched this exchange. "Come on Neeta," said a man, who was one of the organisers of the function, "Stop pestering her, leave Ms. Rati Banerjee alone," and holding his wife by her arm he dragged her away, whispering loudly, "Stop making a fool of yourself in public."

There was a virtual stampede when Rati left the hall and I had to rush Rati out of the door into the car. "I think it went off well," said Rati with satisfaction as she sank into the seat. Somehow I got the feeling that she was not talking of her speech but something else. "Yes, it did," I said, sinking my head into the back rest, "But I wish you would be a bit more tactful." "I don't get you?" said Rati, her voice puzzled. "Well I agree Neeta Upreti was being a pest, but I am sure so are many of your fans, but I have seen you handle them with more gentleness. Couldn't you have pretended to recognize her?" I asked.

'Pretended?' Rati's voice was filled with surprise, "Of course I recognized her. She was in my class from class I to class VII. She was arrogant and spoilt and totally obnoxious."

"You recognized her?" I asked her in amazement. "Then why didn't you acknowledge her?" She closed her eyes and appeared to be deep in thought. When she did not answer me for a long time I thought she had fallen asleep. Suddenly she said, "Do you know, in a way, I owe it to Neeta Upreti that I became a writer." 'What?' I exclaimed, hearing Rati's admission. 'Well,' she corrected herself, "I owe it to her that I can write and speak English so well." I sank my head on the backrest as she began to speak. "I was just five years old when I arrived in Loreto School, Lucknow. I had lived in Agra before that and studied in a Hindi medium school." When I arrived in the new school Neeta Upreti told me, "I like your cardigan. Where did you get it from?" I understood what she said and responded by saying in Hindi, "*Mummy ne khareeda hai*." She sniggered and said loudly, "The new girl in class cannot speak English." "The entire class laughed and since then I became the butt of all her comments. I swore to myself that I would learn to speak flawless English. I began to read Enid Blyton books to begin with and then gradually graduated to more serious reading when I grew older. By the time I had left school I had read many of the classics." I looked at her curiously. I knew that Rati was temperamental. It was now apparent that she was also hypersensitive. "That was certainly insensitive of her," I said, "But she too was only a child."

Rati glared at me. She hated interruptions and she made it clear that she had not finished speaking. "Do you remember her saying that she distributed imported chocolates on her birthday?" she said in a low voice, "Well in the fifth standard she came to class on her birthday wearing a frilly pink frock, accompanied by a servant carrying two big boxes of chocolates with her. We all sang 'Happy birthday,' aloud. Then the teacher asked her to distribute chocolates to all of us. I was sitting in the last row. I know that she saw me but she didn't give me any chocolates. After she had finished distributing them, the teacher asked the class if any child had not received the chocolates. I raised my hand. Neeta Upreti then turned to the teacher and said, "I gave chocolates to all the girls in the class but perhaps Rati has never eaten imported chocolates before and so she wants some more." The truth was that she was the daughter of a businessman and I was the daughter of a postmaster and I had never eaten imported chocolates before. Then Neeta Upreti laughed loudly and the teacher laughed with her. I never got the chocolates. I never forgave Neeta. I never forgot the incident either. "I remembered the chocolates she had distributed," Rati said, fishing out another bar of Lindt chocolates, "I never travel anywhere without them." "For years I have dreamt of meeting Neeta Upreti and snubbing her. I got my revenge accidentally today. Surely, you couldn't deprive me of this pleasure?" she asked.

My thoughts turned to Neeta Upreti who was rich, gross and utterly lacking in class, who must have boasted to all her friends how well she knew Rati Banerjee, the internationally acclaimed, best selling writer, and of her humiliation before the crowd. I realized that there must have been many such characters that must have traversed through Rati's life, whom she had fleshed out in her novels. It was this insight into human nature, which had given her books a ring of authenticity, which in turn had made Rati famous. I stole a look at her serene countenance and realized how little I actually knew her.

□

AMITA'S MOTHER

The most important landmark on Clive Street is St. Joseph's Convent. It's a brick-red building that towers over all the others in the neighbourhood. A tarred road winds its way up to the school, with a gnarled neem tree serving as a halfway mark. Soon after this point, the wrought-iron gates open up in welcome.

How many times have I walked down this road? For twelve long years as a child and now, once again, after a gap of six years, as a member of the staff. I feel like a homing pigeon returning to its nest. The nuns dressed in black and white habits are not strangers, they are family. Wherever I look, I'm swamped by memories. I am no longer Ms. Mehta, post-graduate teacher. I am Smita, who stood in the playfield, watching an eagle swoop down and scoop up her lunch and was destined to go hungry, but for the kindness of her class teacher, Ms. Margaret, who decided to share her thick jam sandwiches with a very hungry seven-year-old. I love to spend as much time in the school as I can. To me each girl is not a roll number, but a name. Not just a name but a bud or a flower about to blossom. Parent-teacher meetings are exciting. I try to pair parents with the pupils. The lady in the peacock blue *salwar* suit is the spitting image of little Snigdha Saha. Mrs. Srivastava, obese and always carelessly dressed, is Mona's Mom. Behind those sleepy eyes she has razor-sharp brain. She always analyses Mona's academic performance accurately. She is a pleasant person and sensitive as well. I once overhead Mona tell her mother, "Why don't you at least dress properly when you come here? My friends call you fat and dumpy." I had seen her mother's face turn pale, a shuttered expression on it masking the hurt she undoubtedly felt. That explained why Mona's good looking father had attended the next two meetings.

Children can be so cruel. Mona doesn't know how lucky she is. She has a mother who cares. Tears prick my eyes, as I think of a lanky school girl who ran races and won prizes, but had no parents to applaud her at the prize distribution function. My parents had one refrain, "We have a nursing home to run." Clearly, I came second. I wouldn't have minded if my mother had been corpulent and my father cross-eyed, as long as they attended school meetings even once. "But Darling," Mummy would say, when I complained, "you always do so well in your class. I am perfectly satisfied with your progress." I had no choice but to share my thoughts and experiences with my school teachers. Mummy was less than satisfied, when I chose to waste, what she called a "Brilliant academic career," to become a school teacher myself.

Now in my first year in school as a teacher, I found myself observing a new girl in my class, who seemed to be a mirror image of myself. Amita was always well-dressed, spoke flawless English, wrote beautiful poems and came first in class. "Is her mother a doctor too?" I wondered. Amita told me that her father was a Marketing Manager in a multinational company and her mother was a housewife. "I have an ayah to look after me," she explained. So had I, at her age, a *dhoti*-clad, beedi-puffing ayah, who was at best, a competent maid, but never a substitute for a mother.

"Why doesn't your mother come to the parent-teacher meetings?" I asked Amita, "She is a housewife." "She has a busy social life. Besides she doesn't need to come for the meetings," was Amita's immediate response, "I always come first in class." The words evoked a sense of déjà vu.

"Shall I ask your mother to come?" I asked her. "No Miss," was Amita's fearful reply, "She won't like it." My heart went out to Amita. She seemed to be petrified of her mother. Yet in her prize-winning essay, "My Mother," she had created the illusion of a warm and affectionate mother! I wondered what kind of life she led, flitting around like a butterfly, leaving her with no time for her own daughter?

I was reminded of my own mother who had held lavish, professionally catered birthday parties, because she had no time to organize them herself. But my mother was a doctor. I had reason to be proud of her. Amita's case, however, was quite different. Yet the fact remained that Amita and I were alike. Both of us were lonely. As a twenty-three years old, I still came back to an empty house. Twelve year old Amita came home to a mother who had time for no one but her friends.

Soon it was time for the Annual Day Function. Amita was to receive a number of awards, for standing first in class, for best essay as well as best actress.

"Do tell your parents to come this once," I urged her. "My Dad is out of the country on tour," said Amita in a wary voice. "And what about your mom?" I enquired.

"She won't come," replied Amita in a mutinous voice. "At least, ask her to come," I urged. "I will," she promised.

The Annual Day came and went, but Amita's Mom did not come. I felt a burning rage within me. It was futile to complain to Amita, so I decided to act on my own. When Amita was away on a school picnic the next day and I was off duty, I decided to confront her mother. Taking her address from the school, I drove Mummy's new Maruti Swift through the imposing gates into the impressive drive. Mrs. Saxena was sitting under an appliqué-work garden umbrella, practically hidden by a semi-circular table stacked with the latest magazines. She was playing solitaire. I had no difficulty in recognizing her. She was an older version of Amita.

"I'm Amita's teacher," I began rather awkwardly, suddenly embarrassed by my unexplained presence. "It's Amita, isn't it?" she murmured, fear leaping into her voice, "She's had an accident." "She cares, beneath the veneer of indifference, she cares," I thought exultantly. My task would not be so difficult after all. I burst into speech. Reassuring her of Amita's welfare, I spoke of her indifference to Amita. "I understand Amita's father is abroad. But you stay at home. Don't you think it's your duty to attend the parent-teacher meetings?" I asked. She tried to reply, but I stalled her quickly, "She may not need your supervision, but she certainly needs your presence."

"How do you know?" she interjected.

"I know", I replied bitterly, "I have suffered the same indifference. But at least my mother had an excuse. She's a doctor. You have none."

"What do you know about me?" she asked pointedly.

"I know enough," I retorted, "I know you're a housewife with plenty of time on your hands. You could have come to the Annual Day Function yesterday, when she got the best actress award."

"She's a clever little actress, isn't she?" said her mother in an odd voice.

"A brilliant actress and student and a good debater," I declared, warming to my subject, "She only needs a bit of your time and presence. Surely, you won't deny her this? You must start attending the parent-teacher meetings."

"Perhaps Amita herself doesn't want me to come to her school," Mrs. Saxena suggested. I looked at her. She had a smooth unlined face, kept glowing by facials and herbal cosmetics, no doubt, I thought nastily. Her hair was perfectly coiffured, with not a single strand out of place. Her hands were beautifully manicured. She wore an expensive, hand-embroidered silk kaftan. I had labeled her a social butterfly, and she fitted the image completely.

'No,' I answered resolutely, "Amita herself told me that she asked you to attend the Annual Day Function, but you refused." That seemed to clinch matters. I thought I detected a curious expression on her face, but all she said was, "Well, if you're sure Amita wants me to attend the next parent-teacher meeting, I certainly will." Waving aside her offer of a cold drink and feeling triumphant at having accomplished my task, I strode out without a backward glance. A strange sound I could not place, made me turn around. It was Amita's mother, maneuvering her wheelchair across the smooth path leading to the entrance of her home.

□

ANTI LOVE

Love, what is it, but a highly over-rated emotion? It decrees a communion of souls. I think that is nonsense. When two hands touch, how can electricity crackle? Most hands I know are flabby, limp, sweaty or calloused. And what happens when lips meet? Most of the time one is only too aware of garlic-laden breath or pyorrhea – infected gums. Love is apt to go out of the window under such circumstances. But people continue to delude themselves. Take magazines for example. An article in a film magazine says, "Why women drool after Amitabh Bachchan." Can you imagine women with their jaws hanging, drooling and sallvating. Shucks. They try to make you believe that love is the be-all and end-all of a woman's existence.

That's bilge. Now take me. I am 22 years old. Height 166 metres, weight 55 kgs. Haemoglobin count-12, pulse-72 per minute. BP 120/80, and I have never felt my heart go pit-a-pat at the sight of a male form. People find that strange. But then I find most people strange. There's Rajesh for instance. Raju to his friends. He once went with me to a public garden, to collect specimens for the botany class. While we were sitting on the grass he said, "You with your large, brown, droopy eyes and a placid expression on your face, do you know who you remind me of?" An image rose before me and the description fitted aptly. "A cud-chewing cow?" I asked. Rajesh thought I was being facetious. Honestly I didn't even know what facetious meant, until I looked up the meaning of the word on my return.

A few days later, I went on the lookout for specimens once again and was trying to climb a tree to look at a tailor bird's nest.

I slipped and would have fallen down, but Rajesh caught me and held me hard right against his chest. "Can you hear," he said, his voice thick, as if he was choking over a fish bone, "Can you hear my heartbeat?" I was trying to hear it when he added, "I am also human, I also have a heart." "Certainly," I said, "Harvey has proved that a heart is essential for blood circulation." "You're inhuman," Rajesh said, as he brushed past me. I found his reaction a trifle strange.

A few years later, when I was in the Medical College, I met another guy, over whom all the girls swooned. "He's handsome," said one girl. "He's got dreamy, brown eyes, with a far-away look in them," said another. "Must be myopic," I said, but they thought I was being flippant, whatever that means.

I met the guy at a party, in a friend's house. He came across the room to me and said, "You're brainy, Medical College and all that, let's see if you can solve this one." He took my hand in his, smoothened my palm and then pointing to the space between the head-line and heart-line he said, "This is a river. Beyond it is the *jungle*. You cross the river in a boat and come to the *jungle*, when the boat drifts away. The *jungle* is on fire. The fire will reach you in half an hour. There are wild beasts in the *jungle*. On the other hand the river is full of crocodiles and you can't swim. How will you escape?" This was really a conundrum. I mulled over the question for a long time and then finally said, "I give up, I don't know the answer." "I don't know the answer either," he said, "But it was a pleasure holding your hand." 'Why?' I asked, looking bewildered, "It has the same amount of flesh and phalanges, tarsal and metatarsal bones as anyone else." "You don't have a romantic bone in your body," he said in a rather nasty voice. That really had me worried. I mean I know the radius, the ulna, the humerus, the tibia, the fibula and the femur, but the romantic bone, which bone was that? I rushed to Sudeep to ask him. "He must be joking," responded Sudeep.

Thank God for Sudeep. He knows all the answers and he is down-to-earth and matter of fact. I mean he is really prosaic. When we met for the first time in the Medical College and he asked me to go with him to the canteen, I was a bit worried, you know, if he said things like— my eyes are like shining stars, or lips are like rosebuds. But no, he did not say anything like that. All he said was, "If you keep skipping meals you will have peptic ulcer." Naturally I rushed with him to the canteen. Sudeep got both of us a carton each of yoghurt, which we ate along with large-sized golden apples. "No caffeine, no additives, complete nourishment, a health food," said Sudeep. It was nice to accompany him for nourishing meals thereafter, like milk-shakes, fruit salads, cheese sandwiches, food which as he pointed out, had no adverse effect on health.

"Don't you watch films?" Sudeep asked me one day. "It's a waste of time," I said. "But it is good for understanding human psychology," he argued, "How will you understand people, if you don't know what moves them?" Put like that, I realized that seeing films had an educational value, though after sitting through a film for three hours, I still couldn't understand why people went to watch films.

So Sudeep decided to take me to see something educational. We went to see a show at the Teen Murti Planetarium. It was really educational, seeing the Solar System and the Lunar System, it was much better than reading a book on the subject. So Sudeep decided to take me to all the different shows, to improve my mind. While returning from a show one day, Sudeep showed me some flowers and discovered that I was still abysmally ignorant about India's flora and fauna. He decided to spend our holidays teaching me about it. I admit I didn't know that there were so many flowers or plants in India, or that so many gardens in Delhi. So he took me to the Lodi Gardens, the Buddha Jayanti Park, the Mughal Gardens and then we spent hours pouring over the encyclopedia to know more about them.

Over the past five years, thanks to Sudeep, my mind has really improved. I am sure if I was called for a General Knowledge Quiz, I would walk away with the prize. But there still are gray areas in my knowledge. In literature for instance. Yesterday Sudeep asked me if I had read Plato's Republic. I hadn't. Sudeep who is also into genetics in a big way, told me that Plato, in the Republic, had envisaged an Ideal State, with three classes, the Ruling Class, the Warrior Class and the Appetitive Class. Plato felt that some were born to rule, and others to be ruled. Music, maths and athletics distinguished the future rulers from the ruled. The best specimen among the ruling class were allowed to mate, so that their progeny could acquire their attributes. Such children were brought up in the State Nursery.

Now Plato's Republic was a Utopia, but the idea of the best male and female specimens mating has some merit, which Sudeep feels we should emulate. According to Sudeep, he is tall and so am I. There is no diabetes in his family nor in mine. We both have perfect vision. There is no family history of hemophilia, baldness and thalassaemia in our families. Our blood group are compatible. And both of us have an I.Q. of 130 plus.

Sudeep then told me the famous story of the actress Isadora Duncan and the playwright George Bernard Shaw. When Isadora Duncan proposed to George Bernard Shaw she said, "Why don't we get married? Our child will inherit my beauty and your brains." George Bernard Shaw replied, "Madam, what if he inherits my beauty and your brains?" "In case we get married," said Sudeep, "It will not matter whose beauty or brains he inherits. He will in any case be a fine specimen."

Put like that Sudeep has a point. As he points out reasonably, my Ma is getting old, she won't live for ever and it will be useful to have a man in the house, to clear clogged drains, to repair the light switch, to drive the car and to ward off men, who keep swarming in with their stupid romantic notions.

Sudeep tells me that he is sure our marriage will be a success. I am sure he is right. After all, we are compatible in every way, where does love come into it at all? Although I wonder why he asked me yesterday, "Don't you feel you are missing something?" And when I started delving into my purse to check its contents he said, "Never mind." And if I didn't know him better I would have said that there was a lost, almost wistful expression on his face.

□

MEMORY GAMES

Old age is debilitating. The trick however, is to know how to adapt to it. I have done it gracefully. Today I am a creature of routine. I love my room in the retirement home where I live. My life is uncomplicated. All I do is eat, sleep, watch TV, walk, take an afternoon nap and then have an early dinner. I have no visitors. That is because people bore me. And now it has become difficult for me to remember their names. I realize that I am getting old. I'm almost sixty-five years old now. I had forgotten my birthday as well. I know it, because I read it on the form Sister filled in yesterday. I doze in my rocking chair and once again I see the same dream I told the Sister about. I see a log cabin on a hill top, with cobwebs covering the teak door with a brass knocker. If only I could clean the cobwebs from the door, everything would become clear once again. Sister comes and wakes me up. "Did you take your pill or not?" she asks me. "I do not remember," I confess. She scowls in turn. "People do forget such things in old age," I argue, "It is not unusual at all. I am sure you must have seen many other patients forget things." What does she think I am suffering from? Alzheimer's? I almost laugh aloud. There is nothing really wrong with me, except slight forgetfulness. I do not trust Sister, ever since she brought that man with curly hair and brown eyes, who took my hand and murmured softly, 'Sunaina.' I shrugged his hand off immediately and withdrew my hand. I stepped back a little, making sure that he would not be able to bridge the distance between us easily. I do not like strangers taking such liberties with me. Undeterred, he took out some photographs of him and me, with a child in his arms. "Try and remember Sunaina," he urged, "For my sake." How could I remember? I was certain I had never met him before. I suspected that he was a fraud. The pictures he had shown me were morphed, of course. I knew that it had become fairly common. The marvels of technology. 'Sister,' I hollered, "Please throw him out." After that I imposed my 'no visitor,' rule.

Of course that was a long time ago. "There is a new inmate in the retirement home," says Sister, "He has joined the retirement home just today." I become wary the moment I hear her. Perhaps he is the fraud in disguise, who had shown me the photograph. Though there are so many things I forget, I have not forgotten him. When I go towards the lawn for my morning walk I see the new inmate in the garden, reading a paper. 'Hullo,' he says on seeing me and gets up immediately. I smile in turn. I am floored by his gesture. I like chivalrous men. He has brown eyes, close cropped hair and looks very frail. 'Mrs. Patel,' Sister introduces me to him. He mumbles his name but I can't quite catch it. I wish he had spoken loudly. I would like to know him better. He is recovering from cancer, he says, his voice a bit louder. That explains his physical appearance. Chemotherapy, I realize, which has robbed him of his hair and made him frail. He starts walking beside me and I do not object. Initially, we walk in silence. I admire the giant chrysanthemums and dahlias. After a few minutes he asks me about my family. "I live alone," I mutter, "What about you?" "I lost my wife," he says softly. He sounds totally heartbroken. 'Oh,' I murmur, clucking my tongue sympathetically, "When did she pass away?" "She didn't die," he explains, "She went away." "Some people can't cope with illness," I murmur vaguely, "It's a pity. The family should rally around a person in the time of crisis." He mentions that he has a son in the US, who is paying for his stay in the retirement home. "He should call you to the USA," I argue, "He should get you a green card so that you can live with him. That is what a family is for." "I do not want to go to USA," he says, jumping to his son's defence, "In case my wife comes back to me. I have very little time left." I frown, as I mull over what he means by saying, "I have very little time left," if he is not planning to go away somewhere. I realize with shock that he is referring to his departure from this world. I feel a sudden pang. I am surprised by my own reaction. I have met the gentleman just now.

It's easy to share confidences with him, maybe because I know that he does not have long to live. I know that he cannot pursue me. "There was a man," I whisper to him conspiratorially, "Who came here once. He insisted that we were married and kept showing me photographs to prove it." He winces slightly, as though in pain and then asks, "What did you do?" "I got him thrown out," I laugh.

He too has a photo in his hand, which he keeps glancing at. But he doesn't show it to me. My curiosity is piqued, especially since he seems to have lost all interest in me. I crane my neck to see the photograph. Seeing my unabashed curiosity he hands it over to me. It is a photograph of a log cabin on a hill top, the same house I see in my dreams. "I know the place," I say excitedly, "I went there for my honeymoon." At last I remember something. I know that if I could only brush the cobwebs away, I would be able to see my husband's face. "When was it?" he asks. "It was a long time ago," I say vaguely. "I know," he murmurs, "It was forty-five years ago." I turn to him in surprise. "How does he know?" I wonder.

□

THE DILEMMA

There are many ways of remembering the dead. Some mourn in silence. Some announce their grief vocally. Some put flowers on the graves of the dead. Others put marigold garlands on the framed photographs of the deceased. Ankita had her own way of remembering the dead. She knelt in the garden, beside the freshly dug flower bed, planted the small rose plant into it with deft fingers and put layers of mud on top of it, careful to water the plant. She then rocked herself on her heels, one hand resting on the ground, to ensure her balance. Her mood was sombre, as she watched the erect little plant. One day, she knew, it would bloom, bearing a profusion of maroon roses. "Bye Bye, little one," she whispered, "Remember that you are gone but not forgotten." She looked at the four rose bushes nearby. No one knew why she had planted the roses once a year and except her, no one cared.

'Ankita,' she was surprised hearing Shekhar's voice, sounding disembodied, beside her. He sounded incredulous as he said, "What on earth are you doing?" "Planting roses," she said matter-of-factly, as she dusted her hands against her *kurta* and got up. She wondered if he would remember what day it was. She looked at his furrowed brow. "Have you forgotten?" he asked, "We have to go to Mr. Sharma's house. It's his son's wedding." She turned a mutinous face towards him. "I can't,' she wanted to say, "Today is Neha's death anniversary." She saw his grim face and lapsed into silence. "How would he react if I said that?" she wondered. "Neha, who?" he would ask and she could not blame him for not knowing. How many fathers, or even mothers grieved, for the loss of a stillborn child five years after her death? "Not many," surmised Ankita. Not many would have named a stillborn child. She had done it only because Neha was the daughter she had longed for. Tears stung her eyes when she remembered that night, five years ago when she had felt the onset of labour pains and Shekhar had rushed her to the hospital. It had been a complicated delivery, with her hypertension remaining uncontrolled and seven month old Neha had been stillborn. Shekhar had been bewildered by her grief. Her tears had given way to her silences and she had spent days staring at the blank walls of her bedroom. She had sunk into a deep depression. It had taken her months to recover.

As Ankita entered her house she began to regain her sense of well-being. She loved her house. It was her haven and her sanctuary. Her mood had lifted, by the time she entered the bedroom. She quickly washed her mud- stained fingers and then slumped onto the bed, unmindful of the mud stuck to her *kurta.* She slept the moment she put her head on the pillow. When she got up it had become dark. Her eyes flew to the wall clock. "Time enough to get ready," she thought with relief. She did not want to annoy Shekhar.

She was walking down the staircase, her hand resting on the bannisters, when she first heard the raised voice, shrill with anger saying, "You killed my son." She caught a glimpse of a man, his face ravaged with grief, as he threw down a brown paper packet and screamed at Shekhar once again. She saw Shekhar's face, completely drained of colour. He hesitantly put a hand on the man's shoulder and said, "I understand you are feeling distraught, but it was God's will." "Not God's will," the man almost spat out the words in anger, "It was your doing. Your drugs never worked. They were spurious. They killed him." She walked down the staircase slowly, her eyes on Shekhar's face. He stood shell shocked. "Do not think I will let you get away with it," the man was raving, "I will drag you to court."

Ankita had reached the last stair and was now standing in the drawing room. "What happened?" she mouthed silently to Shekhar. "Go back," he said angrily, "I'll call you later." The man had meanwhile put his head in his hands and was sobbing loudly.

Ankita stood transfixed. His grief was almost palpable. She could feel it reach out to her. She sank into the nearest chair and asked, “What happened?”

This was the opportunity the man had been waiting for. He caught hold of Ankita’s hand and pressed it with his fingers, seemingly unaware of what he was doing. “My son Rohit had a car accident two days ago,” he rasped, “We bought every medicines from your company, the painkillers, the antibiotics and the life-saving injections. Nothing worked, and he died.” “What makes you think the drugs didn’t work?” Shekhar’s voice had become steely. “The doctors said so,” wheezed the man, “They wondered why Rohit was not responding to either the medicines or the injections.” “It’s a case of doctor’s negligence, not mine,” rasped Shekhar, regaining his normal confidence, “You should blame the doctors and not me.” The man put down his head and began to sob. Shekhar stood there helplessly, not knowing what to do. Ankita got up slowly and put her hand on the man’s shoulder. “I am so sorry,” she murmured, “To learn of your son’s death. May his soul rest in peace.” The man continued to sob for a few more minutes. Then he got up, his head bowed and shoulders hunched. Shuffling his feet noisily he left their house, a man grown old before his time.

Shekhar’s face was still chalk white. He seemed to be bowed down under the weight of the man’s accusations. When she heard the clock chime seven she said, “Shouldn’t we be leaving?” “Make sure that Abir and Sameer have dinner and go off to sleep before we return,” she instructed the servant while stepping out of the house, “They have school tomorrow.”

Ankita and Shekhar returned home early, soon after wishing the bride and bridegroom. The confrontation with the man in their drawing room had upset Shekhar more than he cared to admit. It was visible in the tightening of his lips and his furrowed brow. That is why he had caught her elbow and steered her out of the reception, just after she had finished sipping her coke. As they got into the car, she looked at Shekhar’s profile. His jaw was set, his eyes were dry, but she knew that he was still reeling in shock from the accusation flung against him. On reaching home, she asked the servant Ramu if the children had eaten. "They are asleep," he mumbled. "Sleeping at eight?" she smiled to herself. This was unusual. Normally, they watched television till late and had to be coaxed to sleep. 'Ramu,' she called out to the servant, "We didn't eat dinner at the wedding. Please make something quickly for us." She was surprised when he began laying the table immediately. "The kids have slept without eating," he explained. "Well wake them up," she urged, "You should not have let them sleep without eating." "Let them be," admonished Shekhar, "They won't die of hunger if they sleep on an empty stomach just once." She winced on hearing his words. She wished he hadn't used the word 'die.' The word 'death' was dancing before her ever since the evening.

After dinner she went to the children's room. Abir and Sameer, her eight and seven year old sons, were holding hands and sleeping. She felt a rush of affection towards them, as she tousled their heads and kissed them. They did not even stir. "They seem to be sleeping the sleep of the dead," she laughed to herself, "They must be really tired."

When she went to her bedroom, she found that Shekhar was not in the room. She found that he was in the study reading something. "What is it?" she asked, her voice full of concern. Shekhar's face looked pale as he muttered, "I was reading up to see what action that man can initiate against us." "May I help?" she asked tentatively. She waited for the familiar jibe, "Keep out of it, what do you know of these things?" Instead he asked, "Would you mind fetching the medicines he had thrown on the table downstairs?" She clicked on the light switch and suddenly the bulb was fused. Cursing softly under her breath, she went down the stairs, holding on to the bannisters in the dark. On reaching the drawing room she switched on the lights and the room was suddenly flooded with light. She went up to the table and saw that the newspapers had been carefully folded and kept neatly on one side, the magazines on the other. The silver ashtray lay on the centre of the table and the potted plant stood on the side. But there was no sign of the medicines. "Ramu kaka has been cleaning up," she smiled to herself, as she moved to the sideboard. The packet of medicines was not there either. She moved to the dining table. A fruit bowl filled with mangoes, kiwi fruit, bananas and apples lay at the centre. She moved towards the cupboard and accidentally knocked down a chair. The sound shattered the deathly silence and she waited for Shekhar to come pounding down the stairs. "What happened?" he asked, although anyone, she thought, on seeing the upturned chair, would realize what had happened. "I'm sorry," she mumbled, "I knocked down the chair." He waved aside her apology and asked petulantly, "Where are the medicines, I was waiting for them you know." "I couldn't find them," she muttered. "You could have asked Ramu Kaka," he retorted, his voice rising. She remained silent, afraid that if she spoke it would result in a full blown fight. The kitchen door opened suddenly and Ramu Kaka stood at the doorway. "*Kya hua memsahib*?" he asked. "Ramu Kaka where is the paper bag containing medicines?" she asked, "It was lying on the centre table." "I saw no medicines," Ramu Kaka seemed emphatic in his denial. "Don't be silly," said Shekhar aggressively, "The man who came this evening had flung a brown paper packet containing medicines on the table." Ramu Kaka was equally certain when he said, "I saw no paper packet when I cleaned the table this evening." "Well, look for it," ordered Shekhar, "I need it now." While Ankita searched the drawing room, Ramu Kaka began searching the other rooms. He returned ten minutes later, his face pale, his hands clutching a brown paper bag and two vials, their lid open and their contents half empty.

"I found it in the children's room," he muttered. Shekhar swooped upon the vials and said, "These are half empty, where did the pills go?" Ramu's voice was petrified as he confessed, "There were no tablets on either the floor or the bed. I looked." "What medicines were these?" asked Ankita urgently, "Were they sleeping pills?" Even as she saw Shekhar nod his head she began climbing the stairs, two at a time, as she rushed upstairs. Shekhar and Ramu Kaka followed her almost immediately.

"Wake up Abir, wake up Sameer," Ankita began chanting these words like a mantra. "What is it Ankita?" Shekhar's voice reflected his anxiety. "I'm afraid," she said, her voice breaking, "That they have swallowed the sleeping pills." She saw the look of horror on his face. "My *God*," he whispered, "How many did they take? These were double potency pills."

"Call the ambulance immediately," Ankita ordered Ramu Kaka since Shekhar seemed to have gone to pieces. Within ten minutes both Abir and Sameer were in the ambulance, on their way to the City Hospital. The doctor's face was sombre when he rushed them into emergency. "We can't say anything yet," he said, "We will try a stomach wash." He looked at the bewildered expression on their faces and explained, "We will clean their stomachs of their contents." "It's a good thing you came when you did," he said, "It would have been too late had you discovered this tomorrow morning."

While Shekhar sat like a zombie on the bench Ankita folded her hands in prayer, muttering, "Oh God, please save my sons. Don't let them die. You cannot do this to me. Not again. You took Neha away from me five years ago. You cannot take away my sons from me now. You cannot be so cruel." While she was praying, another emergency case was admitted. A man was being brought in on a stretcher, with his writs slit. He had tried to commit suicide after the death of his son. She looked in horror at the man being wheeled in and realized that he was the man who had come to her house that evening. He opened his eyes suddenly and pointing at them asked, "Why are they here?" "Their children took an overdose of sleeping pills by mistake," explained the doctor. The man's eyes widened in surprise. He then began to laugh loudly. "This is divine retribution," he said. "Don't say that please," Ankita whispered, "Please don't say that." His eyes softened as he looked at her. "Don't worry," he said, "The medicines are spurious. They are not potent. Your sons will live. And their survival will only strengthen my case against your husband's company."

She sat on the bench, numbed by his allegations. "Was it true that India Pharma produced spurious drugs? Was that why the man's son had died? Was that the reason why," she thought, chilled at the thought, "That my blood pressure could not be controlled and Neha was born dead?"

"Oh God," Ankita prayed, "Let this man's allegations be true." She knew that her prayer would spell disaster for her husband's business but it would ensure the safety of her children. She closed her eyes and prayed for the long life of her sons.

□

THE UNWELCOME GUEST

The train picked up speed as it hurtled forward and the old man gazed as buildings began rushing past him. Houses, buildings, trees, lamp posts passed in a haze and the old man realized that he was about to reach Delhi. The train then began to slow down as it was about to enter the station. Standing near the entrance of the compartment, the old man glanced around apprehensively as it reached the platform, which was brimming with life. A sea of humanity seemed to rush towards the compartment as he quickly stepped down, his air bag on his shoulders and the steel trunk by his side. Once his feet had touched the ground he heaved a sigh of relief. It had been his eternal nightmare that he would fall off the compartment onto the track and become crippled for life. He looked around the platform with curiosity. The sight of a man frying bread *pakoras* reminded him of the fact that he had eaten nothing since the last evening. The kiosk selling newspapers and magazines was doing brisk business. A tea vendor, with plastic cups in hand, was selling steaming hot tea to the passengers. Delhi was a strange and unfamiliar city for him and he was afraid to be alone in it. He wished he had informed his son Sudhir of his arrival. His wife Laxmi had urged him to do so but he had told her, "I'll surprise him." The truth was that he was afraid of being unwelcome.

The old man looked at his luggage, which lay by his feet. He knew that he could not carry it all by himself. No coolie seemed to stop near him. Perhaps his simple *dhoti* and *kurta* signalled to the coolie the fact that he was not a wealthy passenger. With great trepidation he called out to a coolie saying, "*Arre bhai yahan aana*." The aged coolie, dressed in the trademark red shirt and white *dhoti*, came to him rather reluctantly, put the steel trunk on his head, and the air bag on his shoulders and threaded his way through the crowd. When they stopped at the *autorickshaw* stand, the old man took out a twenty rupee note and offered it to the coolie, who looked at him in shock "*Aare Kya babuji, yeh kya hai*? I'll not take anything less than fifty rupees." "*Kahan Kahan se aa jaate hain log*," he said, before spitting hard on the pavement, unmindful of the hoarding in front which said that spitting in public was prohibited.

Kahan se aaya tha woh? What could he tell the coolie? He came from a remote village in Etah in Uttar Pradesh where twenty rupees still went a long way, where people did not treat their elders with contempt, where he was not simply an old man, but a respected *Sarpanch* of his village. He broke off from his reverie when the *autorickshaw* man asked him his destination. 'India Gate,' he said proudly. This was his first visit to Delhi. He had never been to India Gate, but he had seen pictures of it. He had also seen India Gate when the Republic Day Parade was telecast. As the *autorickshaw* sped forward he watched the city come slowly to life, the milk vendor on his bicycle carrying metallic containers of milk, a vegetable vendor carrying a load of garden fresh vegetables for sale, children dressed in school uniforms waiting at the bus stop, their tender bodies wilting under the weight of the school bags, the autorickshaw wallahs slowing suddenly at the sight of a potential fare.

Once he reached India Gate he struggled with his notebook, where he had scrawled Sudhir's address. A few minutes later, the autorickshaw stopped before the multi-storied complex called MS Apartments. He looked bewildered for a moment. "All this cannot belong to one person," he thought to himself. Then he realized that Sudhir's address had a house number attached to it. D 305. The man who guided him towards Sudhir's house informed him that there were eight houses on each floor. A few minutes later, he was ringing Sudhir's doorbell.

The door opened after a few minutes. He heaved a sigh of

relief, he had been afraid that Sudhir would be out of town. A strange apparition stood before him, with her hair tied up in a ponytail. As he peered at her, he realized that she was not so strange after all, only he had seen her dressed differently. 'Babuji,' Sudha exclaimed, unable to hide her astonishment, as she bent and touched his feet. "Sudha, who is it?" Sudhir shouted from inside the house. "Why don't you come and see for yourself?" she laughed. Sudhir strode outside and after almost two years the old man saw his son's beloved face. Sudhir looked tired, but the smile on his face on seeing his father was genuine. As he flung his arms around Sudhir and held him in a tight embrace, he felt the rancor of their last meeting disappear. Laxmi had been unnecessarily worried, he thought. She often said, "Our son Sudhir has moved on in life, he has married out of our caste, and now he is ashamed of us." But seeing Sudhir's face the old man knew that his apprehensions were baseless.

"Where is Baba?" he asked Sudhir eagerly. "Babuji, please come inside the room," said Sudha, putting a finger on her lips, "He is sleeping, and mustn't be disturbed." He walked into the bedroom and saw a chubby little baby with the sweetest face he had ever seen, sleeping contentedly in the crib. "He is a carbon copy of Sudhir, he is not a bit like bahu," thought the old man happily.

The old man still remembered the day he had received a letter from Sudhir saying, "Babuji, I know that you will be terribly upset to learn that I have got married." Upset! His anger had known no bounds. He was ready to hit the roof. Laxmi had calmed him down and urged him to read further. In the very next line Sudhir had written, "Sudha and I are coming to seek your blessings."

He had stood at the railway station along with the entire village when the train had arrived. After all the Sarpanchji's son, who was an IAS officer, was coming home. He had hugged Sudhir the moment he had stepped out of the train. But he had been disappointed on seeing Sudha. She was painfully thin, with a wheatish complexion and plain features. She was frankly not the bahu he had wanted for Sudhir. "Why had Sudhir married her?"

he wondered. "Babuji she is also in the IAS like me," Sudhir had written in the letter. It was evident that he wanted a working wife, someone very different from his mother.

After her bath, Sudha had worn the red *zari saree* he had bought for her a day ago. Sudhir had burst out laughing on seeing her and said, "You look ridiculous Sudha." "Hush, don't let your parents hear you," she had giggled.

After some time Sudha had wanted to use the toilet. Sudhir had asked his mother to show Sudha the toilet. Sudha had returned to the room, looking horror-stricken. "I can't stay here Sudhir," she had said loudly, "The toilets are dirty." "The scavenger will come later in the day," Laxmi had said apologetically. Sudhir had turned to his father and asked him what had happened to the money he had sent for the construction of toilets with running water, inside the house and Babuji had explained that he had purchased a pair of oxen with the money instead. "Well, we can't stay in this house, where there are no toilets. I will move to the Guest House nearby," Sudhir muttered and Sudha and Sudhir left that very afternoon. Two days later, cutting short their stay, they returned to Mussoorie.

Suddenly, the bitterness created by their visit was forgotten. The old man had wanted to see his grandson more than anything else in the world, so despite Laxmi's apprehensions he had come to Delhi. As the old man explored Sudhir's house, he realized that it was pitifully small. There was one bedroom, one drawing room and an old *verandah* which had been converted into a bedroom. The house had just one toilet and bathroom. The old man remembered his own sprawling house in the village, especially, the garden where he could pluck guavas straight from the trees. He thought of his mango orchards, where the sweet and sour langda aam grew in abundance and the litchi trees whose lush fruit had him yearning for more. He remembered his fields of mustard and arhar. He felt cramped in Sudhir's house. After sometime, he knew, he would feel distinctly claustrophobic in such a tiny house.

The baby started wailing, interrupting his thoughts. "*Nahi nahi*, don't cry, your bottle is ready," said Sudha to the baby. 'Bottle?' the old man bristled in anger as he saw Sudha put a drop of milk on her wrist and lift the baby in her arms to feed him. “Doesn’t Bahu breastfeed the baby herself?” he asked Sudhir indignantly. “I’m afraid she cannot,” murmured Sudhir, “The baby was a Caesarean and not a normal birth, and Sudha began feeding him two days later. By that time he was hooked on to a bottle. Sudha did try to feed him herself but he remained hungry while she fed him. So he has to be bottle-fed.” The old man had never heard of women who were unable to feed their children. Why, in the village, breastfeeding an infant came instinctively to a mother. And women were healthy enough to give birth to babies naturally. They did not need operations for that. This was yet another black mark against Sudha.

He woke up early next day and went for a walk. The walk near India Gate worked as a tonic and mood booster and he returned home refreshed and hungry. When Sudha served the old man toast and boiled eggs for breakfast he looked at her in bewilderment. Was that all she had to serve him? He yearned for a large glass of buttermilk as well as *jalebi* and *dahi*. The toast and eggs left him hungry.

That night Sudhir told him, “Babuji, I’m calling my boss for dinner. Would you like to join us?” Immediately a shiver ran up his spine. “What would a semi-literate farmer say to a senior IAS officer?” His first urge was to run away from Delhi. He shook his head vehemently and was secretly relieved when Sudhir did not insist on his presence, but told him to have dinner early and sleep in his room.

As he hovered around the kitchen out of sheer curiosity the old man found that elaborate preparations were being made for the dinner. He saw paneer being sliced, chicken being roasted, fish being fried, potatoes being boiled and pulao being cooked. The smell of basmati rice filled the house. The old man savoured the meal in the privacy of his room. By eight o’clock, long before the boss came for dinner, he had gone to bed.

But to his surprise, sleep was slow to come. The old man could hear voices in the drawing room, interspersed with sounds of laughter and of tinkling glasses. “They must be serving cold drinks to the boss,” he surmised. He then heard the food being laid out on the dining table. Soon he heard people moving around the dining table. His small room, an enclosed verandah really, with its single bed, suddenly seemed suffocating and he got up for a breath of fresh air and a glass of water. Clad in a *dhoti* and *kurta* he walked into the kitchen for water. Then unable to contain his curiosity he peeped into the drawing room. His eyes fell on a well dressed gentleman who was smoking a cigarette. The gentleman turned and spotted him hovering by the door. "Who is he?" he asked Sudhir.

He waited for Sudhir to introduce him to the boss but Sudhir suddenly became tongue-tied. "He is, he…" Sudhir seemed to be incapable of completing the sentence. Then Sudhir said, "He is our ser…" The old man realized with horror that Sudhir was going to claim that he was a servant! The old man could have died of mortification. He wished that the earth would open and swallow him up. He remembered the sacrifice he had made in educating Sudhir, the pride he had in Sudhir's scholastic achievements and the overwhelming sense of gratitude he had felt when Sudhir had qualified for the Indian Administrative Service. Then he saw Sudha walking towards him. "He is the 'Sarpanch,' of Sudhir's village, where he is popularly known as 'Sarpanchji' by one and all," she said, without pausing, "But for us he is Babuji, Sudhir's father."

"Come Babuji," she said softly as she led him towards a vacant chair in the drawing room. Turning towards Sudhir's boss she said, "Sir, he is perhaps the best person to tell us about the problems faced by the village panchayats which we were just discussing." Once the old man found that Sudhir's boss seemed genuinely interested in what he had to say, he waxed eloquent on the subject.

When he had finished speaking Babuji stole a glance at Sudhir. He was glad to see that Sudhir was unable to look him in the eye, he was looking ashamed. He then looked at his daughter-in-law, whom he had condemned as being plain and arrogant. This plain looking girl, he admitted, obviously had stronger values and a superior moral fibre than his own son. "Thank you *Beti*," he whispered to her as he left the room.

□

AUTUMN LEAVES

The winter was very severe. It was cold enough to make her shiver even beneath her quilt. It was severe enough to make her wish that she could banish the cold, ease the pain from her arthritic fingers and melt the ice in her bones. She thought wistfully of warm sun rays, which could turn everything golden, and the first blade of grass, which was the harbinger of spring and which could at one stroke lift the bleakness from her surroundings as well as her heart.

The doorbell rang just then. Kartik was back from work. Savitri could hear the maid's footsteps as she went to open the door. She knew that the dog Bruno would put up his legs and lick Kartik on his hands, and as Kartik bent down to fondle him, on his face as well. 'Lucky dog,' she thought, "At least he gets to touch him." She could not recall the last time she had hugged Kartik or touched his face. She wondered how Kartik would react if she did so. Would he stand stoically and suffer her embrace, or would he recoil ever so slightly, trying to disguise his annoyance. She gave a loud sigh. There was so little she knew about her son. Their worlds had drifted so far apart. She instinctively straightened herself and put the shawl around her tightly as though it could protect her not only from the onslaught of cold but from his verbal onslaughts as well.

She knew Kartik would first make a perfunctory stop in her room, before he headed for the bedroom where Smriti would be waiting for him. Savitri was right. He stepped inside, shivered and said, "It's cold. Why didn't you switch on the heater?" "I didn't like to..." she had not even completed the sentence when he laughed and said, "Don't worry about electricity bills, Ma, we can afford to pay them." His words stunned her. Her mind wandered back to the incident, years ago when her husband had lashed out at Kartik for using the room heater the whole day. "We can't afford to pay the electricity bills," he had said. Evidently, Kartik had not forgotten.

She looked intently at Kartik. He was so different from his father, who had been a headmaster. A revered headmaster, she remembered with pride, who had won the National Teacher's Award on Teachers Day but who remained humble to the last. Who, she thought, her eyed brimming with tears, had left behind several tearful students and a heartbroken family. Except, she thought cynically, his son.

Kartik was away in Australia when his father died. He had not been able to return in time for the cremation. Ruma had performed the last rites, much to the consternation of their extended family. "But what could one do?" thought Savitri sadly. One couldn't wait for days for Kartik to return. Kartik had been difficult to contact and having realized that the cremation would be over by the time he returned, had chosen not to cut short his tour. He had come to see her, she admitted to herself, immediately after he had landed in Delhi. "Come Ma," he had said, "Make your home with us." But she could not give up the old house, every nook of which held so many memories for her. This was the house where she came as a bride, where Kartik and Ruma were born, and from where Ruma was married. But not Kartik. Kartik had preferred to announce his marriage to Smriti, after the event was over. Had she been shocked? Savitri could not even recall that. It had happened almost fifteen years ago. A few years later he had left for USA, along with Smriti and his children. They had returned only ten years later. Perhaps she had expected this severing of family ties, for although Kartik had never said it, he had nevertheless made it abundantly clear that he was ashamed of his roots.

But the house where her husband died was her home. It was the only home she had known. She could never leave it permanently. She had not missed the look of relief on Kartik's face when she declined his offer. "You'll live alone?" he had sounded amazed. "Well, Ruma lives closeby and her husband Shiv is like a son to me," She could not resist that tiny barb. However, Kartik had insisted that she come to visit him as soon as possible and that is why she had visited him two months ago.

Two months. It seemed a lifetime. And yet Savitri could not complain that Smriti or Kartik had been unkind to her. It was just that she felt unwanted. If she entered the kitchen to cook something, one of the servants came forward to do it instead. If she tried to dust the furniture, the maid took the duster from her hand. The truth was, she felt redundant.

Kartik sat the corner of the bed, careful to ensure that the crease of his pant was not spoiled. "Did you take your medicines?" he asked her. Savitri smiled. She knew what he would ask next. How was her blood pressure? And her diabetes? She knew it would take them just five minutes, to run through the gamut of questions. Once they had so much to talk about, about his dream of going to USA, the land of opportunity, of striking it rich, of getting out of the lower middle-class rut. Today he kept his dreams and ambitions to himself. Or was it that he had stopped dreaming? Had he had finally achieved each dream that he had chased and had nothing left to dream about?

"I must be off," Kartik said casually over the shoulder, "Smriti and I are going out to attend a dinner." "What about the children?" She asked. "Oh Rohit and Reema are going out with their friends. But the servants are at home. You can call them if you want anything. And you can watch a film on TV," said Kartik.

Before leaving for dinner, Smriti came into Savitri's room. She looked well groomed, as always. "Maji, if you want anything," she said, "just let the servants know." "I want you," Savitri wanted to say, "I want you and Kartik and the children around me, treating me as a part of the family, sharing your day with me. Talking to me, really talking, the way my daughter Ruma and her husband Shiv do." But of course Savitri said nothing.

A few days before Savitri was to return to Kolkata, Kartik

asked her if she wanted to go shopping. Savitri gave a sigh of relief. She didn't think she could have broached the subject of shopping on her own. In her own hometown, she would have gone with Shiv in their car, or with Ruma in a rickshaw, but there she was a part of the family. Here she was merely a guest. "I'd like to buy some woollens," she said. Kartik had paid for her railway ticket, which was why she was able to save five thousand rupees from her husband's pension. She wanted to buy sweaters for everyone, Ruma, Shiv, their two sons and Ruma's mother-in-law and father-in-law. Six sweaters in all.

During the weekend, Kartik took her to the largest shopping complex in the city. They entered a showroom, where mannequins displayed hip-hugging cardigans. "How much do the sweaters cost?" she asked Smriti. Smriti turned the tag and whispered, "One thousand each." She did a quick mental sum. If she spent so much on each sweater, she would not be able to buy all six. She declined to purchase anything. She saw Kartik's irritation grow and Smriti give a tight little smile.

They then entered another shop. "Why don't you ask Maji what her budget is?" Smriti asked Kartik. "Seven hundred each," Savitri said tentatively. "Then this is not the market for Maji," laughed Smriti, the condescension she had struggled to hide for so long, amply visible. Savitri stood fingering a lovely cardigan. It was fawn with strands of brown, yellow and green woven in, just like autumn leaves. It was soft to touch, and she knew instinctively that it would be exquisitely warm. It would be out of her range, she knew. "How much?" Savitri didn't even dare to ask. "Come on Amma," said Kartik, "You can't afford this one. Why, even I didn't buy it for myself when I came here last." "How much?" she steeled her voice and asked. "Three thousand five hundred rupees," said Smriti, in a loud voice. She felt that all heads had turned towards her. Suddenly, she made up her mind. "I'll take it," she said. 'But,' blurted out Kartik, "What about your budget?" "I'll buy just this one cardigan," she said.

As she paid three thousand five hundred rupees, she realized that she wouldn't be able to get any gifts for anyone back home.

She hoped they would understand. But it even if they were disappointed it didn't matter. What was done was done. "Why did you buy it?" grumbled Kartik, "It won't even fit Shiv, he's too fat." She had no answer to that.

That night, as she lay on the bed, she put the sweater by her side. At times she buried her face in its warmth. It was a mad thing to have done. But once, just once in her life she had wanted to splurge, to give into a whim, an indulgence. And it had been worth it, to wipe out that look of condescension from Smriti's perfectly made up face, to see her mouth open and gape like a goldfish. She chuckled to herself. Yes, it had been worth it. Yet that was not the only reason she had bought it, she knew.

The day of her departure dawned soon after. Savitri was ready with all her luggage, long before her train was to leave. "Amma," said Kartik, "have you checked your luggage? I hope you have left nothing behind." "I'm ready," she said and giving the room a last lingering look, she left. "Give me your luggage," he said, taking her suitcase, "I'll put it in the car." While leaving the house, Savitri gave five hundred rupees each to the children and a hundred rupees each to the servants. She saw respect dawning in their eyes. "If only," she thought sadly, "you had not judged me solely by money."

When Kartik returned home that evening he suddenly realized that he missed his mother. He went to her room, where he could still feel her presence. Perhaps it was due to the lingering smell of the sandalwood incense sticks she burnt in her room, which reminded him of her. Or perhaps it was the fragrance of the flowers, which she plucked for her *puja*. But there was a strange sense of peace here, which was missing from the other rooms in the house. He sat by the side of the bed where he always did and felt something beneath the bedcover. He put in his hand and pulled out the sweater, which lay neatly folded. For a moment Kartik thought that she had forgotten to take it. But the next moment he knew it was for him. Amma had bought it and gifted it to him, because of his casual remark that even he couldn't afford to buy it for himself. He wore it quickly and then saw himself in the mirror. The years seemed to have rolled away from him. He thought he looked a decade younger. "Look Smriti," he called out to his wife, "Look what Amma has left for me." Smriti appeared at the doorway, and with a supercilious lift of her eyebrow said, "Surely you can't wear that?" "Why ever not?" he enquired mildly. 'Well,' she said disparagingly, "It's a size too small for you." His face fell. He thought it fitted him perfectly. But he trusted Smriti's judgment more. "Give it to me, I'll put it to better use," she said. Reluctantly, he handed over the cardigan, wondering what she intended to do with it.

'Bahadur,' she called out to their cook, "Come here." When the cook appeared, she lifted the cardigan to hand it to him. For a moment Kartik was stunned into silence. Then he snatched the cardigan from her hand. "No you don't," he said. Something in his voice quelled her. "But it's too small for you..." her voice trailed off. "In that case," he said with deceptive mildness, "I will lose weight." She looked at him uncertainly. There was something in his face she had never seen before. For the first time in her life she began to feel afraid of him. She left the room quietly.

Once again Kartik was alone in the room. His eyes were misted with tears. He buried his face in the cardigan. He understood how much his mother had sacrificed to buy this one cardigan, the cardigan which fitted him beautifully, but which Smriti had disdainfully tried to give away to the servant. He wondered how Smriti had treated his mother in his absence. I haven't been much better, he thought ruefully, I have treated my mother like a stranger. He knew that he had consciously tried to distance himself from his family, but today sitting alone, he realized how empty his life had become. He looked at the cardigan and once again thought of his Amma, who had always thought of others and never about herself. He suddenly knew what he had to do.

As the train entered the railway station, Savitri began peering at the platform. She wondered fleetingly who would be there to receive her. Perhaps Shiv, and perhaps Ruma, and her two grandchildren as well. She wondered if they would be disappointed that she had returned empty-handed. She shrugged her shoulders.

It couldn't be helped anyway. Savitri was startled when she caught the unexpected sight of Kartik standing at the platform, wearing a strangely familiar fawn coloured cardigan. How did he reach Kolkata and that too before her? She knew the answer to that one. He took a flight to the city. But why did he do that? She could not figure that out. The next minute she knew. He climbed into the compartment, perfunctorily touched her feet and then enveloped her in a bear hug. He saw the unspoken question in her eyes and said gently, "Amma, I've come to take you home."

□

NOT ANOTHER SILAS

The house seemed strangely empty. Suddenly, Amba realized why it appeared to be so. It was because there was no sound coming from upstairs, no sound of a raucous cough, no sound of Bhanumati beating the clothes on the stone floor before washing them, no sound of Chachaji croaking 'bahu,' in his reedy voice. "He must be asleep," she surmised. Through the iron grill in the courtyard, she could see a patch of the sky. She saw a kite being flown, a majestic kite, all purple and yellow, with an enormous tail. She wished it would not get cut, not now, not ever. To her, the kite epitomized freedom. It appeared to be unfettered, as it soared in the sky, further and further till it became a mere speck, so different from her own life which was shackled to the old house. Suddenly, she decided to climb upstairs to check up on Chachaji. She did it often these days, ever since he had fallen and broken his leg, which had never healed properly.

She climbed the steep stone steps carefully. Even at the age of thirty-five she had begun to feel the strain of climbing stairs. Besides she could not quite forget that these uneven steps were responsible for Chachaji's fall. She entered Chachaji's room carefully, mindful of the sudden change in the level of the floor. Chachaji lay peacefully on the stringed cot, a handloom bedcover in pastel stripes covering him. Against the wall stood a table, on which lay a tray containing balls of all sizes, which he had confiscated when they were flung onto the terrace, or into the house. "Mean old man, a regular Silas Marner," that is what all the children, including Raju, called him. 'Hush,' she would say, "He is our landlord and he is nice to us, he gives you so many kites and balls." "Nothing he has purchased himself," Raju would reply scornfully. She looked at the wall by the bed, on which hung the kites, which Chachaji had collected when they had fallen on the terrace. The kites hung on nails on the wall in a curious mosaic, completely hiding the plaster peeling on the yellow walls. They reminded her of the kite festival, celebrated with gusto in many parts of India. Or, she giggled to herself, a scalp hunter's booty. She remembered asking Chachaji once, "Why don't you return these to the children to whom they belong?"

"When has any child come to me to ask for them?" he had asked, almost wistfully. People had made him into an ogre, she had realized with sudden insight, when he was just a lonely old man.

She peeped into the kitchen. The steel utensils gleamed on the kitchen shelves. One had to concede, she thought to herself, that Bhanumati did her job well. She picked up the steel container covering the earthen *matka*, to see if it was filled with water, and dropped it inadvertently on the floor. It fell with a loud clang, piercing the silence. She picked it up, dipped it in the aluminum pail lying beside the tap, and wiped it quickly with the end of her *pallu*, waiting for Chachaji to holler in his reedy voice, "What happened?" But he didn't say a thing. 'Strange,' she said to herself, "he is normally a light sleeper." She went up to him and hesitantly put a hand on his head. It was cold.

She felt a sense of foreboding as she touched his flesh. 'Dead,' the realization dawned upon her immediately. She had never seen death at close quarters. She didn't know what to do. She did not even know the telephone number of his relations, she thought hysterically. The knock at the door downstairs brought her back to reality. "Raju is home," she said to herself, relief flooding through her. She rushed down the stairs, forgetting the unevenness and steepness of the steps, and opening the door, blurted out, "He is dead." For a moment Raju was taken aback. He felt a sudden dread. 'Who?' he began to say, and then seeing her point upstairs, he rushed to the *kirana* shop outside and telephoned his father who then took over.

The news of Chachaji's death spread fast. Soon the shop owner returned with Raju. The other neighbours began to troop in as well. The neighbour's wife brought her a hot cup of tea. Raju ran to call the doctor from the dispensary nearby. Chachaji's relatives arrived a few hours later. They brought a *pundit* along with them. She watched Chachaji's body trussed up on the "arthi" before they left for the crematorium. "We will have to get our meals from outside,"she whispered to her husband, reminding him of the old custom, "There has been a death in the house." "But not in the family," he said in a stern voice, "He was no relation of ours, he was merely our landlord."

She shook her head sadly. It was so difficult to make him understand. Chachaji was part of the family, the only family she had in *Kucha Chelan*, in the walled city of Delhi, besides Raju and her husband. She met her own parents, who lived in Gorakhpur, not more than once a year. It was Chachaji who was the elder in the family. Relationships were not always forged by blood, but by association as well. How could she make her husband understand?

The men were back from the crematorium after a few hours. She had nothing to offer them. "Whatever Raju's father may say I won't cook anything," she said mutinously to herself, as a silent protest. Just then the doorbell rang. The *halwai* was standing outside. He was carrying containers of *aloo bhaji*, mango pickle, and *bedbi*, a delicacy typical of the walled city of Delhi, a cross between *dal ki kachori* and *bhatura*. She had often seen it being made at the mithai shop, where the halwai would slap the ball of maida on his bare thigh, before rolling it into *bedbi*, and then fry it in the big black karhai which smoked with oil, till it puffed up completely. It disgusted her, the thought of his sweat on the *bedbi*, but she always forgot about it once she took a bite. "Behenji, You mustn't have cooked today," he mumbled and pressing the earthen container of sabji and packets of *bedbi* and pickles into her hands, he went away.

The *bedbi*s brought back a host of memories. On the last Sunday of every month, the room on the top of the house was full of visitors, when Chachaji's brother, his three sons and their families, came for breakfast and feasted on *bedbi* and *subzi*, followed by '*malai ki baraf*.' The *malai ki baraf* came in two varieties. The more popular, *malai ki baraf*, a creamy concoction which melted in the mouth like *kulfi*, or the seasonal and exotic *aam ki baraf*, made from the juiciest mangoes of the season. 'Chachaji,' his nephews teased him, "*ek aur malai ki baraf dena*," but he would humorously retort, "pay for it yourself." 'Miser,' they all laughed, but after such a hefty breakfast it was obvious that they did not really have appetite for more. She knew that in despite his demeanour, he really loved his brother's family. She knew that this had been his surrogate family, ever since he became a widower.

"Do you have a set of keys to Chachaji's room?" Chachaji's eldest nephew Aseem asked Amba. 'Yes,' she said, displaying a long iron key from her silver key ring. "Will you give to me?" he said, "I'll have to lock it up until the will is read." 'Will?' for a moment she was baffled. Will was something she had associated only with the rich and Chachaji was hardly rich. If he had been, why did he not stay in a hospital, when he had slipped down the stairs and broken his leg? She remembered that Sunday so well. Chachaji was returning after buying the *bedbi*s, when his foot had slipped on a ball, which had treacherously hidden atop the stairs. He had fallen in a heap and his cry of pain had made her and Raju rush up the stairs. Her husband had rushed Chachaji to the hospital. A couple of days later Chachaji had shifted to his brother's palatial house. She remembered her husband's overawed, "Woh ghar nahin mahal hai," as he went on to describe the marbled floor of the chandeliered drawing room, the air-conditioned room in which Chachaji had been put up, the spacious lawns and the retinue of servants he had seen there. "But were the hearts of his relations as big?" Amba had wondered, when Chachaji had returned in just two week's time, saying cryptically, "It wasn't home," when she had asked him why he had returned so soon. She suspected, although she had no way of knowing, that in some way he had been slighted and that his pride had been hurt. His leg hadn't really healed. "Old bones take a long time to mend," the doctor had said and Chachaji was almost confined to the room upstairs. He had begun paying the maid Bhanumati extra money, to look after him and gradually he had taken to his bed.

Occasionally, when Bhanumati was not at home he would shout, 'Bahu,' and Amba would offer him her shoulder, to take him to the bathroom and back. It was always difficult for her frail shoulders to support his burden, but she could hardly complain. It was on one such occasion that her husband, on his way to the terrace, had seen her. He had struck her on the jaw, once they were back in the sanctity of their bedroom. 'Bitch,' he had hissed. She had recoiled in horror, both at his words, and at the blood, which was dripping from her mouth, which seemed to have been ripped apart by the blow. "Your *pallu* had fallen down. Your cleavage was showing," he had screamed. She had been appalled. "What are you talking about?" she had said, her mind in a daze. "I bet he does it deliberately," her husband had sneered, "the old man must be enjoying putting his arms around you." "He is like my father," she had stuttered, too stunned to react. She had seen Chachaji eye her swollen face with compassion and understanding, the next time he had called her. He had started calling her less often. But some kind of perverse defiance made her go up on her own to check up on him, as if to tell her husband that he could bruise her flesh but not her spirit.

Suddenly, she realized that Chachaji would have left the house to someone, his brother or his nephews. It would probably be sold. Why would the men living in a spacious bungalow in Delhi, want to retain this old house in the walled city, within a maze of *gallis*? Sure, she had become accustomed to it all. The narrow *galli* outside her house. The corner *halwai* shop, the fruit juice stall next to it and the stationery shop after that. She had got used to the smell of *pakoras* being fried in mustard oil in the *halwai* shop and the sight of cows ambling lazily in the *galli*. She had learnt to be adept at sidestepping the mounds of cow dung which was inevitable, while making sure that the rickshaw pullers did not knock her down while she walked in the narrow *galli*. But why would Chachaji's relations want to retain the house? According to many people, it was an ill-shaped house, shaped like a lion's jaw, with a wide entrance and a narrow interior. Many, including her husband, had even started calling the house inauspicious. She did not know anything about that. She only knew that for the three months when her husband was without a job, Chachaji had never asked for rent and had surprised her by lending her money to pay Raju's school fees. It was this act of generosity, which had made Amba treat him not as a mere landlord, but as a member of her family. She had returned the money, but she knew that the debt she owed him could never be repaid.

"Where will we go once the house is sold?" she thought to herself, "Where will we get a two bed-roomed house in Delhi by paying a rent of three hundred rupees per month?" Strangely, she had not thought of this even once since Chachaji died. But the mention of the will had made her anxious about her future. "When God closes one door, he opens another," she had often heard her father say. She hoped this was true.

The next day the lawyer arrived, to read out the will. It was quite an event. She saw a small pool of urchins gather outside, when the lawyer's car stopped at the entrance of the *galli*. Chachaji's brother, his three nephews and their wives had arrived already. She was a little taken aback, when the lawyer asked her family to join the meeting as well. "May be has left something for our Raju," said her husband exultantly. "What can he leave Raju, but his collection of balls and kites? He was not a rich man," she retorted.

Amba was wrong. She discovered that Chachaji did not merely own the house, besides his pension, he had also possessed bits of his wife's gold jewellery. The jewellery alone was worth about five lakh rupees. Chachaji's fixed deposits were worth another five lakhs, the lawyer had explained. "Funny, with this kind of money he could have got himself a full-time nurse and spent his last days more comfortably," Amba thought to herself. He need not have depended on just Bhanumati and herself. She was caught completely unawares, when the lawyer mentioned her name. "I bequeath all my worldly possessions to my *Bahu* Amba, whose devotion and care I can never repay."

She was shocked beyond belief, on hearing these words. So were the others. So was her husband. She could see a range of emotions flit across his face. She tried to interpret them, but failed. She dreaded the prospect of returning to her house downstairs with him. Would he hit her once they were in the privacy of their house? Would he accuse her of infidelity? Would he believe her, when she said that the relationship was entirely innocent, it was exactly what Chachaji had mentioned in his will, that between an Uncle-in-law and a Bahu?"

The taunting began immediately after the will was read. "Who could have believed it, she looked so innocent?" muttered Chachaji's eldest nephew Aseem. "She has played her cards really well," murmured his wife. "We should have guessed as soon as he insisted on returning home, that he had someone waiting for him," smirked the youngest nephew Varun. "He wasn't so old, just sixty-five," sniggered the middle nephew, "And she is not a day less than thirty-five." The innuendoes were awful and they hurt her terribly. "Stop it," she wanted to shout, "Stop it. He didn't deserve this. Nor do I." But her throat seem to have dried completely.

She was the first to come down the stairs, unmindful of their steepness, and she almost stumbled when she reached the last step. If Raju had not saved her, she knew she would have fallen in a heap. She returned to her house slowly, the news not sinking in. She then made a sudden resolve. She would have nothing to do with the money. "Let it go to his brother and his nephews," she thought, "They are his blood after all." She was certain that her husband would never touch Chachaji's money. He would consider it tainted.

Steeped in her own thoughts, she entered her room. She felt her husband's hand on her shoulders. She flinched as she waited for him to turn her towards him, she closed her eyes as she waited for the blow. It came as a surprise when he whispered into her ears, "I am very happy today." 'Why?' she said, bewildered by his reaction. "Why not?" he looked at her in amazement, "I don't have to worry about a roof over my head. Now Raju can go to an engineering or medical college when he is older. And finally I may be able to start my own business." There was as usual no mention of her.

"Don't you think that we should not take the money? His blood relations deserve it after all," she said hesitantly. "We didn't ask for it, did we?" he almost spat out the words, "He gave it to us because of the devotion you showed to him, because the care you took of him, like a real daughter-in-law. Where were his relations when he needed them? Where were they these last few months?"

"People will say many things about me and him," she said eyeing him warily. "Not just his relations but others as well." "Let them," he said, shrugging his shoulders, "Mad dogs always bark." Saying this he flopped onto the bed and pulled her towards him. As she felt his hot breath fanning her face, saw desire writ large in his eyes, she closed her eyes. Some perverse desire to hurt him made her say, "What if there was some truth in the gossip?" She thought he would jump up at that, his face contorted with disbelief, and possibly rage. But not even a spasm of pain crossed his face as he said, "I would prefer to let bygones be bygones." She recalled the stunning blow he had given her a just month ago, which had ripped the insides of her mouth. She recalled the blood which had dripped from her mouth and stained her blouse. She recalled his anger and rage, which had been entirely baseless. Where had it gone? And where, more importantly, was his pride and self-esteem? She had thought that she would never forget the intensity of that searing pain. It paled, by comparison, to the pain she felt now.

□

THE HERO

The bus stop was deserted on this winter night. The unexpected downpour had turned the weather chilly. Saurabh could feel the biting wind seep through his shirt. He hated winter, which was accompanied by early sunsets, cold feet and joints, and large shadows looming on the roadside. Winter, Saurabh knew, froze activity and stifled creativity. He peered at the luminous dial of his watch. It was eight o'clock. This was no time to be out on an empty road. He longed to snuggle under the warmth of a quilt. He walked on the pavement, his feet making a staccato sound on the concrete. The bushes by the pavement cast eerie shadows on the road. Somewhere at a distance, an owl hooted. Saurabh marvelled at the fact that the same road, which had a steady stream of pedestrians on a sultry summer day, was totally abandoned on the misty December evening. "All I need now is to complete the picture of desolation, is a jackal's cry," he muttered shakily. His meeting with Shikha had left him perturbed. He had been meeting her clandestinely after office hours for days, his preoccupation with work being his eternal excuse for his late return from office. "And what do I have to look forward to?" he thought to himself. He had nothing to look forward to at home, but for two anaemic children, sniffling, overawed by him, and his passive, boring and predictable wife Renu. She was so different from Shikha, whose sensitive, mobile face portrayed a variety of emotions, enthusiasm over a project, anger at some perceived injustice and sheer delight at some achievement.

His face was suffused with a warm glow as he recalled Shikha's soft, supple and smooth hand, tenderly sweeping away the lock of hair which had fallen across his forehead. Meetings with Shikha rejuvenated him. She was the elixir which held the key to eternal youth. With Shikha he was no longer 38, middle-aged and the father of two. He was transformed into someone young and carefree. But today was different. Shikha was preoccupied. A small frown had appeared on her forehead, her eyebrows had puckered in concentration, and she had asked him the question he had been dreading, "How long can this go on?"

"Forever and ever," he would have liked to answer dreamily. For Shikha's stimulating company always transported him into another world, an exotic and hitherto unexplored world. He knew he was traversing dangerous grounds, a dalliance post-marriage was fraught with peril, but he did not consider it a dalliance. He was truly in love with her. But he realized that today Shikha seemed changed. She had wanted more from the relationship, marriage perhaps. He had not thought this far. Holding hands, a few stolen kisses, he had not progressed beyond that. She had, in an uncharacteristic gesture of violence, flung the coffee cup on the ground. It had dropped with a soft plop on the plush carpet, the dregs of coffee leaving a trail on its silken smoothness. He had picked it up, and coaxed, "Shikha, listen." Suddenly, she had turned her frightened eyes towards him and said, "Saurabh, I must go. I think Manish has seen us." Saying this, she had fled. "Manish," Saurabh thought with a shudder, "Mad, muscular Manish." Saurabh had seen him occasionally in office when he had come to meet Shikha. He was a big man with rippling muscles, who was her self-appointed guardian. "I would not like a showdown with Manish, not if I can help it," thought Saurabh.

He was still thinking of Shikha, as he walked towards the overhead bridge. Near the banyan tree, he suddenly stopped and blinked. Emerging from the shadows, four figures, faces covered with hankies, advanced towards him. "My wallet, that's what they're after," Saurabh thought immediately. It contained the ten thousand rupees he had withdrawn for household expenditure. But the money was nothing compared to his safety and even before they said something he took his wallet out of his pocket and with trembling hands, offered it to them, muttering, "Here take this, but please leave me alone." But the wallet was tossed aside disdainfully, and even before he could register the fact, a blow landed on his stomach, making him double up in agony. He crouched in a kneeling position, trying to lessen the pain, when another blow landed on his jaw, ripping the skin off his cheek, as his assailant's fist grazed it. The pain came in waves. He clenched his hands into fists, and closed his eyes, to blot out the nightmare, but it was not over yet. An arm sailed from somewhere and hit him in the eye and as he reeled under the impact, he felt a well-heeled foot kick him in the abdomen. He lay on his back, his eyes closed, and heard three sets of footsteps walk away from him. The last one stopped. He spat onto Saurabh's face and walked away, victory echoing in the jauntiness of his steps. Saurabh retched on the pavement, the bitter-sour taste of vomit in his mouth, a pale caricature of the man he had been a few minutes ago. He wiped his face with his arm, and his hand came away drenched with blood, which seemed to drip from everywhere, his nose, his lips and his cheeks. Tears rolled down his cheeks and in the dark he rocked himself on his heels and cried. At last he got up, surprised that he could still walk, and had not been maimed for life. All he had suffered were a few blows and the loss of his wallet. As he moved, slowly and painfully on the pavement, his foot struck something soft. He looked down and found his leather wallet, with the money still intact. "Why this mindless violence if not for money?" he wondered. But he realized that there must be some method in the madness. "Who could have done this?" he wondered.

Immediately, the image of Shikha's brother, brawny and big built, rose before his eyes, whom his malicious colleagues like Jatin could have instigated. Jatin,who bore him a grudge ever since Saurabh had bypassed him for a coveted promotion. This could also be Manish's way of saying, "Keep off my sister or else...." Perhaps Shikha had some inkling of what Manish had planned, which would explain her preoccupied air, her anxiety and her fear. Saurabh agonized over the fact that Manish would malign him by telling others about his cowardice and capitulation. But he realized that Manish, the perpetrator of the violence could hardly admit to his own misdeed. By the time he reached his door-step, Saurabh had decided what he would say.

A sleek Hero Honda stood at the doorway. Vijay and Vinayak, his two brothers-in-law, Saurabh grimaced. Then his face brightened. The more of them, he thought, the merrier. The door was opened by Renu. She blanched as she saw Saurabh's face caked with blood. Angry welts stood on his cheeks, making an inverted V, as though for victory, thought Saurabh wryly as he caught sight of his face in the mirror. "What happened?" Renu asked in a strangled sort of a voice. "Four *thugs* were after my wallet," began Saurabh. "Are you sure?" she asked, wide-eyed. "Sure? Of course, I'm sure," he said belligerently, "But I couldn't let them get away with it, so I decided to fight." "Can't you recognize them?" she asked. "I can't," he said, "But though I was alone, I managed to salvage my wallet."

"You're quite a Hero," said Jatin, reclining on an armchair in the drawing room, sipping a hot cup of coffee. So it was Jatin's mobike he had seen outside, realized Saurabh. Jatin seemed perfectly at home. He tried to detect a hint of mockery in Jatin's voice, but his voice was completely devoid of any inflection. "Why don't you call a doctor, Jatin bhaiya?" Renu said shakily, "God alone knows what injuries he has suffered." "There's nothing, which a few days rest won't cure," the doctor, who lived across the road, reassured Renu, who seemed to be ready to burst into tears.

Once inside the warmth of the quilt, Saurabh quite enjoyed Renu's ministrations, which had usually left him irritated. The hot water bottle provided comfort to his aching back, while Renu's fingers moved rhythmically over his arms and legs. The massage produced a soporific effect and in no time, he was asleep.

That night, he had a nightmare. He was back at the banyan tree and the four *thugs* were back again, fists encased in boxers' gloves. And as he stood rooted on the spot, they began beating him, until he turned into a punching bag. He shuddered and remembered the times he had punched Vinay and Vineeta and occasionally his wife Renu. While his children had whimpered and cried, Renu had stood stoically, bearing the violence silently, which only spurred him on. She retaliated by remaining silent for days on end. Saurabh believed that Renu deserved it. But tonight, in a rare introspective mood, he wondered how she had tolerated the violence. Had she ever cried when she was alone in the room? Had she cursed him? Had she wished that he too became a victim of violence? The beating he had received had taught him that it was humiliating and demeaning. It debased a person. He decided that he would henceforth never beat his wife or children.

There was a stream of visitors in his house that weekend. Jatin, Probir, Subir, Nishant, almost all his colleagues visited him. But there was no sign of Shikha. Where was she? And did she know about his injuries? Suddenly, it became imperative for him to see her, to look into her eyes and know if she was party to the violence. If she looked away, he would know. He also wanted to know the movements of his brothers-in-law, Vijay and Vinayak, who always seem to be mocking him. "Where are they Renu?" he asked, "they didn't come this weekend." "They're busy with their semester exams," she said apologetically. He sighed, having lost this opportunity to play the hero before their eyes.

On Monday morning, despite Renu's protests, he was back at work. He saw Shikha dressed in a powder blue *saree*, but she did not meet his eyes. Others however were eagerly waiting for him to recount the tale once again, avid for every little detail. A couple of hours later, his Boss called for him into his room.

"I forbid you to work in office any longer, I order you to go home and rest," he said smilingly.

That is why he returned home that afternoon. Whistling tunelessly, he entered the colony. While he was turning into the lane, he heard familiar voices, laced with laughter. "And Didi," said Vijay, "He gave away the wallet without a murmur. Take it, he repeated, take it, cowering with fear." "You should have seen him," Vinayak chipped in, "deflated like a pricked balloon. Perhaps, now he will realize that he is 38 and a father of two children, before he behaves like a lovelorn teenager." "I wonder how he liked a taste of his own medicine, very free with his fists, isn't he?" said Vijay. The contempt in his voice held Saurabh rooted to the spot. He saw two mobikes zip past, with Vijay and Vinayak, along with two friends riding pillion. "The gang of four," he muttered to himself, trying to whip up a frenzy of indignation.

By the time he entered the house, he was blazing with anger. He was about to say, "I heard everything," when he saw Renu. She was laughing to herself and her laughter tinkled like ice-cubes in a glass. "She is laughing at me," he thought angrily. But the look of triumph on her face turned into one of immediate concern as she saw him. "How are you?" she said, her voice sounding genuinely concerned, "Could you get any clue as to who did it?" While he tottered into a chair, she was back from the kitchen with a glass of cold water. God, she was a superb actress. He wondered what would happen if he told her that he knew the truth. He was afraid of the contempt he would see in her eyes. For she already knew that he was a coward and a brag. Suddenly, he was grateful to her for her pretence. He knew that she had other means of taking revenge. He could imagine Renu in Jatin's arms. Even the thought of that hurt. How long had she known about him and Shikha? Perhaps Vijay and Vinayak had seen him in the theatre with Shikha. Yet not with a gesture had Renu indicated that she knew, she had not confronted him at all. Suddenly, he wondered if he knew his wife at all. Unlike Shikha, who now seemed like an open book, Saurabh realized that Renu had hidden depths to her character. Before her, the Shikhas of this world paled into insignificance. He realized that Renu was not passive and predictable. She was mysterious and majestic. And he was glad that he had a lifetime before him to know her.

□

NEMESIS

Raj sat in the drawing room, enveloped in a haze of fumes, which emanated from the '*havan kund*.' But his mind was elsewhere, soaring along with the kite which he and Kshitij were flying at the India Gate, the kite flying in isolated splendour, having mauled all other kites in the fray. He heard the slow dull monotone of the Swami's voice, but his voice did not seem to penetrate, for Raj's mind was hooked on to the line he had put into the river while teaching little Kshitij how to hold it steady, in order to catch fish.

Smoke was billowing around the room. The smell of camphor, *havan samagri* and incense sticks was cloying. Sudha had begun coughing because of the smoke. "I hope she is not going to have one of her asthmatic attacks," he thought vaguely, as he moved quickly to take a catch off the ball Kshitij had lofted across the field. Images floated in and out of his mind, as he jumped on his feet and shouted, 'Out.' But Kshitij refused to move from the crease. "I'm not," he pouted, his chin thrust out, his face taking on a belligerent look. "I'm not out," he argued, before bursting into tears of childish rage, throwing down his bat and conceding defeat in an abrupt *volte-face* of his earlier stance. He rushed to Kshitij, lifted him in his arms and said, "Don't worry, it's only a game." And so it was, a game Raj played with himself. A game his imagination played with him. A game which fate had played with him by denying him a longed for son.

"You want a son," the Swami's voice penetrated into his conscious. "It does not need divine powers to know that," thought Raj. The puja was being held precisely to propitiate the Gods for this purpose. "And you shall have one," prophesized the Swami. His prophecy surprised Raj. He already had two daughters and his wife Sudha had recently suffered a miscarriage. Another girl. Yet the Swami was insistent. "You will have a son after having seven daughters." 'Seven.' Raj began to laugh dementedly. How could he afford to bring up seven daughters on his salary? The Swami was being ridiculous. But the Swami's next sentence held his attention. "Not all your daughters will survive...."

It was then that the idea came to him. In Indian mythology Kansa had destroyed his sister's children when they were born. Raj knew that in this case he would have to kill his own.

That very evening he saw Sudha smiling to herself. A wave of tenderness washed over him when he saw her. She was still as slender and beautiful as when he had seen her fifteen years ago in her garden, plucking the petals off a rose, her complexion pink like the rose she held. She was the daughter of the Divisional Commissioner and he the son of a lowly government official. But Raj had resolved to have her as his bride and he bridged the social distance between the two families by getting into the coveted Indian Civil Service. Sudha was now his wife. And Shovana and Sakshi were his daughters. They were Sudha's clones, whose spaniel eyes brimmed with tears when he shouted at them, who cowered with fear and hid in a corner while Sudha bore the brunt of his drunken rages. The next day he would be appalled on seeing the purple bruises on her skin, which she would hide by putting a scarf around her neck or by wearing full sleeved blouses.

Why had Sudha never walked out of her unhappy, violent and depressingly sad marriage? He never wondered about that. He knew the answer to that one. It was because of Shovana and Sakshi, who had arrived within a gap of two years. His unwanted, unwelcome and unloved daughters were the bond that tied Sudha to him. The death of Sudha's father meant that she had nowhere to go. Being in the Income-tax Service he was able to provide her with a lifestyle she was used to. "Even when she cries to herself," he thought cynically, "it is in air-conditioned comfort."

Sudha was humming to herself as she brought him a cup of tea. "You seem very happy, is there some good news in the offing?"

he said, in a rare burst of humour. "How did you guess?" she murmured, and he realised with shock that she was pregnant once again. The initial shock wore off as he realised that if the Swami's prediction was true he was closer to his heart's desire. For a few days he was solicitous of her welfare and then he quietly broached the subject of sonography. "I don't need it and I intend to carry the child, be it a girl or boy," she said with determination.

He didn't insist upon the test. He thought he knew of the outcome of the test anyway. The next weekend he decided to drive down to a hill station with Sudha and the kids. This was an unexpected gesture which took Sudha and the children completely by surprise. Their surprise turned into fear as he drove at break neck speed as though demented, travelling through bad roads and jumping over potholes and speed-breakers until they reached the Guest House. That night Sudha cried herself to sleep when she discovered that she had suffered another miscarriage.

Over the next year Sudha became increasingly withdrawn and aloof. Raj was seldom able to touch her and when he saw her grief stricken face he knew she still mourned her lost child. He began watching her bathe through a large crack in the bathroom door and was shamefacedly when Shovana saw him and asked him innocently, "Papa what are you doing?" He laughed feebly to himself. Why was he behaving like a voyeur? Sudha was his wife after all. He knew that a bit of tenderness from him would melt her. And melt she did when he carried her gently to his bed and made love to her that night.

After a few months she seemed as cheerful as before. That is why on that dark, dismal, winter night he was shocked when he picked a file in her almirah and saw a sonography report. Sudha was in the bathroom, brushing her teeth. He walked into it, closed the door behind him and waved the medical file at her. "Who's report is it?" he asked. "It's mine," Sudha admitted. "You're pregnant," Raj said. 'Yes,' she said. " Is it a girl?" he asked. 'Yes,' she said calmly. "We already have two daughters," he argued. "Then undergo a sterilization," she challenged. That stumped him effectively. "I am sure we can manage a third child," she cajoled a little later. "But I don't want a girl," he shouted. "It's too late now," she said, "I'm more than four months pregnant." "Why didn't you tell me?" he screamed. "I didn't want to lose this baby too," she shouted. "I didn't want another miscarriage. I didn't want to feel the pain of emptiness. I didn't want to travel on *kucchha* tracks at breakneck speed and lose my baby. I wanted the child. And I shall have it."

He then lost his mind. He slapped her hard across the face and then kicked her in the abdomen. She fell on the bathroom floor and then got up and came charging at him. Taken by surprise, for she had never retaliated before, he was still able to move aside quickly. As she tried to clutch at his shirt she lost her balance, slipped and fell backwards, hit her head hard against the wall before slumping onto the slippery floor. He expected her to cry out in pain. But she didn't scream. He then looked into her glazed eyes, her lifeless lips and felt her stilled pulse. He was stunned. He had never wanted Sudha to die. In his own warped way he loved her. Then fear replaced grief. If people saw him with Sudha now they would not believe it was an accident. He had to think of himself.

He looked at the watch. It was only 10 p.m. He went to the drawing room and started smoking, lighting up one cigarette after another. He then called aloud for her. Then he walked upto the bathroom and started screaming. The servants rushed from their quarters. He asked one of them to get the doctor. The doctor came and confirmed her death. Minutes later the entire city knew of Sudha's death. The Superintendent of Police, the District Magistrate, and his other colleagues congregated in his house and condoled him. The SP's wife took the little girls home. He nodded dumbly, playing the grieving husband to the hilt.

The next morning a police officer came with an order for post mortem. 'Just routine,' he insisted. Raj then had the first inkling of fear. He looked at Jeevan, the driver. He must have voiced his misgivings to the Police, Raj realized, he had adored Sudha. Raj was sure there was nothing they could pin on him. He was mistaken. The doctors found Sudha's spleen ruptured. "Her injuries do not tally with the story that she just fell in the bathroom and died," said the SP, when he arrested him on suspicion of murder.

Raj told the unvarnished truth about the accident to his lawyer, explaining how Sudha's spleen was ruptured. But Raj had not suspected the hostility of so many people against him. The gynaecologist spoke about his obsession for a male heir and the miscarriages Sudha had suffered. Jeevan and other servants gave evidence about his violence against Sudha. His spirits drooped as the trial proceeded but his lawyer was still confident about the outcome.

The prosecution then claimed that they had an eye-witness. Raj knew that this was impossible. He had been alone in the bathroom with Sudha, having taken the precaution of locking the door. He looked disbelievingly when Shovana came onto the witness box. "I looked through the crack on the door and I saw everything," she said.

Raj heaved a sigh of relief. If she saw everything she must have known that it was an accident, must have seen Sudha charge at him, slip down, hit her head against the wall and die. Shovana said gravely, "I saw my father hit Mummy across her face. Then he kicked her in the stomach and she fell. When she got up on her feet he shoved her and hit her head on the wall and she died." There was a hushed silence in the courtroom after she finished speaking.

Raj looked into Shovana's eyes and screamed, "It's a lie, it's a lie," but he knew that no one would believe him. Only he and she knew the entire truth. "But she is such a consummate little actress that she has convinced everybody about her version of what happened that night," he thought savagely. He suddenly realized that in her eyes it did not matter whether her mother had missed her step and fallen or whether he had pushed her to her death. In Shovana's mind he was responsible for Sudha's death and he would have to pay for it. She wanted justice. Raj remembered that it had taken a Krishna to demolish Kansa but in today's world Krishna had taken a female *avatar*, and suddenly he felt that all his daughters, born and those who remained unborn, were pressing their little fingers around his throat and squeezing the life force out of him.

□

THE REVELATION

The downpour had started. It did a tap dance on the ground, with large drops of rain splattering on the tarred road. Shanti walked back quickly. She had not carried an umbrella with her. Nothing had prepared her for such a downpour, nothing at all. She knew that by the time she reached home she would be drenched. She looked at her *saree*, the blue edge smudged with dirt. The *God*s will have to wait, she smiled to herself, as she watched the water soak into her Kolhapuri *chappals*. The leather sole of one of the *chappals* had begun to open up. She needed to go to a cobbler, she knew.

Shanti walked into the house slowly. "There is no point in disturbing Raman," she smiled to herself. She knew Raman would never have bolted the door. He wouldn't bother. After all, she had thoughtfully put in the secret lock, when she had left home. "What can he do without me?" she smiled indulgently to herself. "What can he, Raman is so dependent upon me," she smiled. "It was stupid," she thought to herself, seeing the wilting flowers in the wicker basket, "To have ventured out without an umbrella."

She slipped the key into the lock and the door opened noiselessly. She opened the umbrella and let it drip in the hallway. She left the wicker basket on the glass table near the entrance. It too needed to dry. She removed her slippers and walked into the kitchen, her feet leaving footprints on the mosaic floor.

She washed her hands in the kitchen sink and went to the wooden almirah in the *verandah* and took out a change of clothes. She then entered the bathroom and peeled off the blouse which clung to her back, then her bra, the *saree* and the *petticoat*.

Scrubbing herself with her towel, she smiled. Once she would have felt shy, but Raman's father was no longer alive. For many years had he pleaded with her, to allow him to watch her change her clothes, but she had never allowed it. "I was too shy," she chuckled to herself as she scrubbed herself with a towel and then wore the *saree* and blouse. After folding the clothes neatly she went towards Raman's room.

She thought she would surprise Raman. His bedroom door was ajar. It was the noise emanating from his room which startled her and stopped her from entering it. Through the door she saw a tangle of arms and legs. She felt if someone had punched her in the abdomen. She began to sway and would have fallen if she hadn't steadied herself by holding on to the doorknob. For a long while she stood still, unable to believe her eyes. She had thought of Raman's marriage for the last many years. He had received many proposals. She had shown him many photographs of eligible girls. He had waved them away, saying that he was not ready for marriage. She had no clue, no clue at all about the reason for his refusal. She should have known. She should have guessed. She had seen the photograph among his clothes just a week ago, but she had never suspected anything even then. She had thought that they were childhood friends and nothing more.

It was Sumit who saw her first. 'Shit,' he said under his breath. She saw the terror in Raman's eyes as he looked up, unable to breathe. "Amma wait," he said, but she had left the corridor, blundering outside the house, unmindful of the rain which had been reduced to a drizzle, unmindful of the *chappal* which had opened up even more, unmindful of the fact that she had, for the first time in her life, forgotten to carry the basket of flowers to the temple.

Once inside the temple she bowed her head before the idol of Lord Krishna, her eyes wet. She felt a searing pain within her, as though she had been branded with a red hot iron rod. She began shivering in dismay and then fright. She began to cry as though the act of crying would cleanse her and end her pain.

"Where did I go wrong?" she shuddered to herself, "Oh God, where did I go wrong?" For hours she sat in the temple, silent, contemplative and stone faced. By the time she returned home Raman had left the house. He had left a note on the refrigerator door. "Ma I am going out, Please don't wait up for me." There was no sign of Sumit.

Shanti sat in the drawing room, on the rocking chair that belonged to her husband. "Where did we go wrong?" she asked him, looking at his framed photograph. "Was it because I dressed up Sumit in Meera's clothes? Was it my fault? Or yours? Or was it not our fault at all?"

Meera's call came just then and slowly she poured out all her pent up hurt and anguish to her daughter. There was a shuddering sound on the other side, followed by a seemingly interminable silence. Once her tirade was over, Shanti began to regret it. She regretted sharing this news with her daughter Meera, she regretted Meera's reaction but most of all she regretted Meera's terse statement, "Amma we are coming to your house immediately." She did not want to see Meera, nor her husband Amar.

Shanti was still sitting on the sofa a few hours later, when the doorbell rang. "The bai," she thought hopefully. She could do with a hot cup of tea. "Meera has really turned obese," Shanti thought dispassionately as she unbolted the door and Meera entered the house. Meera sat on the divan with a thump. "Meera must be at least 75 kgs," she thought, looking at Meera's corpulent frame and her sagging arms. There were hyper pigmentation marks on Meera's cheeks and dark circles under her eyes. "Too many late nights," Shanti thought and then shrugged her shoulders. Meera's life was no longer her concern. She turned towards Amar. His left eye was twitching as usual. His long and pointed nose reminded her of Pinocchio.

Meera's lips were set in a straight line. "Amma tell me all," she commanded her. "There is nothing to tell," Shanti said in a low voice, "I told you everything on the phone."

"No wonder he had been rejecting all the proposals," said Amar, "we never knew he was gay." She closed her eyes. The image of those tangle of arms and legs was etched in her mind. Try as she might, she could not erase it. She could contain her tears no longer. She broke into sobs and continued to sob inconsolably. Her tears swept away with them, the remnants of her dreams for Raman. The middle class dreams of seeing him married and fathering a child. The dream every mother had the right to dream of. The dream of a little boy, a replica of Raman, calling her 'dadi.'

Meera sat ramrod straight on the *divan*. She made no effort to come to her mother and comfort her. "There is no point in crying Ma," said Meera, "Think of what you plan to do." She looked at Meera in surprise. Meera sounded more like a campaign manager than a daughter. Where was the comforting touch she yearned for? "Where did I go wrong?" she shuddered and asked herself.

"We never went wrong," Meera said, "See Ma, I am absolutely normal. If there is something wrong, it is with Raman." She looked at Meera dispassionately and wondered, "Since when had Meera become so judgmental?"

"The question is what do we do now?" said Meera. "I suggest you throw him out of the house," suggested Amar, "If he had any shame he would drown himself in the river anyway."

His words struck her like a slap across her face. The man they were wishing dead was none other than her son, her second born child. He was the painfully thin, premature child she had brought up with infinite care. Waiting for any infirmities, because of his being born premature, she had rejoiced in finding that he was completely normal. Yet it taken Amar just one minute to suggest that Raman should drown himself in the river. She closed her eyes and imagined Raman standing on the banks of the Yamuna, struck by shame because his secret had become known and ending his life in the river. She shuddered as she contemplated this possibility. "I can understand your revulsion Ma," said Meera, mistaking her reaction, "It is revolting. He has disgraced all of us." Meera didn't know that her words had unleashed a sense of fear in her mother's mind. She heard the sound of footsteps climbing up the stairs and then saw Raman enter the house. His head was bowed and his shoulders were hunched. He must have seen Amar's car standing outside the house. As she saw him enter the house she closed her eyes in prayer. "Thank God he is alive," she murmured.

"If Raman had any shame he would drown himself in the Yamuna," said Meera, fully aware that Raman was within earshot. "In any case Ma," she said as he entered the house and then went towards his room, "you should throw him out of the house. The house is in your name isn't it? Why should you let him live here?" "Why not?" Shanti said, steeling herself, "When your Babuji died Meera, where were you and Amar? For the last five years it is Raman who has looked after me and the house. Where were you all this time? Even now, have you even offered once to take me home with you? No it is Raman, my younger child, who has stood by my side, in my hour of need. I will not desert him now."

Meera got up in disgust, just as the bai entered the room with steaming cups of tea. "Ma there is no point in sympathizing with you, you only look for ulterior motives. *Chalo Amar*," said Meera, her voice censorious and her demeanour stiff and unbending. Amar got up as well. "Have a cup of tea," she called out to them as they went out thumping their feet loudly.

She bolted the front door and turned towards her room. 'Amma,' said Raman, "let me explain," 'Don't,' she said, her voice weary, "I saw."

He saw her eyes filled with pain and looked helplessly as tears rolled from her eyes. 'Amma,' he said, putting his arms around her, "Thank you for standing up for me. Thank God you understand." She said nothing as she removed his hand from her shoulder. She had stood by him alright, she thought sadly, and she always would. He was her child after all. But, and she closed her eyes in pain once again, she also knew that she would never be able to understand.

□

NOT BY MEMORIES ALONE

It appeared as a small paragraph in the *Hindustan Times* the next day, the head-on collision between the car carrying a marriage party and a truck, which led to the instantaneous death of all the members, including the bridegroom himself.

She knew nothing about the tragedy. Wearing a thick *Banarasi silk saree* with golden embroidery, she sat admiring the *mehandi* on her hands. The *mehandiwali* had taken almost two hours to apply it. She had been fascinated by the intricate pattern the *mehandiwali* had carved on her hand, after which she had dropped a few drops of lime juice and sugar onto her palm to give it that blackish red tinge. She had waited for many hours till the henna dried and gained colour, before she decided to wash the *mehandi* off. Then her aunt had put in a few drops of coconut oil, before removing the *mehandi*'s dried green crust. She loved it, the smell of henna, the rich maroon red colour, which more than anything else, had made her feel like a bride.

When the news of the tragedy came, she was the last one to know. Sitting in her bedroom, surrounded by her friends, she had heard no loud wails, or any other signs of demonstrable grief. Only her mother had come into the room and clung to her, tears running down her face. She had read the message of doom in her mother's eyes and when the news was told in broken half-sentences, it was not grief but anger she had felt. God could not do it to her, not now, and not this way. He could not betray her like this. He could not let her dreams crash and dissolve into nothingness. After the initial anger she was benumbed with grief. Grief for Sandeep whom she had met just twice, but with whom she had agreed to spend the rest of her life. Life in Hungary, a land that had seemed alien but would become her home, because Sandeep worked as a doctor in Budapest. Grief for Sandeep, who had been just twenty-six years old and for herself, because she had begun to care about him. But finally she felt relief. Relief and a sense of shame. Relief that she had not been his bride, and therefore was not his widow, the stigmatized young widow. And shame at the sense of relief she felt.

In two days time, her house had begun to look deserted. All the guests had left. But there was a difference. Unlike in other homes, here the bride-to-be remained at home and her family members did not celebrate and rejoice, but attended a funeral instead. "There is no one left in Sandeep's family, except his mother," said her father, "his father, sister and brother were all in the car." "How would she live, that woman, who in a matter of a few hours, would have been my mother-in-law?" Sangeeta wondered, "How would she cope with a tragedy which had destroyed her?" Sangeeta had a strong urge to meet her, and was surprised when her parents refused to let her go. Sangeeta realized much later that the tragedy had tainted her as well. Two months later her parents were invited to her cousin's wedding. Why had she naively assumed that she too would attend the wedding, along with her sisters Swati and Surabhi? She had accidentally overhead her mother's conversation on the telephone extension. Her aunt was telling her mother not to bring her along. Something about her bringing ill-luck. "I understand," she heard her mother say wearily. Sangeeta had blinked back her tears. So this is what people had begun saying about her, that she had swallowed up an entire *khandaan*. "Oh God, why didn't the accident take place after the wedding? Then I could have died along with them," she thought despairingly.

She was sitting listlessly in the *verandah* one winter morning, watching the bleak and barren trees with their twisted branches. "Like the shriveled and amputated arms of the beggars at the street crossing," she thought, "But they cannot be bleaker than my thoughts." 'Sangeeta,' her mother's voice broke into her thoughts,

"There is a marriage proposal for you." "Who is he?" she asked, almost indifferently. "It's a doctor, a widower with a child." "Those are the only kind of proposals I am likely to get now, are they? Second hand ones," she said, laughing harshly. Her mother looked shocked. "That's not a nice thing to say." Sangeeta mimicked, "Well has life been particularly nice to me, have people, have you?" She saw her mother cringe. It had become impossible to talk to Sangeeta. Her words always fell like a whiplash. They were aimed to hurt and wound. And yet she had not been like that. "Where has my daughter disappeared?" thought Sangeeta's mother in despair. She looked at Sangeeeta pityingly. She knew that Sangeeta deserved better. "Don't pity me," Sangeeta yelled, seeing the expression on her mother's face, "for God's sake, don't pity me." Saying this, she stalked out of the room.

When Sangeeta met Sumit for the first time, all she noticed about him was his hair, which had begun to grey prematurely and the thick glasses which hid his eyes. Eyes which were called the mirror of one's soul. What kind of a soul did he have? She wondered. "How does it matter," she thought to herself, "I don't have to say yes anyway." But then his little daughter Preeti came and stood before her. There was a look of yearning on Preeti's face. "What is it?" Sangeeta asked her gently. Suddenly, Preeti burst into tears. It seemed the most natural thing in the world to hold the child in her in arms and place her on her lap. Sangeeta guessed why Preeti was crying. She was remembering her own mother. And she was afraid of having a stepmother to replace her, afraid of the pity people would feel for her, afraid of her friends and what they would say if she brought home a stepmother. Sangeeta knew it because she shared some of the anxieties and fears herself. As she hugged Preeti, the little girl clung to her. Then for the first time Sumit spoke to her. "I don't know how you feel about it," he said in an undertone, "But Preeti has made it abundantly clear that at last she has found her mother." She turned towards him in surprise, unable to restrain the inexplicable surge of emotions she felt at his words. He was looking straight at her. She saw that beneath the glasses his eyes looked kind. Kind and experienced and inexplicably sad, as though they had forfeited the right to happiness. She had a sudden urge to remove the lock of hair, which had fallen on his forehead, straighten his tie, and trace her finger across his cheek. "Oh God, what is wrong with me? I don't even find him attractive. Do I yearn marriage so much that I am willing to accept the first man who proposes to me?" she thought to herself.

The astrologer who matched their horoscopes announced to her mother that it was a match made in heaven. "So was the one with Sandeep," she said shortly when her mother broached the subject. "Why can't you forget that, and get on with your life?" asked her mother, irritated by her cussedness. "And think of Swati and Surabhi..." she left the sentence unsaid. Her sisters. Her unmarried sisters who could not marry until she did. "Say Yes," she said to her mother, her voice indifferent, although she wondered if she had said Yes because Sandeep too had been a doctor. "I will," her mother said, a shade too eagerly and almost rushed to her father, not wanting to give Sangeeta a chance to change her mind.

Sangeeta's marriage was a quiet affair. Sumit had been through it once before, while she dreaded the hours before the marriage, afraid every time there was knock at the door, afraid every time the doorbell rang. Perhaps she was destined to stay single. "Perhaps this time too..." unhappy thoughts churned through her brain, the old memories unwilling to desert her. Not until the car had brought her from the airport and deposited her at the doorstep of her new home did she begin to relax.

Sangeeta began to stiffen with fear of a different kind when they entered the house. She didn't even know whom to expect in the house. She knew that Sumit didn't have any parents. He told her that his sister Reema was unable to come from USA to attend his wedding. It spoke immeasurably of the kind of relationship he shared with her. Would they enter an empty house, or would his relations be present?" she wondered. The members of the *baraat* along with Preeti were reaching by train. "At least I will have him to myself for one whole day," Sangeeta thought, looking obliquely at her husband. When they entered the house, home she corrected herself, the first thing which struck her was the life size photograph of Malini in the drawing room. It seemed to crowd out everything else. Till then Malini had just been a name, which she had chosen to ignore, which posed no threat because Malini was dead, had been dead for three years now. Now Sangeeta realized that she could have not been more wrong. The showcase too was full of photographs of Sumit and Malini. Sumit when he looked much younger, smiling and carefree, without the frown lines which now seemed to dominate his face. Sumit, his arm flung casually around Malini. Sumit, looking in awe at the baby in Malini's arms. Each photograph seemed to raise a banner against her saying, "Go back stranger." The photographs had so crowded the room that there seemed to be no place in it for her. The photographs seemed to say, "I will fill all the spaces in his heart. There is no room for you anywhere." "Oh my God," she thought suddenly, "is there nowhere in the house where the ghost of Malini will not haunt me?"

Sumit's Buaji was standing before them, with the large brass thaal for the aarti in her hands. Sangeeta saw a sea of faces behind Buaji. "Cut out all the rituals," Sumit said rather brusquely, "I've been through it before." "But I haven't, for me this is the first time," she bit back the words and followed him. He entered a room to the left. The bedroom, she realized, as she noticed the white silk sheets on the bed, with a sprinkling of rose petals on it. He flung himself on the bed, kicked off his shoes and removed his socks. "God, I'm tired," he said. She looked at him in surprise and remembered that he was at least ten years older than her. "Bahu, come to the puja room," commanded Buaji and she slipped away, half-relieved that she did not have to stay alone with the stranger she had married a day ago. She looked at the unfamiliar faces in the puja room. She did not know how many times she bent down and touched the feet of relations she did not know and was not likely to meet again in her life. She sat through a few rituals, and even managed to smile, when Buaji said in a tone of apology, "Don't mind Sumit, he has been through a lot."

When Sangeeta returned to the bedroom Sumit was asleep. She sat by his side and watched his rhythmic breathing. He snored slightly and she smiled, finding him very vulnerable in his sleep. His glasses were still on his nose and she was wondering whether to remove them or to let them be. Suddenly, he turned towards her and flung his hand across her saying, "Malini, Oh Malini." She stiffened beneath his touch, and tried to move away. The movement woke him up. "I'm sorry," he said, trying to pull her towards him. She slipped away from his hold and stood beside the bed and said stiffly," I…I need some more time." "If that's what you want," he said, and taking of his spectacles, turned his back towards her and went off to sleep.

Sangeeta lay awake by his side for a long time. "That's not want I want," she said to herself. "But I don't want my wedding night to be like this. I don't want to be Malini's substitute. I don't want to be a surrogate wife." But there was nothing she could say to him. She sat staring at his back for a long time, almost willing him to turn towards her and then finally in frustration she slept.

By the time she had woken up he was already dressed. "Where are you going?" she asked. "The hospital," he said laconically, "I have some serious patients I need to check on."

"You'll have to get up early if you want to catch him," Buaji told her, when she came into the kitchen, "His day begins at five am." Sangeeta then learnt of his routine, which began with a one-hour walk in the morning, followed by fifteen minutes of puja and then a bath and breakfast. He spent another hour in his study. Before eight he was out of the house.

The marriage party returned that evening along with Preeti, who rushed into their room and then stopped by the bedside when she saw Sangeeta. "Come here," Sangeeta called out to her, but Preeti went and stood by her father. She saw Sumit's face break into a rare smile at the sight of his daughter. He picked her up and hugged her and she clung to him, while watching her stepmother from the corner of her eye. "Oh God, not this," she said to herself, "I cannot compete with Preeti for her father's affection." Preeti snuggled beside him and was soon fast asleep. "Where does she sleep?" Sangeeta asked. Sumit looked almost guilty as he said, "She sleeps next to me." Sangeeta was glad in a way. It eased the awkwardness between them, by having a child sleep between them. Having Preeti beside her eased the tension between Sumit and her. There was something very reassuring about getting up in the morning, helping Preeti with her bath, combing her hair, giving her breakfast and sending her to school. She liked to go to the bus-stop and stand beside the other mothers. When Sangeeta had gone with her for the first time, Preeti had stood awkwardly with her, till she had nudged her and said, "Preeti won't you introduce me to your friends?" Preeti had stood shuffling her feet for a few minutes and then said, "She is my mother." 'Stepmother,' a fat girl standing next to her mother, corrected her. "What is a stepmother?" a small girl standing by Preeti's side had asked. Preeti had flushed with embarrassment. "It means," Sangeeta had said, "That unlike all of you, Preeti got a chance to choose her mother." Preeti had smiled then, the same tremulous smile which had touched Sangeeta's heart the first time they had met. The ice had been broken and every child had accepted Preeti's new mother, whom Preeti had chosen for herself.

"It's a pity," Sangeeta thought, "That Sumit does not need me the same way." There was something very self-sufficient about him. Everything was well organized in his life, his clothes, his papers, his life and the servants. "He has been a single parent for three years. He has learnt to be totally self-sufficient," said Buaji, "In fact earlier he used to say that he didn't need a wife." "Not just self-sufficient," thought Sangeeta, "Self-contained as well as self-absorbed." He never noticed her nor her efforts around the house. He was so tired after his hospital rounds, that he seldom had time for anything else. He spent the rest of his time in the study. Never since the first day had he tried to come near her. Perhaps Buaji was right. Perhaps he never wanted another wife, he just wanted a mother for Preeti. Perhaps Malini had been so perfect that he had not wanted to replace her with anyone.

That night when he slept Sangeeta looked at Sumit's face in repose. How would it feel to have his arms around her, his lips on her lips.... Tentatively, she put her hand on his shoulder. He didn't budge. "We can't go on like this," she thought looking at the ceiling, "not indefinitely, not forever." "He seems to have forgotten that he has a wife," she thought, indulging in a bout of self-pity. "Since that very first day he has not come anywhere near me." His indifference hurt. It hurt very much. She wondered how she could make him get the message. Then she smiled to herself. She would let photographs speak for her. She hung her wedding photographs in the drawing room. She didn't know what to do with Malini's photographs. She didn't want to bring Malini into their bedroom. She reluctantly put Malini's photographs in Sumit's study. She waited for Sumit's return anxiously.

Sangeeta was totally unprepared for his reaction. He had one look at the drawing room wall and then he asked, "Who removed the photographs from this room?" "I did," Sangeeta said, frightened by the chill in his voice. "Don't ever touch anything in my house without my permission," he said, before walking away. Tears welled up in her eyes. Tears of frustration, of rage and of humiliation. But she blinked them back, she didn't let them fall. She didn't want him to know that he could reduce her to tears, this man she called her husband, but who she didn't know at all. "A servant, that's what he thinks I am," she thought, closing her eyes tight, to prevent the tears from falling. Within a few minutes she had replaced the photographs on the wall.

Sumit's Buaji visited her a week later. "Tell me Buaji," she said on impulse, "Was Malini very beautiful?" Buaji looked at her face curiously. "There is no comparison," began Buaji and for a moment, Sangeeta's heart missed a beat, "You are much better looking." The words took a long time to sink in. 'Child,' said Buaji, "don't torture yourself. Malini was his parents' choice. You are his." Sangeeta did not understand what Buaji was saying. "He did not want to marry anyone after Malini's death," Buaji explained, "He changed his mind only after he saw your photograph."

"She had exaggerated things, just to make me happy," Sangeeta thought, "Otherwise why would Sumit utter Malini's name even in his sleep?" But a burden seemed to have lifted from her shoulders, on hearing Buaji's words. That is why she didn't mind when Sumit took Preeti alone and not her, when he went to attend a wedding in Malini's family. Earlier she would have seen it as another sign of rejection. But now she merely smiled.

She was standing on the terrace, when the first drops of rain started trickling in. Before she could realize it, the trickle had turned into a downpour. Suddenly, she gave a laugh, and swirled around, shedding all tension. The rain fell all over her. She let it seep through her clothes. She shook her head and let the water drip. She laughed. It was so invigorating and so cleansing. It was like being reborn. Suddenly, she saw a shadow. Sumit stood by the door. His eyes were slowly taking everything in. Her hair, which seemed sculpted on her head. The raindrops, which glistened like gems on her forehead. Her blouse, which was moulded onto her body, her *saree* which clung on to her, rivulets of pink colour dripping from the border. She saw his eyes fixed on her cleavage. His voice suddenly turned gruff. "Oh God," he said, his voice breathless, "Sangeeta you're so beautiful." Sangeeta. Not Malini. Sangeeta at last. She couldn't move. He walked up to her, put his hand around her shoulder and slowly they walked down the stairs. "Where is Preeti?" she asked suddenly. "She's in her grandparents' house," he said, pleased that Preeti was not away from her thoughts for long. "Change your clothes," he said, a doctor once more, "or you'll catch a cold." She felt her teeth begin to chatter. For how long had she danced with such gay abandon on the terrace? She didn't know. He was right, she needed to change. She walked into the bathroom and was vigorously drying herself with a towel, when the door opened. He was standing there. 'Sangeeta,' he said, "Your time is up." She turned to him and smiled. She was glad he remembered.

She slept peacefully by his side, clinging slightly to him and he watched her, his eyes gentle. "My wife," he murmured to himself, "My beautiful wife. My beautiful, caring and loving wife, whom I hurt because I in turn was hurt." Tomorrow he would tell her about himself. Tomorrow he would tell her about the burden of guilt he carried. Guilt about the fight he had with Malini, one of the innumerable fights they had had, which had made him drive rashly, which had caused the accident and taken Malini's life. Guilt at having survived, while Malini had died. Guilt and guilt, alone which had given Malini the pride of place in his house. Guilt, which had made him have recurring nightmares about the accident and call out Malini's name in fright.

Sangeeta woke up suddenly and saw that the bed was empty. She was frightened. Sumit couldn't have abandoned her and gone. Not now. Not tonight of all nights. She walked into the drawing room and was relieved to find that he was there. His back towards her, he was putting their wedding photograph back on the wall.

□

THE MEMSAAB

The mango tree stood at the end of the garden, its branches fanning out onto the road, its leaves a lush green, tiny raw mangoes hanging from its branches. A group of boys stood outside, keeping a sharp vigil at the tree. "The owner has gone out," whispered Ramesh. "And the gardener is busy in the kitchen garden," Ramu said softly. It was the right time for attack. In a minute, Ramu had jumped over the fence and was climbing up the mango tree.

Little Armaan stood in a corner, inside the path leading to the house upstairs, a little afraid of the goings on. "Why did you bring him along?" Govind had asked Ramesh, a trifle irritated by his presence. "*Arre*, how could I leave my brother alone?" Ramesh had retorted, unable to explain that little Armaan always tagged along him like his shadow. "Keep a watch on the house," Ramesh bhaiya had instructed little Armaan, "and if you see the gardener coming, simply shout and run." "It was easy for Ramesh bhaiya to say so," thought Armaan, eyeing the pair of rubber slippers on his brother's feet longingly. He was finding it difficult to stand barefoot on the tarred road.

So engrossed was he in keeping vigil that he completely missed seeing the cyclist, who turned the corner, entered the blue gate and jammed his brakes next to him. The next minute he was on the ground, and the world had dissolved into a blur. He saw an unfamiliar face peep anxiously into his, but was unable to focus on him clearly. There was something blurring his vision. He put his finger near his eye and almost screamed when he saw blood.

"*Armaan, tum theek ho na*?" Ramesh's voice seemed to come from far away. How seriously injured was he? And what would Papa say? He saw the cyclist sprint into the house and then return. "He needs to be shown to a doctor," said Ramesh, all of fourteen years, trying to exert his authority. The man looked abashed. He and Ramesh helped Armaan onto his feet. Armaan noticed that he had badly grazed his elbows and knees, but it was the trickle of blood, which dripped from a cut near his eye, which worried him the most. They climbed the staircase leading to the house upstairs. The domestic help then rang the bell. "*Kaun hai*?" a feminine voice hollered back. Armaan shrank visibly when the lady of the house opened the door suddenly.

When she first saw Armaan trying to hide behind his brother, she thought Naresh had caught him breaking a flowerpot. Then she saw the cut near his eye. "Oh my God," she said, as she took her *pallu* and wiped the blood from his face and asked, "What happened beta?" 'Beta?' How long was it that someone had called him beta, with so much affection? Armaan was tongue-tied. It was Ramesh who explained about the accident. "Memsaab," he said, "there is no one in my house at present who can take Armaan to a doctor. My father works as a driver, and my mother is dead. Will you please take him to a doctor?" She appeared to hesitate for a minute, then suddenly her brow cleared. "Find a taxi or fetch a scooter," she instructed Naresh, her domestic help. Armaan wondered why she wouldn't take Armaan in her own car. "Possibly because she is worried that blood will drip all over the seat covers," he thought. Looking at the Maruti Swift standing outside, she said, "It's a pity, but the driver is not at home and I can't drive."

Naresh brought an autorickshaw to the house within ten minutes. She got into the auto, with Armaan sandwiched between her and Naresh. "I also want to go," said Ramesh belligerently, "After all I am his brother." She immediately instructed Naresh to sit in the front, with the autorickshaw driver, and make place for Ramesh at the back.

Armaan was petrified when the autorickshaw swept through the massive gates of the Ram Manohar Lohia Hospital. He clung to her hand as she took him to the Emergency. "What's his name?" asked the man at the Reception Counter. "What's your name?" she whispered to him. 'Armaan,' he said softly. She seemed surprised on hearing his name. "That's a lovely name," she said ruminatively, "Who chose it?" "Ma," he murmured shyly. He was proud of his name. It was so much nicer than Ramesh. He trembled when the nurse took out a large syringe. "Anti-tetanus injection," she said. The thought of an injection scared him. His hands dug into the Memsaab's arm. She winced in pain and he loosened his grip immediately. For a moment he had forgotten that she was not his mother.

"This cut will need stitches," said the doctor, examining his eye. "He is a brave boy, he won't cry," Memsaab said. "How does she know?" he wondered. That is what his mother had said, when he had taken anti-rabies injections after a dog bite. "Is he your son?" asked the nurse. "Oh No," he saw her visibly shrink at the thought. "Then who is he?" the nurse persisted. "He belongs to one of servant quarters," she said quickly. He felt strangely hurt on hearing her. It was as though with her statement she had created a chasm between them. But what had he expected her to say? That he was her son? How could she? She was a Memsaab after all.

When he went in for surgery he was terribly afraid that she would abandon him and leave, but when he returned he saw that she was sitting on a dirty bench, alongwith Naresh and Ramesh. "Did it hurt a lot?" she asked him sympathetically. His lips trembled as he said 'Yes.' "But I didn't cry," he added. 'Good,' she said absently as she led him away. Suddenly, he winced as he stepped onto the tarred road. It was difficult to walk with bare feet in the scorching heat. The journey back was silent.

When they returned to the Memsaab's house he was in for a shock. His entire family had turned up in full strength. His father had been called from his duty. His grandmother, chachi and cousins were sitting on the pavement. 'Memsaab,' said his father aggressively, staggering towards her, "My son is injured in an accident, which took place in your house. I can go to the police and complain." "Oh God," Armaan thought in horror, "Papa is drunk again." He saw Memsaab take a step back. But when she spoke there was a hint of snobbery in her voice. He dubbed it her 'Memsaab' voice. It was the voice the Memsaab, in whose house his mother had worked, adopted while reprimanding his mother. "Your children had come to steal mangoes from the neighbour's house. Hearing Naresh on the cycle they ran helter-skelter. Unfortunately, Armaan collided with the cycle and fell down. It was his fault. Ask your son what he was doing inside my gate? I took him to the hospital out of a sense of compassion, not guilt." "Was that how the accident had taken place?" Armaan was not sure. He did not know whether he had stepped back and hit the cycle, or whether Naresh had hit him. But the sequence of events didn't matter. Her words however, had a strange effect on his father. Suddenly, he became sheepish, "I understand Memsaab," he said, "I'm a driver after all." "Was it how the poor always succumb to the will of the rich?" Armaan wondered. Do the rich always win?

'Look,' Memsaab said, "I understand Armaan does not have a mother. If you want, I will take him for his dressing and for removing the stitches. You may not find time to take him to the hospital." "Thank you Memsaab," said his father gratefully. Armaan wasn't sure he wanted any more favours from Memsaab. He resented his father for abandoning him to Memsaab's care. Memsaab who accused Ramesh bhaiya and him of stealing, who accepted no responsibility for her servant's actions and who put the entire blame on his own frail shoulders.

When Armaan next came to her house she handed him a parcel and said, "This is for you." Then she looked at his feet and her face fell. "Oh you don't need these," she said "you already have a pair of slippers." So she had noticed his bare feet! Armaan opened the parcel eagerly. In lay a pair of white and blue bathroom slippers. "Thank you," he said happily. Maybe he had misunderstood her. Maybe she was not bad after all. "These are borrowed," he lied, only so that he could put the smile back on her face.

The phone rang suddenly. "Come and sit inside Armaan," she instructed as she went into the bedroom. He entered the drawing room cautiously and stood, feeling overawed. His feet sank into the peach carpet which covered the room. He looked at the carved wooden sofa and chairs. There were silk cushions on them. Where could he sit? For a moment he considered squatting on the floor, but decided against it. He was not a servant in her house, even if he was a child from the servant quarters. He was standing indecisively in a corner when Memsaab returned. "Why didn't you sit?" she asked, and ruffling his hair carelessly said, "let's go."

When he came to her house the third time, he saw loads of furniture being carried downstairs. "Are you leaving?" he asked, "No but my servant is," she said, "I am on the lookout for a new one." For one tempting moment he imagined that his family was occupying her servant quarters. Ramesh bhaiya, Papa and he. Just like the old times, without Chachi shouting at them…for sharing her cramped accommodation and beating them up without provocation for imaginary sins. But he knew that was impossible. With Ma dead who would clean, sweep and cook for Memsaab?" They were destined to stay with Chachi, unless of course his father remarried. He dreaded that prospect as well.

When they returned from the hospital, after getting his stitches removed, Memsaab sighed with relief and said, "Now you don't need to come here anymore." The thought of not seeing her anymore upset him a lot. How could he tell her that she was the only woman, who had shown him kindness after his mother's death and that he did not want to lose contact with her? "Will you come to my birthday?" he asked her suddenly, wanting to remain in touch with her for a little while longer, "It's on the tenth of this month." "Give me your address," she said.

On Armaan's birthday, his father bought *sohan papri* and potato chips. 'Hmm,' said Ramesh bhaiya, "The *sohan papri* simply melts in the mouth." Armaan's mouth watered, but he didn't touch his share. His eyes never left the door. He was sure that Memsaab would come. He was sure that she would keep her promise. By the time night fell, he began to lose hope. What had made him believe that she would come? He had forgotten that she was a Memsaab and Memsaabs were Memsaabs.

But somehow he refused to give up hope. Maybe she would come later. Maybe she was out of town. There were hundreds of excuses he made to himself on her behalf. He wrapped the *sohan papri* in a polythene bag and hid it behind the alarm clock on the shelf. He knew it wouldn't spoil for months. "I will wait for ten days. If she doesn't come till then, I will give up," he thought.

A week passed by but Memsaab did not come to see him. The hope he had nurtured in his heart began to dwindle. When she did not come on the tenth day as well he lost all hope.

"I won't wait for her anymore," he thought mutinously the next day while returning from school. The house was empty that afternoon. He pulled a chair and climbed up to reach the shelf. As he stretched his hand he hit the alarm clock, which fell on the floor with a clatter. "Thank God, Chachi is not at home," he thought, as he jumped down and began to pick up the shards of glass lying on the floor. Suddenly, he heard footsteps coming up the house. Chachi had returned. "*Haramzade*," she screeched, lunging at him. Armaan stood petrified, guilt writ large on his face. He knew all too well how Chachi behaved when she was enraged. She pulled Armaan by his neck and dragged him across the room. "Do you know how much the clock cost? Six hundred rupees. Can you get it for me? Or can that drunkard father of yours?" She pulled out the carved stick, which stood by the doorway and began to rain blows at him. He cowered in fear, covering his head with his hands. But he didn't cry. He knew that his silence irritated her. She loved the wails, the tears, and the cries of pain which accompanied her acts of violence. But how could he cry? Hadn't his mother and Memsaab both said that he was a brave boy? "Get out," she said in disgust, kicking him out of the house. He tumbled down and fell at someone's feet. Memsaab. She looked at his mutinous face and then at his Chachi. Hope surged within him. She had come after all. She hadn't forgotten him. He tried to see if Memsaab was carrying a present for him. She wasn't. He realized that she was merely passing that way and had not come to see him. He was deeply disappointed. Her next words took him by surprise. “I am taking Armaan home with me,” she said. ‘Why?’ asked Chachi, looking perplexed. “You are not fit to look after him,” said Memsaab. “This is his home,” argued Chachi. “But it will not be any longer,” said Memsaab, her voice stern. “And if you stop me,” she added, “I’ll report you to the police.” Chachi seemed surprised, on hearing Memsaab’s tirade. She did not know how to react. “When Armaan’s father returns, he will bring Armaan back,” she blustered. “We will see,” Memsaab said, as she held Armaan’s hand and took him away.

That evening Armaan was sitting on the drawing room sofa, watching television when his father arrived. Armaan was glad that his father was not drunk. He began to get ready to go home. He was surprised when his father told Memsaab, “I was told that you took Armaan to your house, I want to know if you intend to give him a home permanently?” “Yes,” she said spontaneously, and then seemed surprised at her own response, as though it was something she had thought of on the spur of the moment.

“What will *Saa’b* say?” His Papa asked her soberly. She pursed her lips. She had not thought of that. Her husband was posted abroad, while she worked in a government department in Delhi. She knew that he would be upset and would strongly disapprove of her decision. But by then it would be too late. She thought of her daughter Juhi, who was now married. She would be appalled and say, “Are you mad, bringing home a boy from the servant quarters? Why?” Neither her husband nor her daughter would understand her increasing loneliness, her yearning for human company and her affection for Armaan. And she guessed that Armaan saw in her a glimpse of his own mother. But how did it matter what her husband and daughter thought? She had lived her life according to their whims for years. Surely at forty-five years she had earned the right to live life her own way?

“Won’t you mind leaving Armaan with me?” Memsaab asked his father curiously. “My wife always had dreams for him.” he said simply, “She made me promise that I would educate Armaan and make him a doctor. I don’t know if her dream can ever come true, but with you he has a chance.”

That night Memsaab led Armaan to the guest room. "This is your room from now on," she said. He was surprised when he saw the room. He touched the bedspread with gold tassels in awe. When she had brought him home, he had expected that she would keep him as a sort of domestic help who would do small chores around the house and sleep on the floor. He had not expected to be treated as a guest. "Tomorrow I will buy you some clothes," she said, as she told him to go to bed. Tucking the sheet around him, she asked him casually, "By the way what were you doing when you broke the alarm clock?" He hung his head in silence but she continued to wait for his response. Suddenly, he began to speak in a rush, "You didn't come for my birthday…." 'Oh,' she said guiltily, "I forgot." He looked wonderingly at the woman who forgot his birthday and yet did not hesitate to give him a home. Now it was his turn to ask her, "Memsaab, what were you doing near my house?" although he already knew the answer. She had just been passing that way. For a long moment she remained silent. Then she spoke. "Don't call me Memsaab," she said, "call me Mother."

'Mother.' The vision of his mother rose before his eyes. His beautiful mother with her long tresses falling over her shoulders, with pale skin and velvet soft hands. "That is a lie," he admitted to himself. He remembered his mother's careworn hands, which had become hard with years of housework and her hair which had begun to grey prematurely. How happy his mother would be to see her son sleeping in this house on a soft mattress!

The next day Memsaab's driver came to take them shopping. Armaan sat gingerly on the edge of the car's back seat. Just then he saw a shadow behind the mango tree, the tree where it had all begun. He recognized the faded blue shirt, darned at the elbows, and the grey pants patched at the knees. But he almost failed to recognize Ramesh bhaiya, his face crumpled with grief. Ramesh bhaiya. How could he have forgotten Ramesh bhaiya, who always shielded him from Chachi's wrath, who had accompanied him to the hospital, whose shadow he had been? Forgetting Memsaab, he pulled the door open, slid out of the car and rushed out. Ramesh emerged out of the shadows, jumped up the fence and hugged Armaan. "*Armaan ab to tu bada admi ban jayega*," he said, with more pride than envy.

Armaan turned to look at the house upstairs, where he had lived for a day. If he continued to live there, the divide between him and Ramesh Bhaiya would never get bridged. It was funny but the day before, wilting under Chachi's wrath, he had forgotten about Ramesh bhaiya. Armaan knew he had a decision to make. But in the end it was no decision at all. He thought of his Ma and her absurd dreams.

He saw Memsaab coming out of the car. She looked questioningly at him and then at Ramesh. She understood. 'Memsaab,' he began to say. This time she did not correct him. "You want to say something?" she said. As he nodded she said, "Let me guess. You want to go home." Once again he nodded his head. She smiled at him. The void his words created would fill in with time, she hoped, as she waved him Goodbye. She saw him put his hand in Ramesh's hand and walk away.

□

THE END

Something bad was going to happen that day. She knew it the moment she saw a shadow in the well, dark and menacing. She little realized that she was merely seeing a reflection of herself. "Bad." Shilpa did not fully understand what she meant by bad. Many things were bad in her thinking. "Sheroo," the stray mongrel, who had bitten her on the leg was bad. Ramu Kaka, who shook a stick whenever she went near his guava tree, was bad. The day her mother fell ill was bad. What happened to her the day her mother went to the hospital was bad.

"*Shilpa bitiya, idhar aao*," she turned back as she heard her mother shout in irritation, although the look on her face was affectionate. Her mother sat on the verandah, her legs stretched apart, the big earthen pot fitting snugly between them, as she churned the buttermilk vigorously, her waist moving in tandem with the movement of the churner, her plait tightly made and pinned carelessly on top of her head slowly coming undone as she moved from side to side. Sometime later, she scooped the cream that had floated on top and stored it in a container. Shilpa came and sat on the steps near her mother.

'There,' her mother said with satisfaction, once all the butter was scooped out, "At least that is done."

As her mother went into the kitchen Shilpa began to bang her head against the wall and began chanting, "Ba…Ba…Ba…Ba… Ba, Ma…Ma…Ma…Ma." Her mother entered the verandah and roared at Shilpa, "*Bus band karo*. Stop this noise immediately." Shilpa stopped her chanting in an instant. "*Idhar aao*," commanded her mother. She dried her wet hands with her *saree pallu* and rolled out the purple and green *chatai*, whose edges had begun to fray. "Come sit here beside me," she ordered as she patted the space beside her. Shilpa hesitated, eying the *chatai* warily, as though it was an object of suspicion. "Come on, no fuss please," said her Ma as she pulled out a large comb with sharp pointed teeth, through which she had strung a piece of thread, in order to remove the lice and nits Shilpa seemed to pick up from God alone knew where, seeing that she seldom left the house. As strands of hair broke from Shilpa's scalp and stuck onto the comb, Shilpa's mother clucked her tongue, picked out the lice, and put them on the nail of her left thumb, killing them expertly with the right thumb.

Shilpa shifted uneasily as her mother oiled her hair, binding it tightly. "Now go inside," her mother ordered, "and sleep. I am going to the Hospital for my check up and will return in a few hours." She wondered if Shilpa understood what she said and if so how much. Shilpa was her mute daughter, who was nearly thirteen, but as yet a child. Did she realize that she was growing up, and growing into a beautiful woman? How would she explain to Shilpa the meaning of womanhood? How would Shilpa cope with the onset of puberty? What could she do to protect Shilpa and for how long?

She choked with anger and frustration at the unfairness of it all. Of Shilpa's father, Bishen dying in a bus accident seven years ago, of Shilpa turning out to be mute and mentally challenged. But for Birju, her brother-in-law, she would have become a destitute. It was he who provided her money from the harvest, enough money to help her survive. It was he who pushed aside his own unhappiness, after the suicide of his wife four years ago and began helping her and Shilpa regularly. If Birju had not been there, could she had gone to the hospital and got operated for her gallstones? "Don't worry," he had said, knowing instinctively that she worried about Shilpa, "*main hoon na*." And he had taken care of his niece. The Shilpa she had met on her return from the hospital looked clean, with a well-scrubbed face and neatly washed hair. "I made her bath everyday *Bhabhi*," Birju had claimed, and Shilpa had indeed smelt of soap and shampoo, and her well oiled hair had glistened and shone.

Shilpa had sulked, looked unhappy and shrank when she had tried to hug her. Then she had suddenly burst into tears, which rolled unhappily across her sullen face. Her mother had shrugged helplessly. She knew that Shilpa felt abandoned. But how could she have explained to her mute and mentally challenged daughter where she was going and expect her to understand?

She picked up the mat and placed it on the floor of her room, put down a pillow and placed a doll beside it. "Shilpa come here and play," she coaxed.

"I have to go to the hospital to get my stitches removed. Birju Chacha will come soon." She wondered if Shilpa understood what she was trying to say. Shilpa stood near the door, unwilling to sit on the mat and play.

As her mother left, Shilpa shivered a little, then closed the door shut and slid the bolt on the door. She put her head on the mat and slept. She was awakened by the sound of someone banging the door insistently. The bolt of the door slid down and Birju entered the room. He quickly bolted the room and she immediately struggled to get up on her feet. "Quick Shilpa," he ordered, as he pushed her on the mat, slobbering all over her, resting his weight over her, making her spread her legs, breathing heavily as he struggled with his *pyjamas*.

She hated it, the pain of it all, the alien intrusion into her, his eyes blood shot, his lips thick and calloused, his tongue wet, darting in and probing the insides of her mouth, one hand holding her mouth and stifling her screams and another hand touching and fondling her breasts. She hated it when he got up, picked her up and made her stand under a tap, to wash away all smell of him, camouflaging it with the smell of bathing soap.

Her Ma did not think Birju Chacha was bad. The day she had left for the hospital for her operation she had said, "Do not look scared girl, Birju loves you like his daughter." She had wondered what this child woman understood about love. She did not know what he had done the very afternoon when she left for the hospital, pushing Shilpa down on the mat, shoving himself into her, uncaring of the blood which had gushed from between her thighs, the pain that had seared through, the sticky wetness between her legs. Then he had shoved her into the bathroom, and from the drum of water filled up a bucket and poured it over her head, soaping and bathing her, his hands resting on her breasts and her hips and lingering over them as he scrubbed her.

Shilpa hated the mat. It was the place where he hurt her. Today too Birju bathed her, made her dress up and then began to leave. Shilpa stood shivering in the verandah, her damp hair making her feel cold. She walked down the verandah towards the well. The shadow still lurked in the well. In fact, it had begun to grow. It had been smaller in the morning. There was something bad inside and it was becoming big. Shilpa began to scream in fright. Birju turned back from the gate. "Why is the wretched girl screaming?" he wondered, worried that her screams would bring some neighbour into the house.

He saw Shilpa standing by the well and sobbing. "What is it?" he asked, irritated by this overgrown child woman, this mentally challenged girl, now that he was sated. She pointed to the reflection inside the well. He peered into it, standing on the elevated mound of loosely piled bricks. Suddenly Shilpa stumbled and fell against him. Birju was not sure whether she had pushed him or he lost his balance and fell into the well. He could see the expression in her eyes as he disappeared into the well, his head hitting a protrusion on the wall before he began to sink into the water. As his head buffeted up he shouted, "Shilpa call someone, ask someone for help." Then he felt utter despair as he remembered that the mute Shilpa was mentally challenged as well. "A rope," he shouted, "Throw me a rope." But Shilpa stood transfixed, as she saw his head, bobbing in the water just a few minutes ago, now beginning to sink. In a few minutes, his head had disappeared and so had the shadow.

By the time her mother returned home it had turned dark. Shilpa was standing by the well and weeping loudly. Her mother looked at her dank and still wet hair, wondering why it had been washed again that afternoon when she herself had washed it that very morning, why Shilpa's dress had been changed and why she was cowering besides the well, sobbing loudly? Shilpa was pointing to the well, where all her mother could see were a few ripples. "Cha-Cha-Cha-Cha," she began to chant as she entered the house along with her mother. Her mother smiled. Till that day Shilpa had only uttered two words, 'Ma Ma,' and 'Ba Ba.' Today she had said, "Cha Cha." There was hope for her. May be some day she would begin to speak.

□

A NIGHT TO REMEMBER

It was twilight, the time he liked best, when time stood suspended between day and night, unable to decide whether to don the cloak of darkness, or to continue with the mantle of light for some more time. Rohit's mouth quirked, smiling at the imagery, as his hands gripped the steering wheel of his BMW, which he drove at a leisurely pace. "Speed, man, speed," had been his motto in his youth, but right now he seemed to have reached the twilight of his life. "Not really," he thought, "Being in one's mid-thirties is to be at the peak of one's life and not at one's decline." But Rohit could not shrug off the mood of despondency. The balance sheet of his life, he knew, would show more assets than liabilities. As the Head of a flourishing pharmaceutical company, having a beautiful wife and two adorable children, he seemed to have it all. Then why was he experiencing a sense of disquietude? Perhaps, a small voice nagged him, because he had got everything in life too easily, too soon, virtually on a silver platter. There were no goals to look forward to. There were no more mountains to climb.

He thought of his marriage, which could only be termed a success. His wife Radhika was breathtakingly beautiful. With her chiseled beauty she seemed like a white marble statue come alive. But perfection could be daunting at times, admitted Rohit ruefully. He could never dare to ruffle her well groomed hair, or leave newspapers littered on the sofa. He could not recall his children ever carrying muddy feet into the drawing room. The price of perfection, Rohit admitted to himself, at times seemed to be too high. Rohit then thought of his business. He remembered the day his Dad had said, "The days of fun and games are over young man. It's time you took over the family business," and the flourishing pharmaceutical concern was his. As its new Managing Director he had his own apartment and chauffeur-driven car. He remembered his blissful, carefree college days with his group of friends he had nicknamed the 'charmed circle.' But maybe, he admitted to himself, the 'carefree' demeanour of his friends was merely a facade. He remembered the final year of college. Vivek, his friend and tennis partner in the Gymkhana Club, had spent all his time in the library, poring over old dusty tomes while preparing for the civil service examinations, in a bid to follow in the footsteps of his illustrious bureaucrat father. While Vivek had topped the university, despite repeated attempts he had failed to enter the civil service. Rohit remembered Sanat, who with his carefree smile and repertoire of jokes, gave the impression of having not a care in the world. But he had quit studies immediately after his graduation, after being offered a prestigious bank job. "The banking industry may not provide one with job satisfaction," Sanat had joked, "But it certainly provides the bucks!"

Amongst his friends, Urmi was the one who was truly like him, who admitted that for her a graduation degree was merely a passport to marriage and nothing more. His thoughts finally turned to Sumita, Urmi's friend, who had stood at the periphery of the charmed circle, who had desperately needed a job when her father died and who had found it so hard to make both ends meet.

His face darkened at the thought of Sumita. "Guilty conscience?" a voice nagged him. He brushed aside the accusation, as he drove along. Although it had turned dark, his attention was drawn to a lone figure standing at a deserted bus stop, illuminated by the street lamp. There was something familiar about her silhouette, perhaps the serpentine coil of her plait, which swung below her waist and almost reached her hips. Perhaps it was her aquiline nose, which seemed even sharper in profile. Surely, he could not be mistaken. It was Sumita. He drove to the end of the road and then took a U-turn. He once again drove past the bus stop. It was Sumita alright, with the same high cheek bones, the mole on her chin and the full mouth. But this time her mouth was red, as though someone had hit her hard across her mouth. She was not wearing her trademark starched cotton *saree*, but something garish, synthetic and flimsy which seemed moulded to her body. His lips tightened, especially when he noticed that she was engrossed in conversation with a motorcyclist. Even from a distance Rohit could see that he was a disreputable character. An ugly scar ran across his face and he was spitting out paan. What on earth was Sumita doing at a deserted bus stop, on a winter night with a man like that? It seemed suspiciously like soliciting. But his mind refused to accept this explanation, until he remembered an old, long forgotten conversation he had with his friend. Two years ago when he had been talking of the "good old days," to Sanat, he had remembered Sumita. "Have you met Sumita recently?" he had asked Sanat, who had nodded. "Where did you meet her and what is she doing?" he had asked Sanat.

Sanat had blushed guiltily and said sheepishly, "I'd rather not talk about it, old chap. I only wish you never meet her under similar circumstances." He had been curious, but on seeing Sanat's obvious distress he had dropped the subject. But now he understood the full implications of Sanat's cryptic remarks.

Sumita. Her name evoked memories of his college days, where his faded denims and baggy shirts disguised their internationally famous brand names and his obvious wealth and the fact that the other members of the 'charmed circle' were not in the same league as him. As for Sumita, she did not even belong to the group, but had remained on the periphery. Sumita spent frugally in coffee houses, never took an auto and maintained that her bus pass was her prized possession. Sumita's crisp, starched cotton *saree* seemed incongruous amongst a riot of jeans, shirts, salwar-kameezes and skirts. Sumita wore her conservatism like a badge and had declined a modelling offer saying, "My parents won't like it." Sumita had never hidden the fact that her father was a mere Inspector of Police. Sumita had been heart-broken when her father had died just three months before her final examinations, leaving her to shoulder the responsibility of looking after her mother, two sisters and a brother. "Five mouths to feed, three persons to educate and a measly pension for support, what will I do?" she had asked Rohit despairingly, as he had tried to dissuade her from quitting her studies. Rohit had then reached out to her, picking her up from home and dropping her back and even paying her college fees. He had helped her in giving tuitions to prospective students. For him it was a novel experience to play the Good Samaritan and he quite enjoyed this dependence of another human being on him.

At the end of the last examination he had returned to the college hostel with Sumita. As she sat soft and pliant in his arms, he had thought that she would yield to his wishes and he picked her up and laid her on the bed. As he bent over her she had said shyly, "Not until our marriage." 'Marriage?' he had said haughtily, his eyebrows knitted together, the word conveying surprise, indignation and even shock. "Marriage with you? Impossible." His silence had conveyed his unspoken words. She had run away blindly, like a wounded bird, and in a way he had been glad, as he had never considered marriage with Sumita and he did not think that a physical relationship should necessarily culminate in marriage. "If that was true," Rohit thought a trifle ruefully, "I would have been married several times by now." He also knew that his parents would never have accepted her as their bahu, but that was a bridge he had never intended to cross. "We were good friends and nothing more," he had said to himself, convincing himself that he was right in not pursuing her and trying to heal the breach.

He had left for Masters in Business Administration in the United States soon after and Sumita had become a closed chapter in his life. After breaking off with her, he had realized that there had been a certain dependence in his relationship with Sumita, which was missing in his relationships later on. Perhaps that was what was missing in his relationship with his wife Radhika, for whom he was merely a husband, but not a friend, a mentor and a guide.

Since the day Sumita had fled from the college hostel, he had never met Sumita again until today. He would not help feeling revolted. Sumita was the girl who wanted marriage above anything else. Ten years had changed all that. Today she was a pawn in the flesh trade, a part of the oldest profession in the world. A whore. He could not get himself to say the word.

But, he said to himself, he had actually seen her soliciting. "There is no excuse, no excuse at all," he thought. "Aren't you to blame?" his conscience smote him, "She had five mouths to feed, and no shoulder to lean on. And you, who could have extended a hand of friendship, withdrew it when she needed it the most."

"But a street walker?" he thought contemptuously. "What about you?" his conscience nagged him. "That was different," Rohit thought, silently condoning his own premarital affairs. "They were for love not money."

Slowly, he was assailed by a sense of guilt. He knew that he was partly to blame and needed to make amends. Although he had driven a few kilometres from the bus-stop, he turned back, hoping to see her there. If he did, he would take her home, get her a job in his company, transfer her out of the city and help her rebuild her life. He decided that even if he didn't find her there that day, he would come again and again, until he succeeded in finding her.

Luck was with him. Sumita was still standing there. Apparently, the motorcyclist's proposition did not materialize, he thought thankfully. He drove slowly towards where she was standing, but she turned away. Did she recognize him? Was she ashamed at meeting him under these circumstances? A thousand thoughts raced through his mind. He sounded the horn so that she could no longer ignore him. She made her way towards him warily. But her face was completely expressionless. She gave no sign of recognizing him. Had he changed so much? It was true that he had put on a lot of weight and had started losing his hair but surely he was still recognizable.

Opening the front door of his car he said, "Come and sit here with me, I want you to come along with me." Suddenly from the end of the lane a blue Gypsy marked, 'Police,' came up. "You are under arrest," said a smartly turned out lady police officer.

"Why, what is my offence?" Rohit stuttered. "Eve teasing," she said succinctly. "But...but I thought she was a street-walker...." He stammered. The moment he said it he realized he had spelt his own doom.

The police officer smiled enigmatically, as he was bundled into the Gypsy. "This is good work Inspector Sumita Saxena," she commended, "Six eve teasers in one evening. You make an excellent decoy, do you know that?"

At the police station Rohit looked surreptitiously at Sumita. Should he try telling them his story? No one would believe it, he knew, least of all Sumita herself. "Would you like to call up your family?" asked the police officer with mock solicitude. He almost shuddered as he declined her offer. He was lucky that Radhika and the children had gone to her parent's place. The maids would arrive only around ten o'clock the morning. Nobody would really worry about him. He would hate it if Radhika learnt about this.

He began to brood about his own plight. What would happen to him? "A night in the police lock-up and a fine," he had once heard Sanat mention. He would contact Sanat the next morning and ask him for money. Sanat could be trusted to keep quiet. Rohit now understood where Sanat had met Sumita and why he had looked so guilty. How he had misunderstood Sanat! He looked at Sumita surreptitiously. He knew he faced a Hobson's choice. If he said that he had not recognized her when he had stopped the car, he would be admitting his guilt. But if he confessed that he had recognized her as his old college mate Sumita and had thought she was a whore,it was infinitely worse. And he could hardly deny that supposition. He had admitted that he had thought she was a streetwalker. Rohit hardly dared to look at Sumita's face. Streetwalker. How he wished he could withdraw those words.

"That is what hurt me most," thought Sumita, "Rohit. The only man I ever loved, who thought I was not good enough to marry him. Today he thought I was a common whore!" Was it possible that Rohit didn't recognize her? 'Impossible,' she said to herself. He had come towards her not once, not twice, but thrice. Everytime she had tried to give him a chance to escape by looking the other way. But perhaps while he considered that marriage was too high a price to pay for her, he did not mind spending a few hundred rupees for owning her for one night. That hurt, that really hurt.

"I may never be rich Rohit," Sumita said to herself, "but I have my pride, my dignity, my values and above all my self-respect. I am the daughter of a policeman, not of a pimp." "He deserves it," she thought, her attitude hardening suddenly, "and he has a long and a seemingly never ending night before him to think about his misdeeds. A night to remember."

□

THE FUTURE IS MINE

It began as a hollow feeling in the pit of the stomach and then began to grow and pervade her entire being. She knew the symptoms all too well. She saw the serpentine queue in front of her and shuddered. Her car had been stuck near Hotel Ashok for the last twenty-five minutes and had refused to budge. She saw the mosaic of cars spread all around Chanakyapuri and groaned. A Volkswagen Vento stood behind a Toyoto. An SX4 stood in the next lane just before a BMW. Big cars, most of them, stood cheek by jowl with each other. This was not a time for traffic jams. "There is a VIP Movement. The Sri Lankan President is passing by," said the driver. His words offered her little solace. She watched the cars stuck to their lanes, without moving an inch, and then glanced at her watch, which was ticking away relentlessly. She tried to ignore the hollow sensation in the pit of her stomach. The phone rang just then. "Aarti, where are you?" cried Tanvi plaintively, "I am waiting for you at the airport." "I am stuck in a traffic jam at Chanakyapuri," said Aarti. "What?Your Bhavan is just there," she shouted, "Have you not moved out of your Bhavan yet?" "I am stuck in the traffic jam," repeated Aarti, as she began to feel sweat break out on her face. She could ignore it no longer. Sweat began to pour down her face, as though she had just come out of a sauna. Her hands, on the other hand, had turned clammy. They were slowly becoming icy. Her chest was becoming constricted. She began to experience breathing difficulty.

She opened the car window panes and took large gulps of air, as though she had been oxygen deprived for hours. She tried to control herself, but could not. Taking a large handkerchief from her purse she began to sob loudly. The taxi driver turned and looked at her with concern. She was displaying all the symptoms of a heart problem. He knew it, as his brother had suffered a heart attack and succumbed to it, since there was no help nearby.

"Don't worry," she managed to say, "I am fine. This is just a panic attack, it will go away after some time." She closed her eyes, visualized an imaginary dot in the centre of her forehead and began to focus her energies on it. Slowly the tension eased. She felt her muscles begin to relax. The tight knot at the base of her neck dissolved, as though by magic. She was once again the Aarti the world knew.

"Where to?" The driver asked her. "Turn back," she ordered, once again in command of herself. There was no way she could reach the Airport if she was stuck in traffic till 12.30.p.m. The gates would close twenty minutes before departure. The distance from Shantipath to the Airport was 30 minutes. There was no way she could make it to the airport, unless there was a miracle. She did not believe in miracles.

Tanvi's phone call came soon after. "Just where are you?" she asked, her voice edgy. "I am returning home," said Aarti wearily, "There is no way I can make it to the flight. I am bound to miss it." 'What?' Tanvi's voice had acquired a note of hysteria, "What about me? How will I cope without you? Where will I stay?"

"Don't worry, Rohit will be there," said Aarti slowly, "He will take you to the guest house. I will try to come tomorrow." "It's only a delay of one day, for God's sake," she added angrily. There was silence on the other end. "Was Tanvi examining the possibility of what twenty-four hours might accomplish?" Aarti thought nastily. She was ashamed of herself immediately. Tanvi had decided to accompany her to Manipur for a week-long holiday, only because she needed a break. "The world in the corporate sector is demanding," Tanvi, who worked in Coca-Cola, had shrugged, "We have targets to meet. We are judged by performance. I need to take a break in order to relax." Aarti had smiled. "Sure. You will have many forms of relaxation. Curfews in the time of agitation. Occasional ambushes and fighting. I would recommend Manipur to anybody who wants to have a peaceful getaway," she had said. Then seeing Tanvi's unnatural pallor she had added, "I am only joking, things are not so bad, I dare say."

As she returned to Manipur Bhavan she began to get stressed once again. Who would get her ticket cancelled? Who would pay for it? Who will get her a ticket for the next morning flight? 'Easy,' she said to herself, "The Protocol Officer in the Bhavan, that's who."

For a moment her hand lingered on her Blackberry phone. She owed it to Rohit to inform him that she had missed her flight, otherwise he would unnecessarily wait for her at the airport. The next minute she decided to keep quiet. She knew that he would not come personally to the airport, but send her office car to fetch her. He would come to know about her delayed departure in a few hours time anyway. Till then she had respite. She knew that Rohit's tirade would begin soon after.

Was this the life she really wanted? A life of subterfuge? Where she could not be herself, before her fiancé? Where she could not discuss her panic attacks with Rohit? Where she had to hide behind the façade of good cheer? she wondered.

She thought of Rohit and realized she was being unfair to him. Rohit was not responsible for any of the things that had led to the onset of her panic attacks. The Departmental Examination she had gone to invigilate two years ago. The ambush on her vehicle when she was returning from the Examination Hall. Her being plucked from the jeep and abducted in a Maruti Gypsy, simply because the Government had not provided her with an armed escort. Her being blindfolded and driven for hours, before being taken into a hovel and dumped onto a stringed cot, God alone knows where.

"Why have they brought me here?" she had despaired, as she had looked at the dog-eaten calendar, the only embellishment on the bare wall. There was no clock in the room. Her wrist watch had been taken away, so that she would lose track of time. Why had they abducted her? She had not deliberately taken action against an insurgent group. In fact she had not even been posted to a Subdivision. She had been made Under Secretary in the Department of Personnel in Manipur, because the powers-that-be did not feel that it was safe for a woman to be in a Subdivision. She guessed that they had abducted her, to try and get some insurgents released. She recalled with fear that a senior woman officer had been kidnapped in a neighbouring state a few years ago. This was a copycat crime. Waves of horror washed over her, as she realized that she had been kidnapped because she was a woman and that made the kidnapping more sensational. Besides, she was single and therefore the insurgents must have figured out that there would be no husband or children to grieve for her, in case she died. In other words, she grimaced, they considered her expendable. She felt a strange rumbling in her stomach. What if the Government did not accept the demands of the insurgent group? What if the government did not care about her life, at least not enough? She was not a local officer. Not a Tangkhul Naga, a Kuki, or a Hmar. She was a Kayastha from UP. Which insurgent group had kidnapped her, the Nationalist Socialist Council of Nagaland (NSCN) or some other group? Aarti thought of the lady officer for whom two insurgents had been released. Would the Chief Minister show the same compassion in her case, or would he be a hardliner, refusing to negotiate with the insurgents, uncaring about her fate?

She was mulling over these questions, when the door had been opened and an old man had come and placed an aluminium plate, with a mound of rice and a pitifully small amount of *dal* and mustard *saag*. He had smiled while leaving, and seeing his toothless evil grin, she had felt bile rise in her mouth, but had quickly fought the nausea. She needed to eat, in order to keep her strength. If she languished without food, she would never be able to escape her kidnappers.

After she had finished eating, she saw the young guard come and pick up the plate. She was surprised to see him. He looked very young, barely sixteen or seventeen years old. Was he a part of the insurgent outfit? She wondered. Did they recruit children in the insurgent movement? "I need to wash my hands," she had said. He had waved at the mug and bucket lying in the corner of the room. "I need to go to the toilet," she had insisted, wondering if they would allow her to leave the room, which would enable her to assess her chances of escape. He had grinned at her, entered her prison and then opened the door to the right. She had seen a toilet, which had been newly constructed for her. There was no chance of escape, she realized. This would be her prison, until the government paid for her release. Or else.

At night, as she lay on the stringed cot, she thought of the unexpected turn her life had taken. She had cursed the day she had been allotted Manipur cadre. But she had no idea that her foreboding and misgivings would come true so soon. She looked at the iron bars on her only window, effectively barring all means of escape. There was no way she could get away from here.

That night, the old man had brought her rice with a large chicken leg. She looked at the chicken with its skin, its claws unremoved, boiled in salt water with whole red chillies, and recoiled. "Eat up," he had said gruffly, "You need to keep your strength." She had looked at him in surprise, unable to get over his revolting smile. She had eaten ravenously, not admitting to herself how hard she had fought to keep the hunger pangs at bay. God, she had taken so many things in life for granted. A steaming cup of cardamom tea after her return from work. Nescafe coffee, beaten with sugar granules, to make a cup of strong, frothy coffee. French toast, done to perfection, as morning breakfast. Waffles, with maple syrup, which she had learnt to make after her trip to Canada, to meet her brother. Cheese balls made with grated Amul Cheese and flour. That was civilization she had taken for granted, as she had the programmes on the TV show, especially *CID* and *Adaalat*, which she loved watching because she had tried to solve the mystery in each episode.

"I want tea," she said plaintively to the old man who brought her food. The next morning, the young guard came with a mug of hot tea, looked at her speculatively and left the mug a few feet away from her, before he locked up her room. She realized why he had done that. He had not wanted her to throw the tea at him and effect her escape. She began to giggle hysterically. As if she could escape from this wretched place, wherever it was. She was not even sure in which district she had been imprisoned. Churachandpur? Chandel? Senapati? Ukhrul? Tamenlong? How could she escape from here all by herself? How many people were guarding her? Was this some kind of Headquarters of the insurgent outfit that had abducted her? Would she ever escape from this prison?

Was Rohit thinking about her? Or had he given her up for dead? What chance or destiny had allotted Rohit, her classmate in college, the same service and cadre as her? Being together in Manipur had brought them close. "Too much familiarity breeds attempt," she had giggled to herself. Rohit had never given her a second glance while in the University, in fact he had been friendlier to Tanvi. But in Manipur she had become the object of his affection. At times he had seemed besotted by her. They had just announced their engagement.

While she was ruminating, she was surprised to suddenly see a shadow loom before her. The young guard was standing at the door and looking at her speculatively. She looking at him wonderingly. Had the leader of the insurgent group ordered her execution? Had the government turned down the demands of the insurgents and had the group decided that she was expendable? Had he come to call her out, so that they could shoot her? Why can't he shoot me here and get over with it? She wondered. Then she saw him look at her *kurta*, which had become unbuttoned. "Clothes," he said as he threw something on her bed and left. She opened the bag excitedly and then closed it with disgust. There was a phanek in it, along with a blouse and petticoat. She had no idea how to wear the garment. Why could they not bring her salwar *kameez* or a *saree*? She wondered. She realized almost immediately that they could not go to the market and buy such clothes without rousing suspicion. She wondered whose clothes had been borrowed. His sisters? He looked too young to have a wife. "I want soap," she shouted. He came back with a bar of Lux bathing soap. For the first time since she was abducted, she revelled in the luxury of bathing with soap. As she soaped her aching limbs and washed herself she felt strangely rejuvenated. The cloak of inertia which had enveloped her seemed to disappear. She felt like a new woman. She wore the *petticoat* and then wrapped the phanek around her waist. She wore the blouse on top. She was surprised to see that she looked almost like a Manipuri.

She saw the guard looking at her with renewed interest. She smiled to herself. The male attention she was getting was boosting her ego. Maybe she could ask him for a comb tomorrow.

That night the old man brought her rice, *lai saag* and *ooty*. (A Manipuri delicacy made with green peas, green leaves, and soda.) She looked at the green concoction of green peas, vegetable leaves and soda and smiled. It was her favourite dish in Manipur. She ate with relish, occasionally clucking her tongue as she ate. After eating, she washed her hands and then shoved the plate towards the door. The old man came and removed the plate. A few minutes later the door opened once again. The young guard entered her room and stood watching her. Suddenly he shoved her on the bed. Her eyes grew wide with alarm. What was he trying to do? Molest her? Rape her? She could not believe it. He seemed to be not more than seventeen. He was a mere boy. He was not a rapist. But something seemed to have gotten into him. He first threw her on the bed and pinioned her. He then began to unbutton her blouse. 'No,' she shouted, 'No, No.' He gave an expletive under his breath and put his hand on her mouth. She thought of Rohit, who had been trying to make love to her and her protestations. She looked at the young guard, who seemed to have become a predatory animal, intent on mauling her. She pushed away his hand with all her might. And then she opened her mouth and screamed at the top of her voice. Suddenly the door opened and the old man entered the room. He saw Aarti's dishevelled appearance, took hold of the gun the young guard had thrown down, and hit the guard on his head with the butt. Taken by surprise, the young guard fell on his knees, clutching his head. 'Run,' said the old man to her, 'Just run.' She looked at him uncomprehendingly. Run? Run where? Where was she? She had just escaped an attempted rape. She wondered what nightmares awaited her outside. 'Run,' he said once again. Perhaps that was the only word in English that he knew, she thought hysterically. She began running into the darkness. A sliver of a moon shone in the sky and Aarti wondered where she was going. She ran until she thought she would collapse and then sat on a mound by the roadside. She took large gulps of air and began running once again, as she thought of the young guard, who might still be in pursuit of her. When she felt tired she began walking. When she was on the verge of exhaustion she dropped on the road, clutched her knees with her hands and began weeping. Once the tears had dried up, she got up and with a sudden burst of speed, started running once again. At last when she felt that she could run no more, she lay by the side of the road and slept. When she woke up she found herself near a police station.

It was then that it all began. The panic attacks. The constriction in her throat. The cold, clammy hands. The need to take large gulps of air while speaking. The imminent feeling of collapse, even after sleeping through the night. It was then that she saw Rohit look at her speculatively. She knew that there were questions that he wanted to ask. Had someone touched her when she was abducted? Was she molested or raped? Was that why she had panic attacks? She had been given a Personal Security Officer while in Manipur. But she had not been offered a cadre change.

"Forget it," Rohit had said gruffly, when he had seen her in distress. Forget it? She had suffered. She had heard a gunshot, after she had run for some time. Who had died? The old man or the young guard? She had no idea. Why was there nobody else, except the old man and the guard where she had been kept captive? At the police station she discovered that she was in Hungdung, not far away from Ukhrul. Maybe it was not a mainstream insurgent group, but a splinter group which had abducted her. Who knew?

After her return from the airport she fell asleep and missed seeing the television news. At six o'clock the phone rang. She picked up the phone on the first ring. "Hullo…Hullo…Hullo…"

Rohit's voice seemed to come from far away. 'Yes?' she said. "Who is that?" she heard Rohit say. 'Aarti,' She said. Suddenly she hear him break down on the phone. "Aarti, you are alive."

She was bewildered by his reaction. 'Aarti,' he said, "the flight you were to take has crashed. I was so afraid that you were dead." Later she learnt that the flight was supposed to land at Imphal but the air traffic control had asked the aircraft to hover in the air for some more time, as another aircraft was about to depart. The plane had turned and crashed into the hillside. Everyone had died. Including Tanvi.

Rohit was still sobbing on the phone. She could hear him utter words of endearment he had not uttered before, " My darling, my love, you're alive, " he said repeatedly, "I cannot believe it."

The news of the plane crash took a long time to sink in. Aarti knew that she would grieve for the planeload of people who had died and especially her friend Tanvi. She was grateful that she was not one of the victims. Aarti closed her eyes and raised her hands in supplication. She had begun to believe in miracles once again.

□

STORM WARNING

They came once again, the nightmares where the lines had blurred so much, that she could not distinguish between dream and reality. The nightmares which reduced her to gibberish, petrified her into silence, parched her throat and made her break out in cold sweat. This time she saw the mountains, which seemed to cave in, just as she had reached the summit, making her plummet from 8000 metres into nothingness. The day before that it had been the ocean, fierce and tumultuous, raging furiously against her boat, as it hit the rocks and splintered into fragments, while she found herself being pulled into the maelstrom. For days she had been seeing nothing but death.

The nightmares were followed by blinding, raging headaches, which made her temples throb with pain. At one time, at such times she would have wanted Avni by her side. But no longer, not after their last fight, when he had stormed off into the spare bedroom, creating a chasm between them which she had been both unable and unwilling to bridge. She dragged herself up to the dressing table, took a painkiller, popped it in her mouth along with a sleeping pill and sought the much longed for oblivion.

The next morning she called for Sarat, her cousin as well as her physician, who has set up practice in the city only two years ago. After her parents death, Sarat was her only family. "Not my only family," she checked herself silently, for there was Avni, who was, or had been her life, her mate and her anchor. Her lips twisted into a grimace. How naive she had been, how unutterably naïve, for she has actually believed at one time that Avni had loved her. She had only to look into the mirror, she chided herself, to know that it was not possible. Wearily she looked at herself the mirror, which hung by her side and grimaced when she saw her sharp, pointed nose which dominated her thin face. Her eyes, her best features, which usually brimmed with life, were as bleak as winter today. Her hair was dull and matted, as though it had not been shampooed for days. Her complexion was distinctly sallow. No one in his right mind would call her beautiful, she thought. While Avni........ She merely had to close her eyes and Avni's face danced before her. His hair were curled around his head, like Apollo's locks. His nose was Grecian. His eyes, large and luminous, were brown with flecks of green. He had a cleft chin. Strong, stylish and sexy, Adonis incarnate, thought Smita dispassionately "Wow, he looks like a Greek God!" her best friend Aarti had said, when she had been introduced to him. Avni had blushed on hearing the compliment while Smita had flushed painfully. While no comparisons had been made, she could almost hear what had been left unsaid. "Maybe he got sick of good looks and decided to settle for a Plain Jane," Adhuna had said unkindly. Ever since that day Smita had looked at the mirror and wondered.

"Wallowing in self-pity as usual?" Sarat's voice contained brotherly candour and Smita unburdened her heart to him, as she had done several times before, pouring out her doubts and misgivings. "Why can't you believe that someone can love you for yourself, your simplicity and your intellect, instead of ruining your happiness by your unfounded suspicions?" he asked, seemingly irritated by her unwarranted fears. Sarat had forgotten one big omission, thought Smita dispiritedly her bank balance, the one factor, she was now convinced, that had tipped the scales in her favour. She was the Motwani heiress, the only daughter who had inherited the millions her father had made in his pearl business, which had flourished unexpectedly at the twilight of his life. The money had been so much more welcome, because it had come after a deprived childhood, due to her father's half hearted business ventures and consequent failures. The absence of money had denied her the medical education which Sarat's father, a government doctor, had provided him easily. Her wealth had enabled Avni to start his own computer business.

She recounted her fears to Sarat once again. "It's all psychological, it's all in your mind," Sarat dismissed her fears casually. "Was it all pyschological?" Smita thought bleakly. Had she misheard the conversation when she had picked up the phone extension and had eavesdropped into Avni's conversation with his Secretary and heard him implore, "How can I let you go, I can't manage without you." Her own misgivings had increased manifold when she had met the lady in question, at a party. Neha was young, and seemed to be in love with Avni, which was obvious from the way her eyes chased him across the room. Neha had looked at Smita and dismissed her at one glance. Smita's fears had been compounded, her tortured mind had thought of the infinite possibilities of Avni's dalliance with Neha in office, especially in view of Avni's seemingly overwhelming preoccupation with work and the late nights he kept due to his business meetings. One day, unable to conquer the demons raging in her head, she had driven over to Avni's office and stormed into his room. She had frozen in her tracks, when she had heard the sound of throaty feminine laughter resounding in the corridor. Avni and the tart, she had thought uncharitably, as she had walked into the room and flung open the door, her mind conjuring up images of Avni and his Secretary in a compromising position. She was shocked to see that she had interrupted a serious discussion, which Avni was holding with four or five colleagues. One of his colleagues, bespectacled and clad in a business suit, was laughing heartily. There was no sign of Neha in the room. Smita's abrupt arrival had been an intrusion, in what had been a serious discussion.

Several expressions had chased Avni's face. Surprise, anger and then contempt, but there had been no affection. There had been no love on his face either. She had stood awkwardly at the door, and then muttered incoherently, "I was just passing by." Avni had guessed her reason for her unexpected arrival and later raged at her, "You are jealous of my Secretary aren't you? But remember she is only an employee, an outstanding one, I may add. For God's sake stop spying on us!" "Then convince me of your love," the words had trembled on her lips and then died. Before she could say anything, he had walked out of the bedroom into the guest room. The Avni whom she had known five years ago would have cradled her in his arms, whispered endearments in her ears and assuaged her irrational fears. He would have read the articles she had written in journals and called her, 'Dear Professor.' But that was in the past, the enviable but long forgotten past. Now Avni had given up his nine-to five job for the unknown travails of business, which kept him away from home for hours, for days and months, while her hours of work as a lecturer in college were not enough to keep her busy throughout the day. Maybe it is me, she said to herself. Maybe I am just restless and hyperactive. Maybe I can never be at peace with myself. Maybe I am self-destructive. After the breach in their relationship, Smita had never found courage to question Avni anymore, however late he stayed at work, or when he went on week - long tours, with his Secretary in tow.

It had not always been like that, Smita thought despondently. When he had first met her in her house, he had found her understated, quiet and tranquil personality appealing. He thought she had depth to her character, which women her age never did. Her scholarship and erudition had impressed him. She half-smiled as she remembered the look of awe on his face, when she had disclosed that she had written two books. He had commented that success sat lightly on her shoulders. She never boasted of the fact that she was a celebrity in her own field. While she, for the first time in her life, had been enraptured by his sheer good looks and the attention he paid her. Avni made her feel that she was the most beautiful woman in the world, notwithstanding her diminutive frame, wheatish complexion and pointed nose. The first few months had been spent travelling around the world, in order to know each other. But that was before she saw herself as others saw her, and that eroded her self-confidence, diminished her self-esteem and made her realize that scholastic achievements and even a sizeable bank balance did not redeem her. She was a plain Jane married to an Adonis. It was only a matter of time, she realized, when the novelty of marrying her would pale and Avni would begin to stray. The time, she realized, had come.

Smita did not mean to unburden her problems on Sarat, but somehow once she began talking she could not stop. It was a relief to know that she could share her pain, her anguish and her doubts with someone else. For in this house, this bleak childless house, she had only herself, Avni and their maid Maria for company, and she knew that Maria held her in contempt, both as a woman and as a wife. "If she had her way," thought Smita, "She would turn me out of her house, she thinks I am not a suitable wife for Avni." "But are you?" a small voice nagged at her. For after five years of marriage they were still childless, although she guessed that Avni thought that it was because she had decided to plan their family.

After hearing Smita, Sarat called her to the Clinic for a thorough checkup. "There is nothing visibly wrong with you," he said with relief, while asking her if she was taking any medicines. "Nothing except some medicines Avni has got me for my acidity and the sleeping pills you prescribed," she said. "I wish you didn't make me do that," Sarat said, "One day you may end up having one too many." "I'll prescribe a tonic for you and you will be alright," he added. And Smita did feel better after that. The lethargy that had enveloped her like a cloak for the past few months seemed to leave her. She began to enjoy eating and her face became animated once again.

But that was before she began to suffer from delusions, memory lapses and hallucinations, which made her forget where she was and what she was doing. If the nightmares had petrified her, the hallucinations had her totally paralyzed. "Sarat, take me away from here," she pleaded, "Before I turn mad."

Sarat's face took on a thoughtful look after hearing her. He said, "If I didn't know better, I would say you were being drugged." Her face blanched on hearing his words. She realized that it was such a simple solution to Avni's problems. If she were to die, the Motwani millions would be his, and he would be free to marry the woman of his choice. She knew who the woman would be.

Neha. She had seen the look on Neha's face as her eyes had followed Avni. She looked like a predatory animal on the prowl. Smita did not want to voice her doubts, as they seemed to be a betrayal of trust. But somehow the words tumbled out. Sarat was astounded on hearing her. "I have made a will in Avni's favour," she said in a low voice, as she expressed fears for her life. "I won't believe that about Avni for a moment," Sarat said, "Avni is not a poor man. In fact he lent me ten lakh rupees, to set up my practice here." This disclosure of Sarat came as a surprise to Smita. She really had no idea how Avni was doing financially. Yet she felt it in her bones that she was right. She knew that she was being drugged, so that the fine dividing line between illusion and reality would blur and she would stretch her arms, and jump out of the window, like so many other drug takers. She suddenly caught her breath. She remembered Avni telling her rather shamefacedly once that he had tried everything in college, including drugs. So he would know all about drugs and their side effects.

Once again she voiced her fears to Sarat. This time he looked thoughtful and then said, "why don't you go off cooked food completely? Why don't you remain on a fruit diet for a few days and stop all medicines?" She agreed to act upon Sarat's advice, but found that Avni looked at her a little strangely when she filled her plate with bananas, apples and oranges. "You don't need to lose weight," he said absently, "If anything you should gain some." Visions of him and his Secretary Neha filled her thoughts. Neha was slim but had curves in all the right places. Avni would never tell her that she needed to put on more flesh. Visions of Avni and Neha tortured her all evening and all night, but, she admitted to herself, her mind was more lucid and alert than it had been for days.

Within a week of her fruit and *salad* diet, she began to feel better, but one day she and Avni had a showdown. Avni was bringing a friend home for dinner that night. "And for once, I hope you will eat food normally, like a civilized human being," he said. "What is so uncivilized about a fruit and *salad* diet?" she blazed. "Why, it seems as if you are afraid that I will poison you!" he laughed. His laughter reverberated in the dining hall long after he had left.

When Avni came home with Chetan, if he was surprised to see Sarat in the house he did not show it. "Forewarned is forearmed," thought Smita triumphantly. With a doctor in the house she had nothing to fear. The meal went off well, right from the cream of almond soup, to the *tandoori chicken* and *paneer masala* and finally to the *Gajar ka halwa*. Smita actually made an effort to talk to her guest. But when they were having coffee, she began to suffer cramps. The excruciating pain in the abdomen had her doubling up in pain. "It's that time of the month," she thought to herself, but as soon as bile rose into her mouth she rushed to her bathroom. Once she had puked she felt faint with relief and was not surprised to see Sarat standing by the door. "Let me take you to your room," he said gruffly and almost dragged her to her room. Closing the door behind him Sarat said, "I'll try to get the contents of the food you ate analyzed. I am sure you were poisoned." "Please don't do that," she said, aware of the scandal it would cause. "Then promise me that you will not eat any food offered to you by anyone, except what you have cooked yourself," he urged. "I promise," she said. She saw him going outside, saying something to Avni before taking his leave. "Had Sarat given Avni a hint that he suspected the truth?" she wondered.

Smita couldn't sleep that night. As she tossed and turned in bed she planned her escape. She decided that she would take a trip to Kolkata, on the pretext of attending a Conference and would not return to this house. She looked at her room carefully. She had chosen each artefact with great care. This was her home, but her haven had now become her personal hell. She would find herself another place where she would be safe. For once she was glad of the fact that she was very rich.

The next day when she woke up she was horrified to see that Avni had not gone to work. He brought her tea in the morning. "I don't want it," she said mutinously. She insisted on eating just an apple and a banana for breakfast. But at lunch Avni was adamant that she eat something. He brought her soup and bread and insisted that she should eat it. "I won't," she asserted. "I prepared it with my own hands," said Avni. "That's why," she whispered to herself. "You have to eat it, even if I pour it down your throat," raged Avni. She suddenly capitulated to his request. "I will eat only if you give me company," she said tremulously. Avni smiled at her and she caught her breath in her throat. He was so devastatingly handsome. How could he be a potential murderer? Avni went into the kitchen and came back with another steaming bowl of soup. It took her one minute to switch the bowls, when his back was turned and then she had the soup and watched Avni finish his bowl. "Now try and get some sleep," said Avni, stifling a yawn, "I'm going to take a nap myself."

The phone rang soon after he had left the room. Sarat was on the phone. "How are you today?" he said. She quickly told him what had happened. "I hope nothing happens to Avni!" he said. She had no idea how prophetic his words were. A couple of hours later Maria came crying into her room. "Saab is very ill," she said, her eyes red with tears, "Please call the doctor quickly." By the time Sarat came it was too late. Avni was dead.

Smita didn't know what she felt, relief or sorrow, when Sarat held her by her shoulders, made her sit on the bed and gave her the news. It had been a close call. Had she not suspected what she did, she would have been dead instead. She had no energy to take care of Avni's cremation. But Avni's office staff took over and informed his parents, his relations and friends. She had no one she could call her own except Sarat. The police arrived in the house, just before Avni's body was being taken for the cremation. "There was no way I could stop them. It's not a natural death," apologized Sarat. Smita was not afraid of the police, she knew she had nothing to fear. But when Avni's body was taken for post mortem, she saw the police officers eyeing her strangely. Soon her family lawyer came and informed her that Avni had made a will in her favor just a month ago. "You may be surprised to know my dear, that in the last three years he had earned a great deal of money. Avni was a very rich man in his own right." Avni had willed his entire fortune to her, not Neha! It made no sense to Smita.

"Why would he do it?" She said to herself. 'Easy,' said a niggling voice within her, "To divert any suspicion from himself." Avni was not expected to die. She was.

Smita was tired of it all, the tension of the past few days and the trauma of the present. Avni's parents, who lived abroad, were arriving the next morning. She knew that when they arrived, the grieving would begin, the tears and the wailing, all the visible display of grief. She could not be party to all that. She took a sleeping pill, leaving Sarat in-charge of the house. When she woke up she saw a policeman standing before her. She heard him charging her with Avni's murder. She began laughing hysterically. "I was the intended victim you know," she began to say. But she was rendered speechless when she discovered, to her horror, that the poison that killed Avni had been in her possession all along, in her medicine cabinet, inside her capsules for acidity. "But Avni had got me the medicines......" the excuse sounded weak to her own ears. She knew her fingerprints were on the soup bowl, from which Avni had taken soup, and the poisoned medicines were in her medicine cabinet. Finally she saw the Police Inspector's eyes rest on Neha, who had come to her house and was wailing loudly. He had supplied himself with the motive. Jealousy.

Sarat? Where was Sarat? Only he could corroborate what she was saying, Smita thought wildly, but Sarat seemed to have disappeared. That was not surprising. He was often faced with medical emergencies. The police officer waved an arrest warrant at her. She could see revulsion in Maria's face, as she stood by her bedside. The nightmare of being imprisoned for years loomed before her. Could she hope for justice? Smita shook her head. She knew that justice was blind. She thought of the scandal her arrest would cause. She would be called a murderess. She would be tainted for life, even if she was given benefit of doubt and left free. "Give me ten minutes to change," she insisted and everyone left her room. She locked the room as she prepared to leave. She thought it was ironic that she was taking this way out..... It took them sometime to break open the door and find her hanging by the fan.

Sarat sat in a hotel room and heaved a sigh of relief, when the news of Smita's suicide reached him through the T.V. news channel. At last it was over. Avni was gone, and so was Smita. Once Avni had gone, as Smita's sole relation, he was the heir to Smita's entire fortune. It had been so easy to play on Smita's insecurities and fears. It had been easy to supply to Avni, the so-called medicine for Smita's acidity, which had brought on Smita's headaches and her nightmares. It had been easy to introduce drugs in her second bottle of tonic. It had been equally easy to control her medicines. It had not been difficult to persuade Avni to give her soup, with just something in it to relax her. He had not expected Smita to switch the soup bowls. He had expected Smita to die and Avni to be arrested for her murder. It was lucky that Smita had taken the easy way out and committed suicide. But it did not matter to him which of them died first, as long as he inherited Smita's fortune. He had manipulated Smita and Avni, like puppets on a string. It had helped, knowing Smita so well and being near at hand, lest his plan threatened to go awry. He had remained tense till the very end, wondering whether his plan would succeed or not. If Smita had gone to jail, his plans would have been thwarted. He now had a right to relax. A fortnight in Hawaii with the woman he loved sounded just right. He reached for the phone and dialled Neha.

□

ONCE UPON A TIME IN MUNNAR

The mountain air is exhilarating. I climb up the hill covered with blue Neelakurinji flowers, running a little, skipping a little, free as a bird which sits on treetops and trills. Ahead of me stands a Nilgiri Thar, silent, curious and brooding. He does not even move when I click his photograph. He has begun to take crowds of visitors in his stride. I want to kick off my shoes and race forward and I do, till I drop on the grass. Sepia coloured images begin flooding my memory. I am four years old and run as fast as my legs can carry me and then I fall and Di runs towards me, cradles me in her arms and we both laugh as we roll down the grassy knoll. Di. I shake my head. Di? I have two brothers and two sisters. Then who is Di? And why did I think of her? Why has the image of Di flashed before me just now? I have no time to brood. Our Group has slowly plodded up the hill and reached the top. The local officials eye me warily. Government officials, especially women officers, are expected to behave with decorum, not loll around on a carpet of grass in public view.

I get up sheepishly, pulling down my *saree* hastily, brushing aside the clumps of grass, which cling on to my *saree* like long lost friends. My ankles and legs begin to itch. Have I picked up some allergy? Poison ivy perhaps? The urge to scratch my ankles and legs is strong, but I maintain a stoic silence. Some things can wait till I reach the sanctity of my own room. This is one of them. Even if it is killing me. I raise my head and see Samar standing before me, a bunch of spinach leaves in his hand.

"Here, rub them wherever it is itching you, it's an antidote," he says. I wonder what is he? A mind reader?

We trudge down the hill slowly. I am lost in my own thoughts.I am thrilled to be back in Munnar. I have spent the first four years of my life here. I can still remember the red brick house where I lived, with its slate roof, a tree house and a well at the back. But it is the first time that I have seen the Neelakurinji, the blue flower which blooms in the hills once in every twelve years. I have never seen them bloom before. I was last here twenty years ago, with Di.

What happened to Di? I frown. I have never seen her photographs in our house. Amma and Papa have never talked about Di. But visiting Munnar has jogged my childhood memory. I remember Amma and Papa saying that Di had fallen off the hill, a month after our family outing there.

Once we climb down the hill, the local officials accompanying us tell us that before returning to our hotel, we would visit the Christian Home and Centre in Munnar, which is run by Roman Catholic Nuns. It is an excellent Centre for Girls Education.

"You will be interested to see what they do for the Mentally Challenged," say the officials. I wonder why this visit figures on our itinerary. We are a group of Indian Audit and Account Service officers and the visit to Munnar is a part of our 'Bharat Darshan.' This visit seems to be unscheduled, but I relish the prospect of being here, as I realize that I can visit the restroom to rub the spinach leaves on my ankles. I have no idea that destiny has brought me here. When I stand outside the building I am spellbound. I seem to be transported to another country, in another era. The building is made of gray stone and has beautiful stained glass windows. I feel I am entering a cathedral. The building is half covered by creeper vine. We stand before an ornately carved door in ebony and press the bell. The door is opened and we are ushered in. The classrooms are empty as the classes are over.The girls have gone to their dormitories. We are then taken to the drawing room. Tea is served to us in style, complete with bone china cups, a silver tea service, slivers of lemon for those who want black tea, as well as milk for regular tea drinkers like me.To my delight we are served flaky and crisp croissants, which seem like layered perfection and simply melt in the mouth, along with red velvet cupcakes. I dig my teeth into one, savour the chocolate flavour, roll it around my mouth, give a loud sigh of delight and shamelessly pick another one.

This institution, tucked into the back of beyond, boasts of a confectionary which can compare to the best in Delhi, Le Meridien, Sugar nSpice, Angels in my Kitchen, and Wenger's.

Soon the girls begin to troop in, five or six of them. Padmini is the first one to enter and she is an ethereal beauty, her hair, naturally curly, flows down her back in beautiful ringlets. She looks like a big Barbie Doll. But her eyes are a dead giveaway. She stares ahead vacuously, with no glimmer of recognition in her eyes. Roli walks in next. She is tall, dark and slightly intimidating. She sits ramrod straight in her chair, staring into nothingness. Lata follows Roli and sits down, touching her face and smiling. She is a Down's Syndrome child, a child trapped in the body of a young woman. She keeps smiling, as all Down's Syndrome children do and occasionally claps her hand and laughs with childish delight. Amisha who walks in next is clearly autistic. She avoids all eye contact and begins banging her head against the wall, while we all watch anxiously, wondering if the headbanging will result in some grievous injury. Smita arrives in a wheelchair as she is spastic. Her hand keeps shaking uncontrollably. She is clearly helpless without her assistant. Five girls, nearly all of them delusional and some of them mentally challenged as well.

Sister Angela, who heads the Institution, enters the room and smiles at us. "The cakes and croissants you ate were made by these girls", she says. That sounds impossible but Sister Angela could not be lying.

And then walks in another girl, small and diminutive, with wheatish complexion and eyes which appear to be too huge for her tiny face. 'Meena,' says Sister Angela loudly as she enters the room. I have to stoop to see her. Someone comes with a foot stool and she climbs on it and then leaps onto a chair. I look into her eyes. They look dead, quite dead. The glazed eyes of a corpse, which the doctor shuts gently, once he pronounces the patient dead, or the eyes of a dead fish on a slab of ice, before it is sliced. The girl before me is really a woman, who must be about thirty to thirty-five years old. She reminds me of someone. It is the eyes that I recognize. I have seen them sparkling with mischief, and blaze with anger as well. But I have never seen them as dead as I see them now. I experience a sudden gut wrenching pain. It couldn't be, but it is her. But twenty years is a long time. And I was only four years old at that time. Maybe I am mistaken.

"What is wrong with her?" I want to know. Sister Angela looks at me in surprise and says, "She is a midget." She is stating the obvious. "But being a midget is not a crime," I begin to say, then lapse into silence. Neither is being a Down's Syndrome Child, Autistic, Spastic or delusional a crime. What I mean to say to is that she is not mentally challenged like the others. "There is nothing really wrong with her, is it, except that she is vertically challenged?" I say, "then why is she dumped here?"

Sister Angela's lips tighten in response. She is a Nun. To her, this home is an extension of God's own abode. And I have dared to call it a dump.

"Her parents left her with us," she says, her voice cold, "And we do not turn away anybody from our doorstep." "We should not be talking about her in her presence," I admonish Sister Angela, "Unlike the other girls she is intelligent and can understand everything." All through this exchange Meena sits silently, not reacting at all. Is she dumb or has she perfected the art of remaining silent? I then feel the warning touch of our Group Leader, Partho Banerjee on my shoulder. This is not the time to argue with Sister Angela. We are guests here, and not an Inspection Team. In any case I have successfully broken up the meeting. It is time for our Group to retreat.

When we finally leave, the other members of our group begin to explain things to me.

"Imagine the plight of the parents," my Group Leader tells me, "They must be having other children as well. If she had remained with them in the same house, the other children would have found it impossible to get married. So the parents had really no choice but to get rid of her."

"What about her?" I argue indignantly, "How did she feel, being plucked from her home and dumped into the Christian Home, into a completely alien atmosphere, simply because she did not grow a few inches taller?" "It must be tough on them, making this choice. They must have done it after much deliberation. They may be having five or six children they had to think of," my Group Leader says.

'Five,' I say automatically, remembering that Di often laughed and said, "We are six." He looks me in surprise. I shake my head. I am in no mood to give explanations to anyone.

I am silent on the way back. Half way to our hotel I turn to Samar and say, "I need to go back." 'Why?' the words are on Samar's lips. But he knows that I will brook no argument. The two of us return to the Christian Home. Everyone else goes back to the Sun View Hotel. This time Sister Angela eyes us suspiciously and is reluctant to talk to me.

"I want to talk to Meena," I say. 'Why?' she asks. "I have my reasons," I say, unwilling to say anything further. She goes inside to call her. After what seems like an eternity, but in reality is only ten minutes, Meena walks into the room. 'Di,' I say, running to her, "I am Madhu." I have no doubt in my mind, I have found my Di.

Di, who Amma and Papa had claimed had fallen down the hill, soon after our family outing there. Di, whose body was never found, but at four years I had not known about death in all its dimensions. Di, about whom no one ever talked in our house. Di, who had spent twenty years of her life in the Christian Home among girls who were not all there mentally. Di, who must have longed for a normal conversation and even more, for love. Who must have yearned to put her head on Ma's lap, as she had often in the past. Who must have dreamt of the home and the family when she grew up. Di, who had raced me up the hill and then dropped in a heap as though her lungs would burst, a twelve year old girl who thought that she owned the world, till her parents discarded her like a pair of old shoes that had outlived their utility. Di, whose hand had a long and jagged scar, because I had once thrown a pair of scissors at her. Di, whose eyes had, once upon a time sparkled with laughter, but had become dead when she realized that she could only survive in this madhouse by pretending to be one of them.

Di, who had taken on the role of the Head Cook in the Home, making flaky croissants and melt in the mouth red velvet cupcakes, walnut cakes and mutton patties, spinach quiche and apple pies, just to be away from the cackle of girls who were lost in their own world. Di, who died a little everyday as she grew older, because her Ma and Papa had decided that she was expendable. Had they ever visited her in the Home? Perhaps they had done so in the beginning. But a year later they had shifted to Kolkata, after Papa had switched jobs, and after that I am sure, Di had never seen any one of us.

'Di,' I say, as I hold on to her legs as I used to as a child, "I am Madhu." She doesn't say anything, but sits silent and stoic, like a rock, on the chair on which she has to leap, with the help of a foot stool. But I just cling on to her legs, as I had done when the pair of scissors I had flung in anger had hit her hand and left a deep and jagged scar.

'Di,' I say, 'Di.' Then five minutes later I feel something hot and wet on my head, the first tear that rolls down Di's eyes. "Madhu, Madhulika," she says. I cling to her tiny compact body, as if it was a piece of driftwood in the river, which would take me to safety, if I hold onto it long enough. I cling to her and cry for her lost childhood and mine, for the sister who would have held me by my hand and taken me across the hills, whose only sin was that she was the innocent victim of a defective gene of my mother or father and did not grow up to be 5 feet 6 inches tall like me, but remained 3 feet 6 inches tall.

'Di,' I say, unable to carry on, leaving everything I want to say unsaid. But Di understands. She understands my bewilderment in losing her, my loneliness in growing up in a house where Ravi